CREED 3

UNDERCOVER

PHOENIX DANIELS

Copyright © 2018 by Phoenix Daniels
Published by Jessica Watkins Presents

All rights reserved, including the right of reproduction in whole or in part in any form. Without limiting the right under copyright reserved above, no part of this publication may be reproduced, stored in or introduced into a retrieval system, or transmitted, in any form by means (electronic, mechanical, photocopying, recording, or otherwise), without the prior written permission of the copyright owner.

This is a work of fiction. Names, characters, places and incidents are either the product of the author's imagination or are used fictitiously, and any resemblance to actual persons, living or dead, business establishments, events, or locales, is entirely coincidental.

❀ Created with Vellum

SYNOPSIS

Catch up with Governor Victor Creed as he battles political foes during a cutthroat gubernatorial campaign, while at the same time doing his very best to help his wife through a life-altering tragedy.

Learn a bit about the life of undercover officer, Donatella Devereaux, as she infiltrates a powerful religious cult with every intention of bringing them to their knees. But will her desire for Lincoln Creed, the governor's sexy younger brother, impede her concentration?

Meet Army Ranger, Colonel Creed; soldier, brother, and overall badass. He is a two-time war veteran with his biggest battle ahead of him: getting the woman that's invaded his every thought.

This novel is dedicated to the memory of Rosemary McMorris, the only person who has truly loved me without condition. I love you, Mommy. Continue to rest in peace

1

DONNA

"Donna!" Marco, her teammate, called from across the room. Donatella Devereaux looked up from the computer screen. She had been checking out her twin sister's social media pages. Since she worked undercover, having a social media page was not an option. However, it was a tool for her to keep up with her family and Donna loved scrolling through pictures of her family.

"Commander Todd wants to see you."

Donatella nodded. She shut down her desktop and stuffed her cell in the drawer. Her commander was cool, but he didn't like to be kept waiting.

She stood and looked around. The rest of her team was seated at their assigned desks, probably checking social media as well. She grabbed an over-time slip from her desk and exited the shared office.

A quick trip down a hall and around a corner led her to the big boss' office. She entered the small outer office and walked up to his secretary's desk.

"The *man* wants to see me," she announced.

Gail, the commander's secretary, looked up with a grin.

"He hates when you call him that." She chuckled.

"Mm-hm. I know."

Gail shook her blonde head and waved her into the commander's office. "Go on. He's expecting you."

Donatella entered her boss' office and placed her palms on his desk. "Wassup, boss man?"

They'd always had a comfortable working relationship, so she was relaxed in his presence. However, the vibe he was giving Donatella was anything but relaxed. His jaw clenched as he chewed on his unlit cigar.

"Wassup?" Donatella asked again.

He leaned back in his chair and inhaled a breath before blurting, "You're going back under."

Donna pushed off of his desk and looked down at her commander with disbelief. With a frown, she asked, "What do you mean?"

Surely, he was fucking with her. She looked around his office as if waiting for Ashton Kutcher to jump out and scream that she had just been Punk'd. Donatella had just completed an undercover assignment that had gone on for more than a year. Not even the big bad police department should expect her to go under again so soon. Not now, when she was looking forward to spending time with her family. She missed them, especially Belladonna, her twin sister. Hell, they'd shared a womb, and Donna's life was incomplete without her.

If she were the lungs, forcing everyone to take a breath, Belladonna was the heart. Whenever Donna was away on assignment, Bella held the family down, spending time with her parents and keeping them from worrying themselves to death.

Belladonna was a homicide detective with somewhat normal hours. Family time was just easier for her. But, for Donatella, the guilt of not being there for her family was overwhelming. As far as her parents were concerned, she was the absentee, inconsiderate daughter. But this was the career path she'd chosen. She was an undercover cop. The job required that she be gone. Sometimes, for very long periods of time.

Donatella walked across the room to the small loveseat and plopped down on the soft leather. "I just helped shut down the biggest dope run in the Midwest. Why would I have to go under again right now? The only thing left to investigate is the Neo-Nazis and the White Supremacists, and I can't work them. So, what do you want from me?"

Commander Todd grabbed a manila folder, stood, walked around his desk, and handed her the folder. Then, he sat on the edge of his desk and waited for her to peruse the contents.

Donna rolled her eyes, opened the folder and flipped through the pages. After reading her assignment, she looked up at her boss. His pale skin had turned red. Clearly, he hadn't wanted to give her the assignment. He appeared extremely uncomfortable.

"What is this? Who is Robert Lee Khal?"

The commander turned his back to her and slowly made his way back to the other side of his desk.

"Who is Robert Lee Khal?" she repeated. "What is this shit?"

He returned to his desk chair and steepled his fingers. "You're being assigned to a federal task force and *Reverend* Robert Lee is the charismatic leader of The Blood of The Chosen religious commune, also known as BOC.

"The *what*?"

Donna had never heard of Reverend Robert Lee Khal or The Blood of The Chosen.

"It's a religious cult. The Feds want you to infiltrate."

Donatella raked her fingers through her hair. "The Feds want me? What the fuck do the Feds know about me?"

"Headquarters recommended you."

Donna hopped up from the loveseat and tossed the manila folder on the desk. "Why?! Boss, I'll never make it past the front door! I don't know shit about no religious cults!"

"You didn't know shit about dope when you first came here, but you're our best UCO."

Donatella folded her arms and glared at her naïve supervisor with narrowed her eyes. "I'm from the hood. What gave you the impression that I didn't know anything about the dope game? Yeah, my parents were working class. But black working class is a lot different from white working class. I knew dope. Trust me...I knew the game."

Todd leaned back in his chair with a pained look on his face and rubbed his temple. "It's out of my hands. The Feds asked for you, personally. The *Gold Stars* already approved it before it hit my desk. I got no say."

Donna blew out a harsh breath and stomped across his small office. She stared out of the window thinking of a way to get out of the assignment.

"I've been under for a long time. I haven't spent time with my family in forever," she declared in a whisper.

"I know Donatella, and I'm sorry."

His tone seemed sympathetic, but Donna didn't care. She had plans. For a year and some change, she'd been out of commission with no social time, family life, or dating life whatsoever. Unless, of course, she counted being a dope boy's bitch, constantly coming up with really bad excuses as to why she wasn't ready for sex. Working undercover, Donna would take the occasional drink, smoke the occasional joint. Hell, she'd even snorted a line once when she thought that playing the good girl would get her killed. But giving up pussy for the Chicago Police Department would never be an option. What Donna wanted, at least for a little while, was a little time with her folks, and maybe a normal date.

Strangely, the governor's brother instantly popped into her head. Governor Victor Creed, once the most eligible and gorgeous bachelor in Illinois had been taken off the market by her sister's friend, Taylor Montgomery. But the good news was the Creeds bred very well. There was another incredibly sexy, though rough around the edges Creed.

Colonel Lincoln Creed (Linc) was everything—tall, handsome, and hard-core. He was exactly the type of man Donna craved when she was alone. They'd shared one incredibly hot night that had left her more satisfied than she'd ever been. The Colonel had soldiered her entire body as if she was his most important mission. Unfortunately, after his brother's wedding, he was deployed and she returned to her undercover assignment. But he'd left his mark on her, and she hadn't been able to go a single day without thinking of him.

Longing for him.

"I ain't goin', Boss," Donna said with conviction, shaking her head. "Find somebody white. Aren't white folks more likely to get sucked into religious cults?"

"Ummm...no." Her commander scoffed as though offended. "Do your research. There are lots of black folks in religious cults."

Donna rolled her eyes with a huff. He might have been right, but so what? She didn't want any part of the undercover assignment, let alone a religious cult.

"I'm black and Native American. Our Native American spiritual beliefs are infused into us at birth. Nobody in that commune is gonna believe I'm conflicted."

Commander Todd leaned back in his chair and glared a Donna. He folded his large arms and narrowed his cool, grey eyes at her. "You and I both know that there are several religions within the Native American community, of which many have Christian elements. Don't talk to me like I'm stupid, Detective Devereaux."

Donna hopped up from the loveseat. "Boss, I—"

"Boss, my ass. I have my assignment. Now, you have yours. You report on Tuesday. So, get your affairs in order."

Donna groaned, tossed the folder on the commander's desk, and stormed out of his office.

"This fucking job," she muttered before disrespectfully slamming the office door.

2

LINCOLN

The Fort Benning MPs saluted as Colonel Lincoln Creed drove through the front gate. He had just under an hour to get from post to the airport in order to make his flight to Chicago. It was his brother's birthday and Belladonna, Luc's cop girlfriend, was hosting a barbecue in his honor.

Lincoln had only touched down on American soil twenty-four hours earlier. He was drained, but he'd needed to make the trip. He hadn't seen his family since his older brother, Victor's wedding almost a year ago, and he missed them. He was also looking forward to seeing Bella's sexy twin. Even in the dry, hot deserts of Syria, he'd found himself thinking about his one night with Donatella Devereaux. Unfortunately, before he could see her again, he'd ended up accompanying three companies on a Middle Eastern recon mission.

Lincoln was an Army officer in command of the 75th Ranger Regiment. Ever since he could remember, he'd always wanted to be a soldier. Unlike his father and Victor, he had no interest in politics. He didn't have a hard-on for business like his brother, Lucas. He wasn't into technology like Alexander, and he wasn't interested in being a pro athlete like his baby brother, Jaysen. He was a Ranger and had been born to be that way.

The shrill ring of his cell phone pulled his eyes from the road to the dash. He smiled when he saw Victor's name. He pushed the talk button on the steering wheel, activating the call.

"Hey, bro," he answered enthusiastically.

"*Linc!*" Victor's booming voice filled the car. His big brother seemed just as happy to hear from him as he was to hear from Victor.

"How's married life, Governor Creed?"

"Everything you thought it wasn't, playboy," Victor teased.

"Playboy? Me? Fuck outta here!"

"Oh, yeah?" Victor teased. "What's the name of the last woman that you had sex with?"

"Name?" Lincoln scoffed. "I don't even ask them if they were born a woman anymore. What the fuck do I care about a name?"

Victor's roaring laughter made Lincoln smile. He was only kidding, but Victor would have no way of knowing that the last woman he'd slept with was Donatella Devereaux.

The night they'd met, both Bella and Luc had been sharing a hospital room after being shot. When Donatella entered the hospital, her overwhelming beauty had made him choke on the stale coffee he was drinking. He'd used every excuse known to man to be near her, drawn to her like that thirsty ass moth to the flame. He encountered beautiful women all the time. But, in all his travels, he'd never seen a woman more exotic and intriguing. Her flawless skin was a blend of copper and crimson, her dark brown eyes slanted, both reflecting her African and Native American heritage. And her sharp cheekbones and plump lips only compounded the perfection.

Although she looked identical to Bella, her short, sassy hair, tribal tattoos, and the fire behind her eyes set them apart. Donatella was more than pretty. She commanded attention. Her charisma was the giant magnet that pulled him, almost against his will, right where she wanted him. Thoughts of the night they'd shared invaded his thoughts.

. . .

LINCOLN PUSHED the door open and entered the hospital room. He was expecting to see his injured older brother and his brother's debilitated detective girlfriend. But the first thing he saw was a beautiful woman with Belladonna's face, but so much more.

When she looked up at him with sensual brown eyes, he was ashamed that all of his brotherly concern for Lucas went out the window. His brother and his lady had become secondary. All he saw was Bella's fiery, tattooed clone. Their faces were identical, their auras, attitudes, and personalities contradictory. Donatella's presence was alluring and alluring, for Lincoln, was saying a lot. Being a soldier, he'd had access to women from all around the world.

"Is he up?" Lincoln asked, entering the hospital room.

The first words from her mouth were a lie.

"Yes," Donatella fibbed.

"No, he's not, Lincoln," Bella interjected. "But you can come in."

Lincoln walked across the hospital room, never taking his eyes off Bella's gorgeous sister. And it hadn't escaped him that she was watching him too. He'd hoped the attraction was mutual because he instantly wanted her. Yeah, he had been around the world, but Victor and Lucas seemed to always be surrounded by drop-dead gorgeous women. In love, his brothers had been very lucky.

Taylor was a strong, dynamic beauty. Bella was gorgeous, headstrong, and ridiculously intuitive. But Donatella was... fierce. Even though she was a fraction of his size, he somehow knew that she was a giant.

After an hour of 'kumbaya' moments, everyone was satisfied that Luc and Bella were going to make it. Family and friends slowly began to leave the hospital. When Donatella said her goodbyes and left the room, Lincoln hugged his big brother and kissed Bella's forehead before running out behind her.

He caught her down the hall. "Donatella," he called from behind.

Her steps halted. She turned around, locked eyes with him, and smiled. Her smile was disarming. Her full lips framed crisp white teeth, and her eyes lit up like the Eiffel Tower at night.

"Yes? Did I leave something behind?"

Lincoln slowed his steps to a stalk. He moved as close to her as he could without being creepy. "Yes, you did. You left me behind."

He stood over her, forcing her to raise her head, and inhaled the sweet scent of honey and spearmint. His dick swelled, and there was a tingle to his skin that almost threatened his manhood. He was a big, bad Army Ranger, but Donatella was reducing him to a teenage boy who couldn't control his hard-on.

He shifted, hoping his growing cock would land in a comfortable spot.

"I left you behind?" *she asked with a sexy smirk.*

"Yes."

She batted her long lashes and shifted her weight to one leg. No matter what she did to conceal her desire, her demeanor indicated that she was just as hot for him as he was for her.

Lincoln scratched the bristly hairs that covered his jaw and worked to figure out his next words. Thankfully, before he could come up with a sufficient line, she asked, "I'm still on duty. My partner dropped me off. Can I get a ride back to my job?"

Lincoln wrinkled his brow. "On duty? Are you a cop too?"

"I am. You didn't know that?"

"Actually, no. I knew Bella had a twin, but I didn't know you were a cop too."

"Oh, well... yeah, I am. But I work undercover, brother-in-law. So, don't tell anybody."

Lincoln grinned. "It'll be our little secret, officer."

"Detective," *she corrected.*

"My bad, Detective. Come. Follow me. I'll drop you off."

She grinned and raised a brow. "I asked you to give me a ride, not drop me off, Colonel Creed."

Lincoln lowered himself and leaned closer to her. "Ah, Detective. I see you've done your research. You know my life."

"Well, I am a detective," *she reminded with a smirk.* "I'm paid to be nosy."

Lincoln laughed and placed his hand to her lower back, mainly because he wanted to touch her, and guided her toward the elevator.

∼

A FTER A TWENTY-MINUTE DRIVE FILLED *with stimulating conversation and a whole lot of flirting, they were on the west side, making a left turn on Fillmore. Less than forty feet from the corner was a guard shack manned by a uniformed Chicago police officer. Lincoln drove until he was in front of an automated guardrail. He looked over at Donatella, disappointed that he'd reached the end of the line. But after one wave to the cop, the rail rose.*

Lincoln drove past the checkpoint. Donatella guided him to a parking lot protected by privacy fence with barbed wire.

"Park here," she told him, pointing to a parking spot facing a huge concrete wall.

Once he parked, he looked over at her and waited for further instructions.

"Wanna see where I work?"

Truthfully, he didn't. He'd rather see where she lived.

Lincoln looked up at the old, brick building that surely had asbestos issues and wondered why the city of Chicago didn't treat their cops better. However, he'd been in worst shitholes. If he had to hang a bit in order to get closer to her, he would tour her workplace.

"Sure." He did his best to seem enthusiastic.

Donatella chuckled. She was an intuitive woman. She surely knew he was full of shit.

"I'm just going to grab some stuff from my locker. It won't take long."

Victor nodded and turned the engine off. He hopped out and walked around to open her door, but she was already climbing out.

"A gentleman, huh?"

"At first," Lincoln admitted through a chuckle.

She laughed and grabbed him by the arm, pulling him toward a tiny door in the corner of the building. Once they reached the door, she entered a code, and they entered the small lobby. They passed the cop sitting behind a window and made their way to a turnstile. Donatella placed her hand in a palm reader. When the lock clicked, she pulled the door open.

"Shit, this is like going into the Pentagon," Lincoln quipped.

She laughed and held the door open for him. "This is the Organized

Crime building. It's where all the undercovers work—vice, intelligence, narcotics, and so forth. That's why everything is so secretive. Years ago, this was a Sears warehouse. At one point, it was very covert, but now every thug in Chicago knows what this building is. They'd love to get a look at the undercovers. That's the reason for the guard shack, the covered fences, and the high-tech security."

"I see. So, will you get in trouble for bringing me inside?"

Donatella smiled and gestured for him to follow her down the hall. "Well, Colonel, I would suspect that you have higher governmental clearance than anyone in this building. You could probably ban me from this place if you wanted."

Lincoln couldn't help but laugh. Donatella was not only beautiful, but she was clever and witty.

"You might be right, Detective."

"Do me a favor. Call me Donna. Everybody calls me Donna."

"Naw. I ain't everybody. I like Donatella."

"Don't mean I'll answer," she scoffed.

Lincoln grabbed her forearm, tugged her around to face him, and placed his hand against the small of her back. He pulled her close his body and looked down at her, into her beautiful eyes. "I'll teach you to answer to it."

When she reached up and placed her soft hand to his jaw, his body instantly reacted.

She pushed herself against his manhood. "I love to be taught," she whispered seductively. "I'm like a sponge, more than willing to suck... in all the knowledge that I can."

Lincoln raised a brow. "You are quite brazen, Donatella Devereaux."

She grinned and moved even closer.

God, she was sexy.

"No, what I am is a grown-ass woman. Life is too short for me to pretend that my virtue won't allow me to have something I want."

"And you want?"

"An hour or two," she responded.

Lincoln was a bit thrown off and definitely turned on by her brash response. Donatella seemed to know herself, didn't bother putting on any airs. She oozed confidence, and he found that incredibly attractive. Shame-

fully, he only had one night to give to women that tried to play at being coy.

"An hour or two? Is that all you require?"

"For now," she replied with a wink.

She stepped out of his grasp and continued down the hall. And like a dog in heat, Lincoln followed, watching the bounce of her beautiful ass along the way.

They took an elevator to the 2nd floor. She walked over to what she called the 24hr desk and spoke to a plain-clothes cop with super long blonde hair. The woman was staring at him past Donatella throughout the brief conversation. He would've assumed she was just doing her job until she winked and licked her lips.

Lincoln cleared his throat and looked away. He spied a trophy case and walked over to it. Inside were a few 1st and 2nd place trophies for the police versus the fire department in softball, football, and boxing tournaments.

"Wait here, Colonel. I'll be right back," Donatella called out before pushing through a set of double doors.

He nodded and returned his attention to the trophy case. Behind one of the boxing trophies were two photos that grabbed his attention. In one, Donatella was sporting boxing gloves, posing with a trophy in her arms. The very same trophy on display in the case. The second was a photo of her in a bikini holding a number card over her head. Lincoln smiled. Her versatility was intriguing.

The sound of the double doors pulled his attention from the photos.

"Come on. The coast is clear," Donatella called out from the doorway.

Lincoln frowned and followed her through the doors down a long hallway. "The coast?"

"Yeah, this is where the undercovers work. We're not supposed to bring civilians in here."

Lincoln scoffed. It was strange being called a civilian, but in Donatella's world, he was. In his world, she was the civilian.

"Well, aren't you the rebel?" he joshed.

She grabbed his hand. "That's me."

She pulled him down a hall. She took a left, and then a right. It was like being in a maze. After a minute or two of walking, Lincoln realized it would take a while if he tried to get out on his own.

"Where are you taking me, lady?"

She looked up at him with a grin. "What? This is your tour."

"Of walls?" Lincoln mused.

She giggled.

"We're almost there," she assured.

After a few more turns, she was entering a code on, yet another, keypad. After she was granted access, they entered into what looked like an outer office. It was a large room covered with institutional beige. There were about ten desks spread out about the room, some in cubicles.

Donatella led him to a cubicle. "Welcome to my corner office," she joked.

Lincoln chuckled. "Why is it so empty here? Where is everyone?"

"Well, Narcotics works in shifts. The night shift has already hit the streets, the bosses work days and have weekends off, and so do the civilian administrative staff. So, it's just you and me, Colonel." She smirked. "You scared to be alone with me?"

"Hardly." Lincoln scoffed, looking around the tiny cubicle. "But I have a feeling that I should be."

Judging by the pictures on the wall behind her desk, she really loved her family. Lincoln moved closer to peruse candid shots of her, Bella, and a couple he assumed was her parents.

Donatella moved to take a seat in the chair behind her desk. It didn't go unnoticed when she purposely brushed up against him, rubbing her soft tits against his back. Before she sat, Lincoln was able to get a whiff of her perfume. It was light and feminine. He found himself grinning, but he didn't turn around.

"Good looking family," he mused aloud.

"Thanks. So is yours."

"You think so, huh?"

"Ain't seen an ugly Creed yet, Colonel," she muttered through a chuckle.

Lincoln abandoned the wall of photos and took a seat in a chair next to her desk.

"Well, thank you, Detective Devereaux."

"Mm-hm." She opened her bottom drawer and pulled out a bottle of Jameson Irish Whiskey. "Can I offer you a drink?"

Lincoln was surprised by her choice of drink. He didn't see any ice nor anything that could serve as a chaser. So, he assumed she planned on drinking it straight.

She grabbed two plastic cups from the same drawer and placed them on her desk. She took the top off and poured herself a sizeable portion.

"Well?" she asked, holding the bottle over the other cup.

Lincoln nodded. After the night they'd had with his brother and her sister getting shot, he could definitely use a drink. And...there was no way he was about to let the tiny woman outdrink him.

After pouring his drink, they toasted to family and tossed them back.

A few drinks and a lot of laughter later, Lincoln was really enjoying Donatella's company. She had a fun, easygoing disposition, and a raunchy sense of humor. It was like drinking with one of the guys, except for one gigantic difference. The more time he spent with her, the harder his cock pushed against his zipper. He was certain that never happened when hanging out with the fellas.

In a short amount of time, Lincoln had found himself more than content spending time with her. He had absolutely no expectations as to where the night would lead. But he definitely wasn't disappointed. Because three-quarters of the bottle later, he was cock-buried deep in her tight pussy, fucking the little rebel on top of her commander's desk.

Lincoln had worried that the night shift would return to their office, but Donatella was insatiable. She loved to cum, and he loved making her cum. And he did over and over until she finally collapsed across her boss' desk.

After a brief rest with very little conversation, she showed him to the men's room where he could clean up. It didn't take him long because he'd been planning to go back to Lucas' for a shower. And, if he were to be honest, he wasn't exactly eager about scrubbing the sweet scent of her arousal from his face and cock. So, he took a piss, washed his hands, and left the facilities.

He entered the hall and leaned against the wall while waiting for Donatella. When she finally emerged, she'd donned the sexiest of grins. No bullshit, after all the work he'd put in, he was actually fighting another hard-on. And the fact that she rushed into his arms, pushing her body against his, didn't help.

"Wow, Colonel," she gushed breathlessly.

"Wow, Detective," Lincoln countered, gripping her by the waist, pulling her closer.

"We gotta go. The team will be up any minute, and so will the commander. I don't wanna be here when he sees the mess we made of his desk."

"Come on. I'll take you home," he told her.

"Nah. My car is in the lot. I'm good. Come on. I'll show you out."

Donatella grabbed his hand and led him to the elevator. Once they reached their designated floor, she directed him through the maze and out the same door they'd entered. He was still holding her soft hand as she led him to her car, a black Dodge Charger with dual exhausts. He wasn't surprised by the car she was driving. It said a lot about her—stylish, powerful, and unapologetic.

She used a key fob to open the door, tossed a backpack in the back seat, and hopped in the driver's seat. "Will you call me?" she asked.

Somehow, Lincoln got the impression that she wouldn't have cared either way. If he wasn't so sure that he'd put it on her the right way, his ego would've been severely damaged.

"Of course, I'll call. I missed that beautiful ass as soon as you planted it in the seat."

Donatella smiled and closed the car door. She turned the key and revved the engine. Lincoln figured that was his cue to walk away. He went back to his car, wondering if he'd ever hear from Donatella Devereaux again.

He didn't.

THE NEXT THREE DAYS, he'd called her several times, only to be sent to voicemail. He'd even stooped so low as to call her sister. It was only then that he found out she'd been assigned to a long-term undercover mission, and she would be inaccessible.

Lincoln could have located her. After all, he was a high-ranking soldier with a security clearance that very few had. However, he'd never had to chase a woman before, and he wasn't going to start with Donatella. Ultimately, it wouldn't have mattered. He was deployed to the Middle East on a recon mission. There would be no point calling her if he was unable to see her, unable to reenact their night of explosive sex.

Lincoln didn't know if she was still unreachable because of some bullshit undercover mission, but he hoped like hell he would see her at the barbeque. He wanted another whiff, another taste. He wanted, badly, to be buried in her warmth once again.

3
DONATELLA

"Thanks, babe," Zach said, accepting the plate Donatella made him. "Your sister is an amazing cook."

"Please," Donna scoffed. "Bella couldn't cook her way out of an oven. Her friend, NiYah, the medical examiner, cooked all this shit."

"Medical examiner? Ewe. That's dark," he remarked with a frown. "Don't matter anyway. As long as Bella is as fine as you, she ain't never gotta cook."

Donna rolled her eyes. Zach was acting like a typical twin chaser. His behavior was bordering pathetic and unattractive. Other than their physical appearance, she and Belladonna had absolutely nothing in common. Admittedly, Bella was more grounded. She was the *good daughter* that had dinner with their parents at least once a month. Bella got married when she was expected, to a handsome, strong, reliable black man. As far as Donatella was concerned, Bella was taking up the slack. Her sister was the perfect daughter that she couldn't be for her parents. She deserved to be happy.

But sadly, the fairytale hadn't worked out for Bella with her husband. No matter how handsome and perfect on paper he was, it didn't change the fact that he was gay. So, she winded up falling in love with the governor's baby brother, a white dude from corporate America.

Donatella laughed out loud at her hypocrisy. She, herself, was feeling a privileged white boy. She had also spent some time with the governor's brother. Lincoln Creed had blown her whole fucking mind. It was not at all what she expected from the West Point graduate, the *All-American soldier.*

They'd only spent a few hours together. Yet, he was able to rock her world in such a short amount of time. The conversation flowed effortlessly and his enormous dick was like a wand that created beautiful magic. She'd hoped to see him again, feel him again. He'd promised to call, and he did. Unfortunately, she was sent under the very next day. Now, she continuously found herself scanning Bella's backyard, hoping to see him.

"Donna!" her sister called from behind.

When she turned, Bella was waving her over. Donatella stood and mumbled, "I'll be back."

"I love the hair," Bella complimented when she made it over to her.

"Thanks."

Donna's hair had grown out of the pixie cut into a chin-length bob. Unlike Bella, whose jet-black hair was always long and straight, she frequently changed her hairstyles. Whereas her sister's look was always traditionally Native, her looks changed depending upon whatever criminal organization she was trying to infiltrate.

"Nice party." Donna discreetly scanned the yard again for Lincoln. "The yard looks amazing. When did you do all this?"

"I didn't," Bella admitted. "Lucas did all the landscaping."

Donna narrow her eyes in suspicion. "You mean, he paid somebody."

"Noooo, girl." Bella chuckled. "Lucas and Dean did all this shit."

"Weird," Donna muttered. "Only you can get your current man and your ex-husband to do shit for you. Hell, none of my exes even speak to me."

"There's no competition between Lucas and Dean. They ain't got no beef. *And*, speaking of exes..."

Donna followed Bella's line of sight and her eyes landed on Victoria Price. She was still so beautiful. A quick flash of their short fling caused a tiny smile to escape before she could stop it. She hoped her sister hadn't noticed.

"I thought you hated her," Donna pointed out.

"We've worked out our differences."

"Whaaaat? I'm shocked. Your ass can hold a grudge forever."

Bella laughed. "Maybe I've matured."

"Maybe. Mm-mm-mm, girl, look at her man though. He is so fucking fine. What I wouldn't do!"

"What you wouldn't do for what?"

Donna startled and turned right into Lincoln. He was a sight, tall and muscular with a face that could give sight to the blind. If she were the type, she would have swooned.

"A Klondike bar," she responded with a smirk.

"I got your Klondike bar," he mouthed.

His cheeky response sent chills down Donna's spine. Her entire body responded, remembering how she'd cried out when his thick dick was filling her completely.

He grinned and moved closer to Bella. "Hello, beautiful," he greeted with a hug.

Bella's smile was filled with excitement. "Linc, I'm so happy you made it. Lucas was worried that you wouldn't be able to get away."

"I worked it out. After all, he is my favorite brother."

Bella lips pursed. "I've heard you say that to all of your brothers."

Lincoln grinned, displaying perfect white teeth. "Keep that to yourself," he said with a wink.

"Will do. I'm gonna go find Lucas. He'll be so happy to see you."

Donna watched as Bella hurried away in search of Lucas. She knew Lincoln was watching her because his gaze was searing her skin. She turned slowly and looked up at him. His glare glimmered with an emotion she didn't recognize.

"Hi," she greeted in a weak voice.

"So, when you said all you wanted was a couple of hours, you meant it, huh?"

Her breath hitched. His question had caught her by surprise.

'Damn! Just jump right into it.'

"Um...no. Lincoln, I'm sorry. I got an undercover assignment the next day. I only recently just wrapped it up."

"There are no phones undercover?" he questioned with a frown.

"It's complicated."

"Who's the guy?"

Surprised again, Donna blinked rapidly. She'd been standing with her sister when he arrived.

"How do you know I'm with a guy?"

"I've been here a while, Donatella." When her brow wrinkled, he said, "I'm trained to be invisible."

"Good to know," Donna scoffed.

"The guy? Who's the guy?"

"Just a guy. As a matter of fact, he's a guy I've abandoned. Don't wanna be rude. I'll see you later, Colonel."

"You will," he muttered as she walked away.

Donna made her way over to Zach, hoping that was a promise.

"Hey, isn't that the governor?" Zach asked, smiling as if he were a groupie.

"No. That's his younger brother."

"Oh. They look just alike."

Donna took a seat in the lawn chair next to his and found herself comparing Zach to Lincoln. Zach was definitely a good-looking man. He was tall with a nice build and a great smile. Although he was half-white, he had a beautiful milk-chocolate complexion. The two of them made for a nice photo. However, appearance-wise, his looks couldn't hold a candle to Lincoln. Lincoln's masculine jawline, full luscious lips, and striking green eyes were worthy of a magazine cover. He was stop your heart, quicken your breath fine as fuck. In addition, there was a ruggedness about him that Zach, the ambitious prosecutor, didn't have.

"Is the governor coming?"

Donna rolled her eyes. "Your slip is showing," she muttered. "I'll be back. I'm gonna go grab a drink."

She stood and left. It was no wonder he practically begged for an invite to her sister's party. Zach had big plans for his future in the State Attorney's office, and he thought Donna was his link to the governor. He was an exceptional prosecutor and she didn't mind helping a brother out. However, she did mind that he thought she was unaware she was being used. She laughed inside because Zach was oblivious to the fact that he was being used as well. There was no way she was showing up to a party full of Creeds without a handsome man by her side. Hell, Lincoln could've shown up with a woman on his arm. She wasn't about to be looking all lonely in front of him.

Donna weaved through the small crowd in the backyard and entered the house through the patio door just as Lucas was palming Bella's ass.

"Y'all got company," she scolded.

"Our company is out there and we're in here," Lucas pointed out with a smirk.

"*I'm* in here."

"Then, get out!" he blurted through laughter.

Donna folded her arms and leaned against the wall. "Nope," she quipped. "I ain't going nowhere."

Lucas grinned and raised an eyebrow. "Then, stay here and watch me play with your sister's sweet ass."

"Ughh! I'll pass. I gotta go vomit."

She pushed herself off the wall and left the kitchen. She had to admit, she loved the way Lucas and Bella interacted. Her sister seemed genuinely happy and Lucas seemed to care a great deal about her. Maybe it was a twin thing, but when Bella was happy or sad, her emotions seemed to wash over Donna. As she walked down the hall, thoughts about all her sister had gone through during her divorce and how happy she was now, made Donna smile.

She continued on to the bathroom and was only a few feet from her destination when she felt an arm grab her around her waist.

"What the fuck?" she exclaimed.

As she was being pulled through the pantry door, she was unable to see who'd grabbed her. But she definitely recognized his scent, a mixture of clean linen and testosterone. She would always remember being bathed in his scent as he fucked them both into a cooling sweat.

"Lincoln, what are you doing?" she asked when he pinned her against the wall.

He narrowed his eyes, giving her a stern look. "Who's the guy?" he gritted, pushing his bulge against her stomach.

"H-he's nobody," she said through a breath.

"*Nobody?*" He raised the hem of her long, black maxi dress. Along the way, he allowed his fingers to glide along her outer thigh.

"Lincoln, what are you doing?"

Her voice turned husky. Her skin began to tingle, and she could actually feel the blood rushing to her swelling genitals.

"Lin—"

"Shut up!" he commanded. "You have the nerve to treat me like a piece of meat, ignore my calls, and show up here with a man." His cobalt glare turned menacing. "Oh, sweet Donatella, you have to pay for that."

"I—"

Cutting her off, Lincoln grabbed the back off her head and slammed his lips to hers. Donna immediately went limp, but he held her firm by wrapping an arm around her waist. She moaned into his mouth when their tongues entwined.

Lincoln braced her against the wall and pulled the fabric of her dress over her hips. He was less than gentle when he tore the thin lace from between her thighs and tossed it to the floor. His breathing increased, but he didn't break the connection of their kiss as he worked the buckle of his belt and the button on his fly.

Once he freed himself of all barriers, he pressed his fingers to her engorged clit. Donna gasped and threw her head back, severing their link. She looked into his hooded green eyes as he massaged her pussy with expertise. She saw determination; his determination to make her cum. Using one foot, he pushed her legs apart. With only his fingers, he was working her pussy into an orgasmic frenzy.

"Ah, fuck!" she cussed, pulling his mouth to hers.

He kissed her with immense passion through an explosive and much-needed orgasm.

"Fuck!" she gasped against his lips.

Her breathing was erratic as she collapsed against the wall. Through her own hooded eyes, she saw his mischievous grin.

"Oh, no, baby doll," he chuckled. "I'm not even close to being done with you."

Lincoln pulled a condom from his pocket. Donna pushed herself off the wall, prepared to push past Lincoln. After all, they were in a pantry. Was he planning to fuck her on a shelf with the canned green beans?

As it seemed, that was indeed the plan. In less than a second, he had lifted her off of her feet and guided her legs around his waist. He reached under her and positioned the thick head of his dick near the mouth of her very wet pussy.

"Lincoln," Donna protested. "There is a house full of—"

Her protest was stifled when he impaled her with his super-hard, massive dick.

"Aghhh!" She cried out as her body struggled to accommodate his size.

"Shhh," he urged as he eased out and pushed back in.

His invasion was so overwhelming, Donna was no longer thinking about being quiet. If Lincoln wanted to be discreet, maybe he shouldn't have shoved his giant dick in her. Maybe he shouldn't have cupped her ass and fucked her with the skillfulness of a porn star.

Donna clutched his back and bounced up and down, matching his rhythm. With each stroke, she swallowed as much of him as she could into her pussy. Her fingers dug into his back, his finger dug into the globes of her ass, and between the grunting and heavy breathing, neither of them were all that concerned with discretion.

Donna's entire body trembled as her orgasm washed through her like a tsunami.

"Oh, God!" she exhaled.

As she was hit by wave after amazing wave of ecstasy, her pussy throbbed, clutching his dick. The sensation must've elicited his own release. He wrapped an arm tightly around her waist pushed into her with feverish ambition until he was groaning and pumping warm semen into the plastic barrier.

"Goddamn it!" he blurted through gritted teeth as he poured into her.

He pressed his forehead to the wall and peppered sweet kisses along her collarbone.

"Damn, Donatella," he whimpered breathlessly.

Damn was her sentiments exactly.

After allowing himself a few seconds to catch his breath, he steadied her on her feet. He fixed his pants, buckled his belt, and retrieved her torn panties from the floor. He stuffed them in his pocket and watched while she adjusted her dress.

Donna was confused by the frown etched across his face. They'd just had amazing sex and ridiculous orgasms.

"What? What's wrong?" she asked curiously while finger combing her hair.

"Not a thing, doll. But you better get going. *Nobody* might be getting thirsty."

Before she could respond, not that she had a response, he opened the door and left her alone in the food pantry.

4

TAYLOR

Taylor tossed the used paper cups in the trash and hurried out of the kitchen. She was finally headed to the bathroom. Every attempt she made to get to the bathroom, someone stopped her with questions about the upcoming gubernatorial election. As she hurried down the hall, she thought she was home free until she bounced off a wall that turned out to be her brother-in-law.

"Linc!" Taylor screeched.

He caught her by the shoulders, keeping her on her feet. "I'm sorry, sis. I didn't see you."

"Clearly," she scoffed. "What were you doing in Bella's pantry anyway?"

Before he could answer, the door flew open. Donatella stepped into the hallway. Her dark, slanted eyes widened like a deer in headlights. Taylor looked from Donatella to Lincoln. Whereas she looked horrified, he was wearing a Cheshire cat grin.

"Excuse me," he said to Taylor. He then turned to Donna and placed a hand on her shoulder. "I'm gonna go check on your date. He may be feeling a little lonely."

Donna narrowed her eyes and slapped his hand from her shoulder. Lincoln chuckled and walked away.

"*Hey, Donna.*" Taylor's greeting was accusatory.

"Taylor, it's not what you think. We were just—"

"Mm-mm, I don't care. Not my business. I gotta piss."

Taylor hurried off to the bathroom, but when she turned the knob, she discovered that the door was locked.

"Damn!"

Taylor was doing the "pee dance" by the time the door opened. On the other side of the door was Bella. She bunched her brows as if studying Taylor as she bounced up and down on the other side of the threshold.

"Move!" Taylor shouted. "I gotta pee!"

Bella dried her hands slowly with a paper towel and raised a brow. "You gotta go bad, huh?" Bella stalled.

"*Bella,*" Taylor warned with narrowed eyes.

"Okay, okay." She giggled and stepped out of the bathroom.

Taylor was grateful. It seemed the closer she got to the toilet, the harder it was to hold it.

She hurried into the bathroom and went to close the door, but a big foot in the way prevented the door from closing. Taylor grunted out of frustration. She was tempted to sit on the toilet regardless of the foot in the door. Thankfully, it was Victor's foot.

"Babe, I was thinking—"

"Close the door," she ordered, quickly cutting him off.

Before she heard the lock click, Taylor had already raised the hem of her dress above her hips. She pulled her panties down, elated that she was finally able to get relief.

"Taylor, wait."

"Wait? Victor, I am about to piss on myself!"

He pulled a small rectangular box out of his pocket and opened it. It was a pregnancy test. He handed it to Taylor. "Pee on this," he instructed.

Taylor stared at the little stick, but only for a second as she snatched it from his hand and sat on the toilet. She positioned the test under her and pissed like a panther and released a loud sigh as she emptied her bladder. Once she was done, she removed the stick from under her.

"What's up with this?" she asked as she handed it to Victor.

He smiled and placed a paper towel on the sink and sat the test on top of it. "Well, baby, you've been spending a lot of time in the bathroom. And your tits..." He chuckled, spread his large fingers in front of his chest. "Babe, your tits are massive."

Taylor frowned and reached for the toilet paper.

"Don't get me wrong. I'm definitely not complaining," he assured with a grin.

As Taylor cleaned herself and fixed her clothing, she tried to remember when she last had her period. After thinking about it, she realized she hadn't missed a period. She didn't feel sick. Her body was giving her no indication of pregnancy. Maybe her breasts were getting bigger because she may have gained a little weight. Wishful thinking on Victor's part was what she concluded.

VICTOR

Victor stuffed his hands in the pocket of his slacks and tilted his head at his baby brother. The way he was staring at Bella's sister indicated he was up to no good.

"What's up with that smile, bro?" Victor probed.

"What's up with yours?" Lincoln countered.

"Answering a question with a question? Oh, you're plotting something." Victor chuckled. "Donatella?"

Lincoln grinned with a nod and scratched his beard. "*Man,* look at her."

"I see her. She's gorgeous. I also see the man standing next to her," Victor pointed out.

"He's nobody," Lincoln snorted.

"Whatever, Linc," Victor dismissed while searching the yard for his wife.

Lincoln's shenanigans were of no concern to Victor. His mind was preoccupied with the fact that he was going to be a father. He couldn't have been more pleased. Truth be told, he'd been trying to get Taylor pregnant long before they married. He was overjoyed at the thought of tossing a ball with his son or having a tea party with his little princess. Taylor had given him everything he ever dreamed of.

"What are you boys up to?"

Victor turned toward his mother's voice. Lincoln moved quick to swallow her up in a suffocating hug.

"You're killing my mother," Victor muttered.

Linc was definitely a "mamma's boy." He had been from the very beginning. Although Victor adored his mother, he'd spent more time being groomed by his dad. However, Linc spent most of his time with their mother. It was no wonder why he was an excellent cook and kept an immaculate house. He often said being away from her was the hardest thing about deployment.

"I'm sorry. It's been so long since I've seen this beautiful woman. I've missed you, Mom." He planted a sloppy kiss on her forehead.

"I've missed you too, my love. How long are you here?"

"For a while. I'm not sure how long."

"Where are you staying?"

"At Victor's."

"Wait! What?" Victor jumped in.

Lincoln gave him a lopsided smiled that reminded him of when he was as a little boy. "Oh, I didn't tell you? My bad. Taylor said that I could crash with you guys while I'm in town. She wouldn't hear of me staying in a hotel."

"Hotel? Why can't you stay with Lucas? You hate all the security around me."

Lincoln shrugged. "Don't want to. I want to spend time with my big brother."

"Aww, that's sweet," Tabitha Creed gushed.

Victor glared at his brother. He wasn't buying the "I miss my big brother" bit. But it didn't matter. His family was always welcome in his home. And, if he were being honest, he missed his brother. Because of the upcoming election, life for him had been so hectic that he missed all of his brothers.

"Yeah, sweet," Victor mumbled, feigning irritation.

Once more, Victor did a quick scan of the yard. He was looking for Taylor. Instead of laying eyes on his beloved pregnant wife, his eyes landed on Jeffrey Morgan. He grunted louder than he intended.

His aggravation was no longer feigned when he saw his sister-in-law's bootlicking, ass-kissing fiancé. It was bad enough that he had to put up with the annoying bombardment of praises from Donna's date, the ever so ambitious prosecutor, Zach Barnes.

"What's up, bro?" Linc asked, eyeing him curiously.

"Nothing. Just wanna be you for a day." Victor sighed.

"Oh, good." Linc coughed. "That means I can be you. I can sleep next to that goddess every night." He pointed at Taylor who was having a seemingly rambunctious conversation with Bella and Donna.

"Watch yourself," Victor warned, his eyes still trained on Jeffrey.

In his peripheral, he saw vigorous movement. He turned. It was Gregor, his head of security, Kena, his assistant, and Renee Griffin, his press secretary. Victor folded his arms and waited for news he knew wasn't good.

Gregor said something to Jeffrey that sent him in the other direction as Renee approached.

"What is it, Renee?"

She frowned and reached into her briefcase. "It's the Times."

Victor groaned and waited to read what was sure to be a disturbing headline. Renee pulled the paper from her briefcase and handed it to him. On the front page was a picture of him from Taylor's birthday party in a laughing huddle with Jack Storm and Luca Savelli. The headline read: ANOTHER ILLINOIS GOVERNOR LINKED TO ORGANIZED CRIME.

5

DONATELLA

Donna stood in front of the glass doors looking up at the FBI building. As usual, she'd arrived early. After getting through a ridiculous amount of security, she clipped the visitor's pass onto her t-shirt and headed to a bank of elevators. Minutes later, she was ascending to the seventh floor.

When the doors of the elevator separated, Donna stepped off and right into a mousy brunette with dark-rimmed glasses. Her hair was pulled into a lazy bun and she had a pen tucked behind her ear.

"Detective Devereaux?" she asked in a timid voice.

"Yes."

Donna looked over her wrinkled blue pantsuit and wondered what she looked like off duty. She had a pretty face, but there was no way to tell what her body looked like with the oversized clothing.

"I'm Special Agent Helen Cassidy." She held out her hand as she introduced herself.

As Donna shook the agent's hand, she noticed that she had striking grey eyes. Framed by thick, dark lashes, they seemed to sparkle like silver. She smiled nervously under Donna's scrutiny.

"You're early," she chuckled anxiously.

"Always."

"Good to know. Follow me."

She turned and headed down a hall and Donna fell in step behind her. After a few turns, Agent Cassidy was pressing her ID to a keypad that led to an outer office. Several people were moving about the busy office. The agent spoke to no one as they headed down another hall where, halfway down, she opened a door of the left and entered.

Donna followed her inside and was surprised that several agents were sitting at a rectangular conference table as if they were waiting for her. And she was thirty minutes early.

"Please, have a seat, Detective." Agent Cassidy waved her hand toward a seat just to the left of the head of the table.

Donna sat and got another surprise when the agent sat at the head of the table.

"Everyone, welcome Detective Devereaux. The CPD brass swears that she's one of the best undercover officers in their department, and they've been kind enough to loan her to us."

As mutters of welcome floated around the room, Donna realized that Agent Cassidy wasn't as timid as she had initially assumed. At least, not when she was surrounded by her peers. Her words came out clear and confident. She even seemed taller.

Donna was a people watcher. She studied the mannerisms of everyone she came into contact with. In order to do her job without getting made, she had to pay very close attention to her mark's body language. She had to gauge their mood as well as their temperament. Misreading someone could be a deadly mistake. It was a habit. Occupational, but a habit nonetheless.

Agent Cassidy slid a stack of papers over to Donna. She picked them up and flipped through the first few pages. It was the criminal history of Robert Lee Khal, the leader of a religious commune in Springfield, Illinois, known as The Blood of The Chosen, or BOC.

"Study him. That's your mark," Cassidy informed, handing her a large folder filled with papers.

Donna nodded. That was the easy part. She already started her own research on the charismatic cult leader.

"Study fast. You go under in three days," the agent added.

Donna's eyes jumped from the folder to Cassidy's icy eyes. "Three days? Are you joking?"

Cassidy slowly shook her head. "Unfortunately, it's our only window. Every year the commune conducts a huge membership drive. It's the only time outsiders are welcome in their world."

"It's a religious community, right? What exactly am I looking for?"

"Religious community." Cassidy scoffed, frowning in disgust. "You'll be looking for evidence of polygamy, human trafficking, incest, and illegal firearms. Detective, this is no religious community. This is an army."

Agent Cassidy picked up a glass of water. As she sipped, she pointed to a man with blond, shoulder-length hair and a full beard. He looked more like a surfer than a Fed. She returned the glass to the table and cleared her throat. "This is Kelly, Kelly McClain. He's your handler."

Kelly nodded, but Donna was feeling uneasy. She didn't like working undercover missions without her team. She trusted them. They'd worked together for years and she felt safer knowing they were looking out for her. She had her own partner, Joe Preston. Other than her dad, he was the only man she fully trusted.

"I'd prefer my own partner to be my handler. Can't you have him detailed here?"

"Umm-mm." Cassidy shook her head. "Not gonna happen. Kelly is already on the inside. We don't have time for your partner to work his way in."

Confused, Donna tilted her head and frowned. "How is my handler on the inside? And, if he's already on the inside, why do you need me?"

Cassidy steepled her fingers and smiled. "Detective, this case is a little different from most drug cases. Yes, Kelly is in, but he can only get so close to Robert Lee. But *you*...we believe you can penetrate his circle. Once you study his profile, you'll see why."

She handed Donna another folder. When she opened it, there were reports held together by a paperclip. Clipped to the pages was an Illinois Driver's License with her picture and the name, Kateri Montoya.

∼

TWENTY-MINUTES LATER, Special Agent Cassidy was walking Donna to the elevator. When they arrived, she pushed the button and turned to Donna. Just as the elevator arrived, she said, "This is a *bad* man, Detective, and he's about to do bad things. Read carefully."

Donna nodded and stepped into the elevator. She turned to face the agent and clutched the large packet to her chest. When the doors closed, she leaned against the wall and groaned. Loud.

6

LINCOLN

Lincoln stepped off the elevator and pushed through the double doors of CBI, Creed Brothers, Incorporated. He walked down the cool grey hall, decorated with contemporary light installations, and rounded a corner. "Madeline, how are you gorgeous?" Lincoln flirted.

Madeline, the receptionist, looked up from her desk and pursed her lips. "I am blessed and highly favored, Mr. Creed."

He grinned. "Good to know."

Lincoln loved teasing Lucas' receptionist. Madeline was a no-nonsense, middle-aged, extremely religious African American woman who had been working for the company for over twenty years.

"It's good to see you back in one piece," she offered.

"Thank you, ma'am. He in there?" He walked toward Lucas' office door.

"Yes, but now isn't a good time. Please, sir, have a seat."

Lincoln squinted at the receptionist. She'd never curbed him before. He was always able to walk freely into his brother's office.

He glared at Madeline. Even with her darker skin, he could see a blush crawling her cheeks. Something wasn't right. "Madeline?"

"Trust me, Mr. Creed, you'll wanna have a seat."

"Ooo-kay," Victor acquiesced with a frown.

Lincoln was still curiously eyeing Madeline when he walked over to the waiting area and took a seat. She quickly dismissed him and returned her attention to whatever she was working on. He sat for fifteen minutes before he decided to leave.

Just as he stood, the door to Lucas' office opened. Bella emerged with a disheveled ponytail. Her wrinkled t-shirt was tucked into her jeans and her gun belt was missing a loop. Lincoln chuckled softly as he made his way over to her.

"Hey, Bella. What's up?"

She startled a bit and turned to face him, brandishing the guiltiest of smiles. "Oh, hey, Linc. Does Lucas know you're here?"

Lincoln smirked with a tilt to his head. "I don't think he'd care. Are you on duty, Detective?"

Bella tucked one of many loose strands of hair behind her ear and nodded.

"Well, if I were you," he moved closer, "I'd find a mirror."

Bella recoiled and self-consciously ran her hand over her hair. "Excuse me?" she asked, feigning offense.

"Girl, you got that whole 'post-coital chaos' thing going on."

Bella's face was awash with embarrassment as she turned to see if Madeline was paying attention. She wasn't. Or, she was pretending not to be.

Lincoln pressed his lips together and tried hard not to laugh.

"Shut up, Linc," she scolded in a hushed tone.

Bella turned on her heel and walked away, leaving him standing alone. Lincoln shook his head and chuckled as he entered his brother's office where Lucas was walking out of the bathroom, drying his hands with a towel. When he looked up and noticed Lincoln, he tossed the towel on his desk and smiled.

"Hey, baby brother," he beamed.

Lincoln chuckled and closed the office door. "You're in a good mood."

"I'm having a good day."

"I believe you." Lincoln smirked. "I ran into Bella."

Lucas ignored the comment and walked over to a closet. He pulled his suit coat from a hanger and slipped it on. "You wearing that to dinner?" he asked, appraising Lincoln's attire.

"Yes. What's wrong with what I'm wearing?"

Lincoln was comfortable with his black V-neck and blue jeans. Hell, he had on a jacket.

"Nothing. But we are going to a five-star restaurant."

"And? Look, *you* are the businessman, and Victor is the governor. You actually have to wear those monkey suits. I, on the other hand, am a soldier. I don't have board meetings, and I'm not in the public eye. Therefore, I can wear whatever the hell I want."

Lucas laughed and snatched his keys from his desk. "Oh, little bro." He shook his head. "You own a sizeable percentage of this corporation that you and your brothers leave me to run. So, technically, you are a businessman. And right now, you're not pissing in some desert. It's time to dress the part."

"Fuck you," Lincoln muttered. "Can we go?"

"Yeah." Lucas chuckled. "Victor's meeting us there."

VICTOR

Victor entered the Roundhouse Café surrounded by his security detail. He nodded and waved to a few constituents as he made his way over to the table where his brothers were waiting.

"Nice of you to join us," Lucas jibed between sips.

"Sorry. Got caught up at a budget meeting." Victor unbuttoned his suit jacket and sat. "I see you got started without me."

"Only drinks and appetizers," Lincoln informed. "I ordered you a bourbon on the rocks. It's on the way."

Gregor and the three other men charged with Victor's protection, took a seat at the table next to them. Two more stood by the bar.

"What's the plan?" Lincoln asked, tossing a copy of The Times on the table. "How are we gonna handle this?"

"*We*?" Victor chuckled. "*We* aren't going to do anything about this. I have people that deal with shit like this."

It didn't surprise him that Lincoln was ready to dive right in. He was a problem solver, not at all accustomed to allowing someone else to fight battles he considered his. Victor, on the other hand, had learned to delegate. Renee Griffin, his press secretary and publicist, was nothing if not competent. It was her job to curb the bad press, and she was very good at her job.

"Victor, I would normally agree," Lucas chimed. "But look at this picture. It was taken at Taylor's birthday party. This was a private party—no press, no photographers. One of the guests had to take this picture."

"Exactly," Lincoln agreed. "We have a traitor in the midst."

"I'm aware. It's being handled."

Before either brother could respond, a waiter approached the table and placed a rocks glass filled with ice and brown liquor in front of Victor.

"Thank you."

"It's my pleasure, Governor," the waiter responded, wide-eyed with a big, toothy smile. "I'm honored to serve."

"Oh, please." Lucas scoffed humorously. "Can we order already?"

"Hater," Victor muttered under his breath.

"Yes, sir," the waiter said, pulling a notepad from his apron. "What are you having?"

After placing their dinner order, the waiter hurried away, promising to return with fresh bread. When Victor was finally alone with his brothers, he couldn't help the almost goofy grin that spread across his face.

"What the hell is up with you?" Lucas asked. "You've just been linked to the mafia. Why are you so giddy?"

"Giddy?" Victor frowned. "What am I, a fucking school girl?"

"Today," Lincoln remarked facetiously.

Ignoring his asshole brother's comments, Victor blurted, "Taylor is pregnant."

Lucas and Lincoln turned to each other and shared looks of astonishment. Then they turned back to Victor, both smiling from ear to ear.

Lincoln raised his glass. "Good shit, bro! Congratulations!"

"Yeah, congrats! I'm happy for you guys," Lucas added. "I'm gonna be an uncle."

"Yep. My baby is having my baby," Victor beamed.

He couldn't have been more pleased. To be honest, he'd never thought much about having children. His marriage to his first wife had been a calculated political ploy. Although he cared for Rosemary, he was never motivated to have children with her. Victor wasn't even sure she would have been willing to have children. She was a good person and a great lawyer, but maternal? Not even a little.

"When is Taylor due?" Lucas asked.

"December. We have some time."

"I'm happy for you, bro."

"Thanks. I'm gonna assume that you're next," Victor responded with a grin. "When are you gonna make an honest woman out of Bella?"

Lucas snatched the glass from the table and gulped down a large amount of what Victor assumed was Scotch. His irritation was evident.

"What?" Lincoln asked, confused by his brother's demeanor.

"Not that I'm ready to get married, but even if I was, Bella has made it clear that she's not open to the idea of marriage. She just doesn't trust the institution."

"Because of Dean?" Victor asked.

"Maybe. I'm thinking that after what went down with Dean, she swore off holy matrimony."

Lincoln wrinkled his brow and raked his fingers through his dark beard. "Is that what she said? Or, are you just assuming that's how she feels?"

Lucas shrugged. "We don't talk that much about it, and that's fine for now. We're in a great place."

Victor nodded and sipped from his glass. Lucas and Bella hadn't been together very long. There was no need to rush into marriage. Not that he and Taylor were together long before they married, but every couple was different. He knew from the moment he saw Taylor that he wanted her. And when he had her, he knew he wasn't going to be willing to let her go.

"Take your time, Luc," Lincoln told him, relaying Victor's sentiments. "There's no rush,"

"Exactly," Victor agreed. "Besides, you—"

Before he could complete his sentence, there was a loud boom. The earsplitting sound of an explosion.

Victor covered his ears and looked around to see where the noise had originated, but the only thing he could see was Gregor's six-foot-six, three-hundred-and-fifteen-pound body flying toward him like Brian Urlacher.

In seconds, he had him tackled to the floor and pulled under the table. Gregor was shouting orders to his security detail, but Victor couldn't hear a thing over the frantic screaming coming from the restaurant patrons. From underneath Gregor, he could see Lincoln pull a firearm from the back of his pants while yanking Lucas behind him.

Victor shoved Gregor. "Get the fuck off me!" he gritted through his teeth.

He knew the man was just doing his job, but there was no way he was about to cower under a fucking table while his little brother stood in his defense.

Gregor resisted but Victor was no weakling. He was able to move his bodyguard enough to free himself. He got to his knees and pulled his own weapon from its holster. Since being stalked by an assassin, he never went anywhere without his .45 pistol.

He stood and scanned the room for the threat, but all he saw was hysterical patrons fleeing the restaurant.

"Governor, please let me do my job," Gregor implored.

"Take care of Lucas," Victor ordered.

"That's not my job," Gregor calmly refused.

Victor glared at him, ready to give him a direct order. After all, Lucas was the only one of them that was unarmed. Or so he thought. After looking his brother over, he noticed the gun in his hand. Seconds later, Jagger Barr, the bodyguard positioned at the bar, was running toward them.

"Boss!" he called out breathlessly. He was speaking to Gregor. "It wasn't a bomb."

Out of habit, Gregor stepped in front of Victor. "What?"

"It wasn't a bomb."

"Then what the fuck was it?" Gregor questioned.

"M-80," Lincoln offered.

"Yeah," Jagger confirmed.

"M-80? Are you serious?" Victor asked.

Lincoln nodded. "Yeah, if detonated indoors, it sounds just like a bomb."

Victor didn't question Lincoln's explanation. He was very familiar with all things incendiary.

"What the hell? Kids?" Lucas asked. "Did anyone see who did it?"

Jagger shook his head. "No. Someone just tossed it through the door. We'll pull security tapes once we secure the governor."

"Was anyone hurt?" Victor asked, concerned about the stampede of bodies struggling to get out of the restaurant.

"No. Nothing serious, sir. Let's get you out of here."

Unable to figure out why someone would throw or leave an explosive device more so meant to make noise in a restaurant, Victor turned to Lincoln and Lucas with furrowed brows. "What the hell was that all about?"

They both shrugged. Since no one was hurt, Victor could only assume that it wasn't a terrorist attack.

"Are you riding with me?" he asked.

"Hell, no." Lincoln chuckled. "Folks are throwing bombs at your ass. I'm riding with Luc."

"Fuck off! That shit might have been for you, GI Joe. ISIS might have followed your ass back to the US."

"Victor," Lucas interjected. "We'll meet you at the penthouse."

Victor agreed and allowed Gregor and his security detail to escort him out of the restaurant. Once secured inside the vehicle, Jagger sat in the driver's seat and Gregor slid in the backseat next to him. He was glaring angrily at Victor when he asked, "Why the hell do you even keep me around?"

"Your sparkling personality," Victor muttered, fastening his seatbelt.

7

DONATELLA

FBI Special Agent Kelly McClain threw his arm over Donna's shoulder and leaned into her. What looked like intimate whisperings in her ear was really intel on each member that crossed their path.

Together, they made their way across the large, crowded field until they were close to the main stage where a band was playing upbeat, sacred music. Hundreds of people wearing loose-fitting clothing were praise dancing and singing along with the band. As she looked around at the smiling faces, it all seemed sickeningly Stepford. Almost nauseating. She'd smiled so much since the hour and a half she'd arrived; her face was beginning to hurt.

"Here is good," Kelly said, dropping his backpack to the grass. He removed the small blanket that he had thrown over his shoulder and spread it across the grass. "You're in the perfect position to be seen. He'll definitely notice your fine ass."

Donna frowned and placed her purse on the blanket. Apparently, their entire case rested on whether or not Robert Lee took notice of her and invited her into the fold. In order to make that happen, she wore a tight crop top that showed her pierced belly and a long, flowing, hippie skirt. The packet had indicated that

Robert Lee was fascinated, almost obsessed, with Native America and Native American women, or women that look Native American.

Kelly sat on the blanket and began to clap and sing along. He raised a brow at Donna, encouraging her to play her role. On cue, she started waving her arms and swaying with the music as if she was having the same spiritual experience as the rest of the believers. When she felt a hand on her shoulder, she stopped dancing and turned around. In front of her was a young woman, maybe in her late twenties. Her blonde hair with green streaks was pulled into a messy ponytail. She was pretty, but it was hard to see behind the dark eye makeup and heavy foundation.

"Here you are, hon," she said with a big smile.

She held out a tambourine. Donna looked at the instrument. Not knowing how to play it, reluctantly, she accepted it.

"Thank you."

The woman must have gauged her reaction because she held up another tambourine and began to demonstrate how to play, tapping it against her hand to the beat of the drums.

"It's easy," she assured. "Try it."

Donna smiled and mimicked her actions. Once she had the hang of it, she and the woman turned toward the stage and created their own music with the metal jingles. They danced joyfully, clapping the tambourine until the music gradually tapered off.

"I'm Vera, Vera Holt," the younger woman introduced with her and held out.

Donna accepted her hand. "Kateri Montoya. Nice to meet you." She turned to Kelly, who was stretched out on the blanket. "This is my boyfriend, Cameron."

"I know Cam." Vera giggled childishly. "Everybody knows Cam."

"Is that right?" Donna asked with a raised eyebrow, playing the jealous girlfriend.

"Oh, it's nothing like that," Vera assured with a nervous smile. "He...well, he's a perfect gentleman. It's just...well, he's very handsome."

A deep blush covered the woman's face. She appeared uncomfortable and a bit embarrassed.

"Aww, he's alright." Donna chuckled, trying to ease the woman's discomfort. "Since nobody's actually from Springfield, where are you from?"

"True." Vera grinned. "I'm from the Bay area. You?"

"I'm from St. Louis."

Kateri Montoya, half black/half Native Americana from a St. Louis ghetto was her covert identity. She'd been a waitress in a rowdy strip club in a shitty part of town, and Cameron was her on again, off again drifter boyfriend who'd fled to find the meaning of life. He eventually found The Blood of The Chosen. Supposedly, it was a profound and enlightening experience. So, he eventually convinced her to quit her job and follow him to salvation.

"Welcome, brothers and sisters," resonated from various speakers placed throughout the park. "This is the day the Lord has made; we will rejoice and be glad in it."

"Amen," the crowd choired.

Donna looked toward the stage. Behind a microphone was a forty-something man with dark brown hair and thick, horn-rimmed glasses. He was thin and fairly tall. Kind of a geek. To her, he seemed the type to easily be swayed into worshiping a better looking, more magnetic man as a god. It was probably his only way of being part of the "in crowd."

"Brothers, sisters, you are among the blessed. You are among a privileged few to have witnessed the return of the Messiah."

Amidst the crowd's harmonious accords and the jingle of several tambourines, the announcer continued.

"Behold...*The Prophet*."

Roaring cheers and thunderous applause caused Donna's brows to wrinkle. She turned and studied the crowd with disbelief. When she turned to look at Kelly, he was jumping up and down, throwing his fist in the air, and screaming, "*Yes!*" at the top of his lungs.

Donna stared at him, wondering if he had been drinking the proverbial Kool-Aid. However, to her relief, his gaze landed on her for a split second before nudging her to play along. So, she did. She joined the cheering followers and furiously slapped the tambourine to her hand.

The nerd backed away from the microphone just as Robert Lee Khal stepped into view. *He,* on the other hand, was very easy on the eyes. He had thick, wavy blonde hair that bounced when he moved. He was tall and strategically dressed in a tight, button-down shirt. No doubt to show off the fact that he was physically fit.

"Good afternoon, my children," he said into the microphone.

It was easy to understand how he was able to hypnotize the gullible. His deep, rich baritone was nothing if not alluring. Donna sighed when Lincoln immediately invaded her thoughts. He too had a voice that could lure like the Pied Piper.

"It says in 1 Peter 5:14 that we should greet one another with the kiss of love. Let us obey."

When the audience began to kiss each other freely on the lips, even men with men, Donna moved closer to Kelly. She tucked her face into his chest and felt the rumble of his laughter.

She glared up at him with narrowed eyes. "What you laughing at? You kissing these dudes?'"

"Naw." He chuckled. "This ain't my first rodeo. Take a look around. I'm surrounded by women."

Donna looked around. Sure enough, in front, behind, and on each side of Kelly was a woman.

He winked and pulled her close. Before she could resist, he kissed her on the lips. She didn't put up a fight. Even though she didn't really know him, she figured kissing Kelly would be better than kissing some random man.

She closed her eyes and fantasized about the last time she'd shared a kiss with Lincoln. Of course, she didn't feel the same spark, but at least Kelly held the kiss long enough for the kissing session to be over.

When they heard clapping, she and Kelly separated. She quickly looked to the stage when she noticed his lingering gaze.

"Hear me!" the preacher shouted. "God said that he should send his one begotten son to lead the wild into the ways of the man. Follow me! Eat my flesh, flesh of my flesh."

"This muthafucka," Donna scoffed. She moved close to Kelly in order to whisper, "This motherfucker ain't Christ born again. He's fucking Tupac."

Kelly chuckled and nudged her with his elbow. Apparently, they were the only two, in a crowd of hundreds, who noticed that their messiah was quoting lyrics from *Hail Mary*. The whole preacher bit was a crock of shit. Nonetheless, she had a job to do, so she copied the young blonde by clapping enthusiastically while jumping up and down.

Sadly, Donna had to suffer through three hours of faking jubilance while listening to a snake charmer butcher Bible verses before she was able to capture his attention. After ending his sermon with a closing prayer, Robert Lee looked up and locked eyes with Donna. His gaze quickly roamed from her head to her toe, bathing her with a feeling of disgust. For sure, he was undressing her with his eyes. Apparently, Kelly noticed as well.

He leaned over and whispered, "Looks like you're in."

8
VICTOR

"Good morning, Governor," Kena greeted as Victor entered the outer office. She was standing in front of his office door carrying a pile of papers that she must have been getting ready to put on his desk.

"Kenyatta," Victor muttered, a little grumpier than intended.

"Good morning, Governor," she repeated as if expecting a better greeting.

Victor smiled. "I'm sorry, Kena. I didn't get much sleep last night. Good morning."

It seemed as soon as Taylor's pregnancy was confirmed, the all too frequent vomiting spells started. Someone needed to change the term "morning sickness" to all-day-and-all-night sickness. Taylor's bouts with nausea didn't follow a specific schedule. She had suffered a night full of sickness and urgent trips to the bathroom. Yet, she was able to get up, get herself together and, despite his objections, go to work.

"Governor, is everything okay?"

"Yep. Just a bit tired. No biggie. What's my day looking like?"

"Busy. You have a meeting with the Illinois Police Union president at 10 AM. At 11:30, you're speaking at a brunch hosted by Wives of Fallen Officers, and you're expected at campaign headquarters by two. After that, you're back here for a staff meeting at four."

"Damn," Victor murmured. "Anything else?"

"Yep. Renee is in your office."

Victor looked at his watch. It was just after 7 AM. Since he'd hired Renee as his press secretary, she'd never beat him to his office in the morning.

"This can't be good."

Kena nodded in agreement.

"Shall we?" She nodded toward his office.

Victor held the door open and followed her inside. Renee was sitting at his conference table going over her own pile of papers.

She pulled her reading glasses from her face and looked up.

"Morning, Governor."

Concern was etched across her face.

"Good morning, Renee. What's up?" he asked on the way to his closet.

After hanging his suit jacket, he walked around his desk and took a seat. Judging by her demeanor, he felt he wanted to be seated for whatever bomb she was about to drop.

Renee fished something from a folder, walked toward him, and placed it on his desk. It was a photo.

Victor picked it up and squinted, looking closer. It was a picture of him and his brothers in the restaurant. He and Lincoln were both pointing guns. Behind Victor, Gregor was crouched down wearing a scowl while reaching for him. In the background, he could see a few frightened patrons. On the photo, written in red marker, was: MOB HIT ON GOVERNOR?

"Fuck me!" Victor swore.

It was the second photo that alleged he was involved in organized crime.

"Who the fuck is doing this?" he asked, more to himself.

Renee stuffed her hands in the pocket of her slacks and shook her head. "I don't know, Governor Creed. But I promise you that I'll find out. I've got a few meetings with some media insiders. I'll find out something. In the meantime," she pulled the picture from his fingers, "I've already squashed this with the papers."

"Good." Victor sighed.

Unfortunately, his relief was short-lived.

"However, I can't stop whoever is disseminating this BS from posting it online, but I'll cross that bridge when I get to it."

"Thanks, Renee. Say, do you have plans Friday night? Taylor and I are having a dinner party at the penthouse to celebrate Gregor's birthday."

Renee's brow rose as if she was surprised by the invitation. "Really?"

"Yes, really. What?"

"You're having a fancy dinner party for your security guard?"

"Head of security," Victor corrected. "And I may not be his favorite person at the moment, but he and Taylor have bonded."

"I see." Renee giggled. "I got no plans. I'll be there."

"Perfect. Come casual. Dinner's at eight. Feel free to bring a plus one."

"Plus one? Please." She snorted. "As busy as you keep me, I might as well be married to you."

Victor laughed. Unfortunately, she was right. Lately, a good scandal was always just around the corner.

"Kena says the same thing. You exaggerate."

"Hmph! If you say so, Governor."

When she walked over to the conference table and gathered her paperwork, Victor silently approved of her sleek, blue business suit. Her dark skin was smooth and creamy, and she had a figure that was curvy and feminine. Victor concluded that it had to be her job that kept her from finding love. He made a mental note to insist that she take a vacation.

"Don't forget that you have a photo shoot at 5:30," she reminded.

"Ugh!" He had forgotten. As a matter of fact, he'd forgotten just how hard it was to run a campaign, now even harder since he was already in office. Together, his run for re-election and his gubernatorial obligations were running him ragged.

"Where is it?"

"Here. Kena and I have put together a wardrobe, including your wife's favorite tie and hanky combo."

Victor smiled at the mention of Taylor. She made him feel like a giddy, teenage boy, excited to be with a girl for the first time. However, he tried to play it cool when he asked, "Will she be there?"

"Yes, sir," Renee responded with a smile that let him know that he hadn't, in fact, played it cool. "She'll be there."

When she left, closing the door behind her, Victor pulled his phone from his pocket. He pushed a button to speed dial and waited for an answer.

"Creed."

Victor rubbed his temple. He could feel a headache coming. "Linc, we're all Creeds."

"Yes, but I'm the only Creed with the phone number. What do you want?"

"That shit at the restaurant was a set-up. Can you meet today?"

"Not today. I'm on a mission."

Victor knew all too well what that meant for the Army Ranger.

"When will you be back?"

"I have no way of knowing."

"Well, be careful, little bro."

"Will do."

"I'll check back and forth with Mom."

No matter what country, jungle, or sandstorm Lincoln was in, he always managed to call their mother, if not every day, then every other day. Although the family worried a great deal about Lincoln and his chosen profession, they'd gotten accustomed to him leaving to places unknown for long periods of time.

Victor pushed a button to end the call and dialed another number. He groaned when Lucas answered with, "Creed."

9

TAYLOR

"How many?" Taylor asked, leaning against a wall in the hallway.

She and Gloria, the District Manager, were discussing the number of graduating recruits that were to be assigned to her district. As the commander's secretary, it was her job to place them.

"Seven," she responded with a huff. "Seven fresh out of the academy, wet behind the ears, know every damn thing, thirsty ass rookies just for us."

Taylor laughed. "Damn, girl. Why so mad?"

"Please," Gloria scoffed. "You know why. When you were on the street, didn't you have to work with 'em?"

"Hell, at some point, I was one of them. We all had to learn and the only way to learn was to work the beat."

"Hmph...whatever," Gloria responded with an unflattering lip purse.

In Taylor's opinion, it took a lot of nerve for Gloria to criticize. She was a civilian. She'd never made the decision to risk her life on a daily basis in order to make the streets a safer place. Her entire career was spent behind a desk, criticizing police officers. Taylor knew all too well that the department couldn't function without its civilian workforce. However, that didn't give them the right to shit on hardworking cops.

"Why are you so worried?" she asked. "You don't have to work with 'em."

Gloria's lips parted as if she was about to respond, but she quickly pressed them back together. Maybe she'd sensed Taylor's annoyance with her negative attitude. But then her eyes widened, and she looked beyond her.

Taylor turned around and peered down the hall. Her heart fluttered when she saw her gorgeous husband taking powerful and purposeful strides toward her, wearing a navy-blue pinstriped suit and a crisp white shirt. Of course, he was surrounded by his security detail, headed by Gregor.

He smiled as he approached, showing off perfect white teeth and cratered dimples just above a strong, masculine jawline.

Taylor frowned. It wasn't like Victor to show up at her job in the middle of the day. She instantly began to worry that something bad had happened.

But since he was still smiling when he snaked an arm around her waist, she relaxed a bit.

"Hey, sweet thang," he whispered in a deep sexy voice, pulling her close.

He held her protectively and tight and kissed the top of her head. Judging by his behavior, something was definitely on his mind. Work or not, she wrapped her arms around his waist and inhaled the fresh, manly scent of mint and sandalwood.

"Honey, what are you doing here?" she whispered against his chest. "What's happened?"

He gripped her shoulders and took a step back. Taylor looked up and gazed into his intense emerald greens. Despite the smile on his beautiful face, she could see conflict swimming in his expressive eyes. She'd read The Times. She had a pretty good idea what was bothering him, but she didn't want to be the one to bring it up.

"Everything is fine, sweetheart. I had a meeting nearby and I wanted to see my lady."

"Must be nice." Gloria muttered, sarcastically. Taylor had completely forgotten her negative ass was still there.

She turned without actually facing her. "Yep," Taylor dryly affirmed. "Very nice. I'll catch you in a minute."

Gloria eyed Victor up and down before slithering to her office.

"Who's your friend?" Victor asked.

"That's Gloria. I wouldn't call her a friend. She's the District Manager here. But...are you okay?'

Victor smiled again, showing off his sweet dimples. "Yes, ma'am. I'm fine, just missing my beautiful wife. How are you feeling? Did you eat?'

Taylor smiled and rubbed his back. "Yes, love. I've eaten, and I'm feeling just fine."

"Good to hear."

He turned and nodded at one of his guards. The officer stepped forward and handed her a basket.

"I picked up some pomegranates. The doctor said that they're good for morning sickness."

Taylor happily accepted the basket. "Thanks, babe. I love pomegranates. But really, I'm feeling pretty good. As a matter of fact, it's almost time for lunch. Wanna grab something?"

"Oh, I can't, sweetness. My schedule is a wreck today. But I will see you at my photoshoot later, right?"

"Yes, sir." Taylor nodded. "I'll be there. Now, if you don't have time to feed me, get your goons outta here. People are staring."

"What people? Fuck them." Victor scoffed, looking around. A small band of blue uniforms had gathered down the hall. "The *only* person I see is you."

"Go, sweetheart." Taylor grinned. "Start chipping away at that crazy schedule of yours. I'll see you at your office later."

Victor placed his large hand to the small of her back and pulled her closer to his solid frame. He kissed her forehead and then used his finger to raise her chin enough for her lips to reach his. After a slow, sweet kiss, he pulled his lips from hers and gazed into her eyes.

"I love you, lady," he confirmed with an alluring baritone.

"And, I love you."

Victor took a step back and gifted her with a full-dimpled smile that made her heart flutter.

"Have a good day, babe. Be safe."

"Yeah, I'll try not to get a paper cut," Taylor joked.

∽

TAYLOR WAS UPDATING crime stats for the district when Commander Evans emerged from his office.

"You ready to take a ride?" he asked with a smile.

"Let's do it."

Taylor saved her work and signed out of her computer. She walked over to her filing cabinet, grabbed a couple of radios and her Kevlar vest, and glanced over at his crisp white shirt. "Where's your vest?"

"It's in the trunk." He tossed her a set of keys.

As usual, at the end of the shift, Commander Evans would go on patrol as a street supervisor, oftentimes providing backup to his beat officers. As his secretary, Taylor's duties also included being his personal driver.

As they walked the halls of the 26th District, Taylor had to endure a number of fake ass greetings from officers and supervisors who were only so eagerly polite in the commander's presence.

After exiting the back door of the station, they walked over to his designated parking spot. When Taylor unlocked the doors, he slid into the passenger seat. She popped the trunk and grabbed his bulletproof vest before hopping into the driver's seat.

"Forget something, Boss Man?" she asked with a raised brow.

He didn't answer, only smiled. She was constantly reminding him to wear his vest. As a boss, he didn't spend much time patrolling the streets. It was common for a person who'd mostly been confined to a desk to become lax. But not Taylor. She had seen entirely too much to assume that shit wouldn't go up like a Roman candle in a matter of seconds.

Commander Evans slipped the vest over his head, connected the Velcro at his sides, and looked over at Taylor with a wry smirk. "Can we go now, Boss?" he asked sarcastically.

Taylor nodded and started the engine. No sooner had she backed out of the parking spot, the dispatcher assigned a burglar alarm to one of the beat units.

"Let's take a ride on this call," the commander instructed.

Taylor nodded and headed toward the location which was only about five minutes away. She reached for the radio on her shoulder and keyed in.

"Squad, show 2600 taking a ride on that burglar alarm."

"10-4, 2600. I got ya going."

That was Taylor's way of warning her fellow officers that their boss was on the street and he would be observing them on their job. Her boss was no fool. She suspected he knew exactly what she was doing. After all, he had been a beat cop once.

"So...how's your sister?"

Taylor laughed, ignoring him as she took a left. Ever since he'd met her sister at a fundraiser for the Boys and Girls Club, he didn't even try to hide his attraction.

"Well?" he prompted. "How's your sister?"

"Engaged," Taylor reminded.

"She can do better," he muttered under his breath.

Taylor couldn't agree more. Jeffrey Morgan, the Chicago Water Commissioner, wasn't her favorite person. She couldn't quite put her finger on it, but she felt uncomfortable whenever he was around. Something about him read dirt bag. However, since she had no proof of any wrongdoing, she never shared her feelings about her sister's fiancé. Yet, it was obvious, especially when Victor was present that Jeffrey was a thirsty, overly-ambitious, kiss ass. Nicole would have to be Hellen Keller not to notice.

The more Taylor thought about Commander Evans' interest in Nicole, the more she thought he'd make a far better match for her than Jeffrey. He was young, handsome, single, and successful. Well-liked by the powers that be, and he was still on his way up the ladder.

Taylor could very well see him as superintendent in a few short years. Maybe she would invite him to more events where Nicole would be present.

"Up here on the right." He pointed to a house with a squad car in front. "Go around to the alley. We'll check out the back."

Taylor nodded, reached for her shoulder strap, and spoke into the radio. "2600," she announced.

"Go ahead, 2600," the dispatcher responded.

"Who caught the burglar alarm on Wentworth?"

"2632 is responding."

"10-4, Squad. Let 'em know we're coming up the rear."

"10-4, 2600. 2632," the dispatcher confirmed. "2632, did you copy? Take caution. 2600 in the rear of the property."

"10-4. Copy, Squad."

After a quick search of the property and a brief conversation with the owners of the house, Taylor and the commander were on their way.

"Commander?"

"Taylor, why don't you call me Bob? We've been working together for a while now. Why so formal?"

Taylor laughed out loud, causing the commander to look at her like she was a crazy woman.

"What's so funny?" he asked with a frown.

"Your name is Bob Evans!" Taylor blurted. "Every time I say it, I get hungry."

"Haha, Officer. Commander Evans is just fine," he dismissed with a pout.

After her short fit of laughter, she calmed and looked over at her commander. "No, but seriously, *Bob*. Do you have plans for Fridays? Victor and I are having a dinner party for a friend."

"Whaaaat? Dinner with the governor? Ain't I the lucky one?"

"Ummm, forget the governor. You, sir, will be enjoying the privilege of tasting my famous lasagna."

"You still cook?" he asked curiously.

Taylor looked over at him to see if he was serious. It seemed as though he was.

"Yeah, I still cook. Why does that surprise you? I still work," she pointed out.

"I guess," he mumbled. "I don't see why, though. You clearly don't have to. Your husband is rich, and I'm sure you have cooks and maids."

"Where we actually live, we have *one* housekeeper and *one* chef, but Victor and I do a lot of our own cooking and cleaning."

"Mm-hm," he doubted with pursed lips.

"For real!" Taylor insisted through laughter. "I kid you not."

"I'll just bet you—"

The commander's words were stifled by the dispatcher's voice. "2612?"

A female voice responded to the dispatcher's call. "2612."

"Stand for the final cast...units in 26, and units on the citywide, there's a call of shots fired at 10659 South Halsted Street. Anonymous caller says that they heard seven to eight shots coming from the currency exchange. Caller states that one offender fled from that location, a male, white, about six feet, wearing a blue jacket, blue jeans, and a black baseball cap. The offender fled eastbound on foot from Halsted. No further information in the 26th district, Zone 15. Radio is clear."

"Show 2612 en route, Squad," the female officer responded.

"10-4, 2612."

"2610 en route," a male voice chimed.

"10-4, Sarge."

"2622, hold me down for the assist," a familiar female voice added.

Recognizing her best-friend Maria's voice and her beat number, Taylor didn't wait for the commander's instructions. Without hesitation, she hit the MARS lights and flipped on the siren. She drove as fast as she could to the scene. Maria had been shot while on duty before, but Taylor had taken off that day. So, secretary or not, she would be there to have her friend's back.

Commander Evans reached for his own radio. "2600," he called.

"Go, Boss," the dispatcher responded.

"En route to the shots fired."

"10-4. Gotcha going."

Taylor turned the corner and proceeded down Halsted. She was three blocks away when she heard someone on the radio shouting. "Emergency!"

"Standby, everybody! Who called for the emergency?" the dispatcher asked urgently.

"2612! Foot chase!"

"Where ya at, 12?"

"Southbound. On... on Emerald... from... 108th." The officer's breathing was labored as he ran, but he continued. "Male white, long hair..." The officer took a breath. "Blue hoodie...gun!"

"2622, coming up Emerald, Squad!" Maria shouted.

Taylor's heart was racing as they turned the corner on 109th. She slowed to a creep so she and the commander could have a look around. They were searching for the officers in pursuit of the armed offender. As they crept down the side street, the radio went eerily silent. She fought a panic attack when she couldn't locate Maria or the other officers.

"There!" the commander blurted.

Before Taylor could see what he was talking about, or even come to a complete stop, her boss had jumped out of the car and fled down the alley.

"Commander, wait! Commander!"

Either he didn't hear her, or he was ignoring her.

Taylor slapped the gear shift into park and hopped out of the still running squad car. She keyed the radio. "Squad, 2600 is in foot pursuit. He's running southbound through the east alley of 109th Street."

"2612, Squad let 2600 know I'm coming from the other end."

"Copy, 2600?" the dispatcher asked.

Taylor waited, hoping that Commander Evans would respond. When he didn't, she did.

"Does anyone have eyes on the commander?"

When no one responded, Taylor pulled her weapon from the holster, keeping it ready to fire as she ran down the alley in pursuit of her boss. She wasn't halfway down the alley when she heard shots fired, about five. She slowed and jogged along the garages, using them as shields. She passed a garbage can, and that was when they came into view.

Both her commander and the offender were pointing guns at each other, but it was her commander that fell to the ground.

Taylor fired, striking the assailant, but he didn't fall. Instead, he grabbed his shoulder with one hand and pointed his weapon at her commander's head with the other.

"*No!*" Taylor screamed, running toward him, firing her weapon.

She was hitting the offender center mass. When his body jerked, but he remained on his feet, she realized that he was also wearing a bulletproof vest.

He fired, shooting her commander in the head. Taylor gasped and fell to her knees. She fired a round and hit the offender in the neck, but that didn't stop him from raising his weapon to her. When she pulled the trigger again, her weapon went into slide lock.

She was out of ammo.

The ruthless assailant smiled and fired another bullet into Commander Evans. Taylor could hear sirens over the radio, the frantic transmission of other responders. Unfortunately, there were none in sight. If she was going to survive, she would have to save herself.

She pulled a fresh magazine from the pouch on her gun belt and dropped the empty magazine to the ground. With an almost unnatural speed, she stuffed the full magazine in the weapon and racked the slide. Taylor aimed and fired, just as the offender was firing at her. All of a sudden, she was stung by what felt like a jolt of hot lightning piercing her left shoulder. The pain was familiar. She'd been shot before.

Taylor cried out in agony and lurched backward before stumbling to the ground. She could hear the footsteps of the shooter approach. Thankfully, she was right-handed. She mustered every bit of energy she had to raise her right hand and fire a bullet into the offender's cheek.

He still didn't fall. It was like a goddamned zombie apocalypse.

What would it take to drop his ass? The motherfucker was inhuman. Or, so she thought until he was hit by a volley of bullets. He took so many rounds that pieces of his head spattered unto Taylor's face. Even then, it took about five long seconds for him to fall.

"Tay! Tay, are you okay?"

Taylor finally exhaled at the sound of Maria's voice. But she needed to make sure the shooter was really down.

She raised her head just enough to see the brain matter that decorated the alley's dirty pavement.

Taylor winced when Maria pressed her palm to her wound.

"You're okay," Maria promised. "You're okay." She yelled in the radio while adding pressure to the wound. "Squad, roll fire! We got an officer down."

Officer down? Commander Evans!

Taylor struggled to raise up, but Maria held her down.

"What are you doing? Wait for the ambulance."

"Commander Evans?" came out in a whisper.

Just saying his name out loud left her with a feeling of dread. Even if she hadn't seen him take a bullet to the head, the sadness in Maria's eyes was confirmation that he was gone.

Her breathing increased erratically as blinding tears pooled in Taylor's eyes. "Oh God, no."

10

VICTOR

All the extra bodies buzzing around his office was beginning to get under Victor's skin. He was more than ready to be done with his photo shoot. As a matter of fact, he was more than ready for a conclusion to the entire campaign. As far as Victor was concerned, November 6th couldn't come soon enough.

"Kenyatta," he shouted over the babble.

She looked up, and instead of talking over the other voices, she crossed the office. "Sir?"

"Has Taylor called? She was supposed to be here forty-five minutes ago."

"No, sir. Maybe she got caught up at work. I'll put in a call."

"Thank you."

Victor managed to tolerate the photographer, the stylist, and their assistants for fifteen more minutes before he was on the verge of completely losing his patience. Kena blew into his office just as he was about to, less than politely, ask everyone to leave.

"Everybody out!" Kena ordered.

"What?" the photographer shrieked. "We're all set to go."

"Get! Out! Now!" she shouted.

Without any more words, folks were tripping over each other as they scrambled out of the office. Victor had never heard Kena's raised voice. Hell, even he was tempted to leave.

Once everyone was on the other side of the door, she closed it gently and slowly turned to face him.

"Governor, Superintendent O'Conner called." Her solemn tone gave him pause.

"And? What did he want?"

"It's Taylor, sir."

Victor's heart nearly stopped. He rose to his feet but held on tight to the edge of his desk. If Kena was about to tell him that he'd lost his wife, he would surely die where he stood.

"What about Taylor?" he asked in a shaky voice.

"First, she's okay."

Victor heard her words, but her demeanor was still a concern. "Oh, God. Is it the baby?"

"*Baby?*"

"Kena! What the fuck did the superintendent say?!" Victor snapped.

"S-sorry," she said, blinking back to the reason she was there. "She's been shot."

"What?!" Victor roared. "She works at a desk! How did she get shot?"

"I'm not sure. It was some kind of robbery."

"Did they rob the fucking police station?! What did he say?!"

He could tell she was flustered, but he needed her to be clear.

"All he said was that she got shot during a robbery, but she's okay."

Victor was confused as to how his pregnant wife, who worked as the secretary to the commander, got shot during a robbery. But he wasn't going to get answers talking to Kena.

"What hospital?!" he shouted as he ran out of the room. Kena ran out behind him. Not surprisingly, Gregor was waiting for him just outside his office. Victor turned to Kena for an answer.

"She's at Northwestern. I already called your driver. The car is waiting downstairs."

"Call the hospital. I want an update by the time I get to the car," Victor ordered.

"I'll call from the car. I'm coming with you."

Victor didn't argue. Having Kena close by in an emergency had always proven advantageous. Instead, he dialed Taylor's parents. He didn't want them finding out what happened to their daughter on the news.

∼

It was like déjà vu when Victor rushed through the sliding doors of the emergency room. It was like a horrible reoccurring nightmare when he approached the desk. Only, this time, he didn't have to say a word. Every employee behind the desk knew exactly why he was there and who he was there to see.

Just like before, the place was filled with cops. More cops than patients. The chatter from their radios filled the emergency room with loud, white noise. Victor ignored the huddle of higher-ups, including Superintendent O'Conner, and focused on the people behind the desk.

"This way, Governor," said a woman that appeared in the hall.

With Kena, Gregor, and his security detail in tow, Victor followed her down a hall.

"You are?" Victor asked.

"I'm Dr. Suzanne Greer. I'm treating your wife."

"And?"

"And…your wife is resting comfortably." She looked over at his entourage, spoke softly. "Should we speak in private?"

Victor shook his head. "Won't be necessary."

There was no point in keeping secrets from Gregor or Kena. Other than Taylor, they were the only people he saw damn near every single day of his life.

"Well, Sir, it's like I said. Officer Creed is recovering well."

It irked him to no end to hear the doctor refer to his wife as

Officer Creed. With a passion, he hated her fucking job. Whether she liked it or not, she was done.

"Go on," Victor urged in a harsher tone than he intended.

"She was shot once in the shoulder. Thankfully, it was a through and through, no damage to any major arteries or organs. However, Sir, since your wife is pregnant, I was more concerned with the trauma from two shots that she took in the vest. Even though the vest stopped the bullets, the impact could be equivalent to a car accident."

"But Taylor is okay, right?"

As excited as he'd been when he'd found out that Taylor was carrying his child, at that very moment, the only thing that mattered to him was the well-being of his wife. Right or wrong, if given a choice between her and having a baby, he would choose her every day of the week.

"So far, everything looks good. I'm very optimistic," she encouraged with a smile.

For the what seemed like the first time since he found out Taylor had been shot...*again*...Victor was able to exhale.

"Thank you, Dr. Greer."

"There's no need to thank me. Your wife is strong. However, I'm going to keep her here overnight so we can monitor the baby."

Victor nodded and turned to Kena. "Find O'Conner. Get details."

Kena smiled and placed her hand on Victor's shoulder. "Congratulations, Sir. I am so happy for you and Taylor." Her voice was soft, and her words were sincere.

Victor placed his hand over hers and gave it a gentle squeeze. "Thank you," he responded in a whisper. "Now, go."

"On it." She softly chuckled before hurrying away.

Victor returned his attention to the doctor. "I'd like to see her."

"Of course, Governor. Right this way."

She led him to a room at the end of the hall and gestured toward a closed door.

"Your wife has a private room," the doctor stated proudly.

Victor tilted his head at the doctor. Of course, his wife had a private room. Would they have housed her in a ward? Was there a ward for First Ladies of Illinois-slash-cops that got shot in the line of duty?

Dr. Greer cleared her throat as if embarrassed. "I'll give you some time, Governor."

"Thank you, Doctor."

Once the doctor walked away, Gregor stepped closer. "I've rearranged your security detail, Sir. Please tell Taylor I will be right out here at all times."

It wasn't at all like Gregor to forego a duty that he took so seriously to a subordinate.

Victor grinned and slapped his bulky shoulder. "I'll let her know she's in good hands."

Gregor nodded, folded his massive arms across his chest, and pressed his back against the wall next to the door to Taylor's hospital room.

Victor entered the room. Since it was just reaching dusk, the setting sun released rays of orange into Taylor's room. She was curled into a ball so, when he approached the bed, he thought she was sleeping. But her weak, broken voice, calling his name let him know that she wasn't.

He rested his hand gently on her hip. "Hey, sweetheart. How are you feeling?"

"I-I'm okay," she whimpered.

Her tone was alarming. The last time she was shot, she'd been frightened but angry. Now, all Victor heard in her tone was sadness.

She slowly rolled over on her back. The anguish in her expression was painful. If he could, Victor would've pulled her close and held her tight until she felt better. Since he didn't know the level of physical pain she was experiencing, he needed to be as gentle as possible.

He leaned over and ran his thumb across her hairline.

"Commander Evans," Taylor whispered.

"I know, honey. I heard."

With fresh tears pooling in her eyes, Taylor shook her head

dramatically while sobbing. "H-he shot him right in the head. Right in front of me."

Victor's heart ached for his wife. She was hurting. And when Taylor hurt, he hurt.

He leaned over the bed, careful not to cause her more pain, and covered her with his love and protection. She clutched his arm and allowed herself a good cry.

"I'm so sorry," Victor repeated softly, over and over again, not knowing what else to say.

11

LINCOLN

"Come on, bro. What else did Bella say?" Lincoln probed.

"Nothing," Lucas muttered nonchalantly before shoving a fork full of distressfully rare ribeye in his mouth.

"Ugh!" Lincoln grunted, leaning back in his chair. He had asked his brother to do one thing: get him some info about Donna's undercover detail. She'd been unreachable and he at least wanted to know when the detail would end. "I expected better of you."

Lucas chuckled and forked another piece of bloody steak.

"Why don't you just run up to the fucking cow and bite it in on the ass?"

Lucas stuffed the meat in his mouth. "You're in a mood," he mumbled with a mouthful.

He was. He hadn't seen Donna since their tryst at Bella's house. She hadn't reached out to him, and he'd been unable to reach her. Admittedly, he felt as if he was chasing a woman that didn't want to be caught. Seemingly, the only time she seemed at all interested in him was when he was standing in front of her. Out of sight, out of mind.

Lincoln had never had to chase a woman, especially if he'd already slept with her. It would have been so easy to chalk Donna up as a loss. But she was so fucking captivating. Smart, funny, and absolutely stunning. Not to mention, her beautiful body and her snug, wet pussy weren't making it any easier for him to walk away. And it was a damn shame too. Donatella Devereaux was mutilating his self-esteem.

"What's up with you, Linc? You don't seem yourself. Don't tell me my sister-in-law put in on you like that," Lucas teased through laughter.

"Sister-in-law my ass," Lincoln mocked with his own laughter. "That woman ain't gonna marry you."

"Ha-ha-ha," Lucas fake laughed with a frown. "We'll see. Anyway...I'm not the one with the level three security clearance. Find her yourself."

Lincoln grabbed his glass from the table, sipped his bourbon, and glanced around the restaurant. His spine straightened and the hairs on his arms stood at the sight before him. Heading in his direction was a beauty he hadn't seen in over a year.

Tahira Raji was an Egyptian born, American CIA operative who was turning each and every head as she walked through the swanky, downtown restaurant. Even in a simple navy-blue pantsuit and matching hijab, concealing her hair, she was beautiful. Although her attire was meant to be modest, there was absolutely no way for her to hide the curves that lay beneath. She was a very well-formed woman with dangerous curves.

When she made it to the table, she took the seat next to Lucas. "Lincoln, it is so good to see you again," she said with a smile.

"Tahira," he responded dryly. It wasn't that he didn't like her. He was just waiting for the other shoe to drop. Tahira's presence could not be good. It never was.

When she turned her smile on Lucas, he reached for his napkin to wipe his mouth. "Hello," he greeted with a raised brow.

Lucas was polite, but Lincoln could see the questions in his brother's eyes.

"You must be...Lucas. My goodness, you guys look so much alike. It's hard to tell you apart."

Lucas frowned, but before he could respond, Lincoln asked, "What's happened, Tahira? Why are you here?"

Ignoring him, she remained focused on Lucas. "You should get to Northwestern. Your sister-in-law has been shot."

"*What?*" Lincoln breathed.

"Wait...what the hell did you just say?" Lucas sneered, leaning close enough to make a normal person feel uncomfortable. Tahira, however, was no normal person. She was unfazed.

"Don't worry, dear, she's okay. But you should be with your brother. And you," she turned to Lincoln, "I was sent to bring you in. I can brief you on the way."

Lucas pulled his phone from his jacket pocket and, assumedly, dialed Victor. When he didn't get an answer, he hopped up from the table.

"I told you, she's fine. Try to stay calm."

Lucas leaned toward Tahira and glared at her with angry narrowed eyes. "Lady, who the fuck are you?" he snapped.

Lincoln hopped to his feet and placed his hand on his brother's shoulder. "Luc," he hushed calmly. "Go and see about Taylor. I have to take care of something."

Lucas looked from Tahira to Lincoln, and he could only speculate about the inner debate going on in his older brother's head.

"Go," Lincoln urged. "Call me and let me know what's what."

Although he seemed reluctant, Lucas agreed with a nod. He gave Tahira a look of warning before hurrying toward the exit.

"That's a beautiful man," she remarked. "But, all of you are. The Creed genetic pool has got to be filled with an unlimited amount of testosterone."

Lincoln grumbled. He didn't have time for Tahira's banter. He needed to check with his brother and find out for himself if Taylor was truly okay.

"What do you want, Tahira?"

"I told you. You're being called in."

"*You* don't call me in. I don't work for the CIA."

Tahira chuckled and sat back confidently. "Keep telling yourself that. Everywhere you go, the CIA has a hand in sending you there."

Lincoln grabbed his glass and defiantly leaned back in his seat. He took a sip, looking at her through skeptical, narrowed eyes. Without his permission, his gaze lowered to her full, ill-hidden breasts. Covered or not, she had to be aware of what she was working with. He was still staring when his cell phone began to ring. His gaze landed on her pretty face. She was wearing a smirk of, *"Told you."*

Tahira stood and pushed her chair to the table. "I'll see you in the situation room," she told him before sauntering off.

Again, turning every head in the restaurant.

DONATELLA

Kelly stuffed the last bit of his clothing into his duffle bag. "So, it begins," he whispered, throwing the bag over his shoulder.

Word had just come down that coed living quarters in The Blood of The Chosen compound were to be no more. Even the married couples were to separate.

Robert, or Bobby Lee as some of the others called him, had delivered a sermon the night before, stressing the need for total submission to the Lord, quoting 1 Thessalonians 4:3-5.

"For this is the will of God, your sanctification: that you should abstain from sexual immorality; that each of you should know how to possess his own vessel in sanctification and honor, not in passion of lust, like the Gentiles who do not know God."

According to Robert Lee Khal, sex was a distraction, pulling one's love and attention from God. In twenty-four hours, several gender segregated dormitories had been formed within the commune.

Donna and Kelly had only been there a few days, but they'd already received several coveted invitations to dine with the prophet. On every occasion, he seemed fixated on Donna. So much so that she was invited, along with a handful of women, to stay in one of his private houses. It was supposedly a privilege and, hopefully, a huge change from the overcrowded dormitories with inadequate bathroom facilities. Compared to the dorms, Robert's private quarters were rumored to be like the Four Seasons.

Kelly handed Donna her backpack. "Remember, you know exactly where I am. If you need to get out of there, get out. Fuck the case. Your safety comes first. Do you understand?'

"Yes, Kelly, for the thousandth time, I understand," Donna assured. "I'll be fine."

Kelly was obviously worried. Surprisingly, more worried than she was.

"You okay?" she asked. "You still here with me, right?"

"Yeah. I just don't like this fucking guy. I don't trust him. But, try not to worry. I'm always watching."

"I'm not worried." Donna chuckled. "You try not to worry. I can handle myself. And, if need be, I'll run like a track star."

Kelly smiled for the first time since he found out that they were to be separated.

"Okay. I'll never be too far."

"I know. Come on. Let's go drop this bag off at the big house." Donna grinned. "We don't wanna be late for church."

"*Church*!" Kelly scoffed. "Can't be late for that shit."

"Blessed be," Donna mocked.

"Yeah, okay. Just don't drink the Kool-Aid."

∼

Two hours after an extremely boring, self-serving sermon, Donna was entering her new living quarters. After turning down two long hallways, she was led to a large bedroom with two king-sized beds, positioned opposite each other. A door next to a large window suddenly opened. Vera, the girl she'd met at the rally, peered around the door.

"You made it!" she exclaimed with a huge smile. "The first time I saw you, I knew you would be chosen."

She entered the room and plopped down on the bed. Donna raised a brow at the woman.

"Chosen? What exactly have I been chosen for?"

Vera laughed. "Look around. You've entered paradise. You've been handpicked. You'll wed the Messiah."

Donna frowned at the goofy, young chick. She, for sure, had drunk the Kool-Aid. She was downright giddy, definitely delusional. Paradise? It was a freaking bedroom with dooky-green walls, an old schoolroom desk, and a tiny window.

"You and I are gonna be roomies," she announced with overexaggerated enthusiasm.

Donna stared at the woman, wondering what could have possibly happened in her young life to make her so easily susceptible to cult-inspired brainwashing.

"And, you?" Donna asked. "Are you to wed the prophet?"

"*Yes!*" she screeched, bouncing up and down on the bed.

Donna smiled, doing her very best not to look disgusted. However, when Vera stopped bouncing around, Donna feared that she hadn't been able to hide her disdain for the so-called prophet.

Vera squinted at Donna as if *she* were the weirdo. "What?" she asked. "What's wrong? Are you worried about Cam?"

"A little," Donna played along.

"Cam will be fine. He'll follow the Lord's instruction. Don't worry. Your coupling with the anointed one has been sanctioned by God."

The chick is off her nut!

Demented or not, Donna couldn't help but pity her. There had to be something very important missing from her life. She was the perfect target for people like Robert Lee Khal. He was a predator that preyed on those who were lacking, whether it was love, family, affection, or spiritual direction. Essentially, he was nothing more than a conman. A charismatic, good-looking conman, but a conman nonetheless.

Donna tossed her backpack in the chair next to what she assumed was to be her bed and sat down on the hard mattress. "When will you marry the prophet?" she asked.

Vera's giggle was a touch demented. "Oh, silly, we'll all be married at the Enlightenment Festival. The prophet's birthday."

The festival was in a few months, so Donna would have to work fast. Fake ceremony or not, she would not be exchanging vows with Robert Lee Khal.

12

VICTOR

While his security team kept hungry reporters at bay, Victor helped Taylor into the SUV and slid in beside her. Thankfully, she was doing well. The bullet didn't hit any major organs. Through and through meant no surgery and her unborn child had been protected by body armor.

Victor glanced over at Taylor. She didn't seem to be in much pain. He was relieved that she was physically intact. However, her mental state was another story.

"Sweetheart, would you like to recover in Springfield? We could spend some time at the Governor's Mansion."

Taylor only shook her head. She was visibly shaken and hadn't spoken a word since she was released from the hospital. Victor didn't know how to help, so he reached over and covered her hand with his and held it until they reached their Chicago home.

Soon, they were pulling to the curb. Victor waited as his security detail, mixed with the state police, created a path to the entrance of Storm Tower. When Gregor opened the door, Victor climbed out and reached for Taylor. She placed her hand in his and stepped out of the SUV. When he noticed that she was shaking, he was enraged. He wanted to tear down the world for making his wife feel unsafe in it.

Reporters shouted questions as he shielded her along the path. Focused solely on Taylor, he ignored the chorus of stupid inquisitions. When they finally reached the door, one question captured his attention.

"Governor Creed, how do you feel about the Illinois Attorney General's investigation into your connection to the mafia?"

Victor turned and glared at the reporter. It was Brent Trainer, the bitter reporter Taylor had rejected the night of the State Dinner, where they met for the first time. The motherfucker obviously had a bug up his ass for him, but he was a flea in the world of things important. Taylor would always be Victor's first concern. He would get her to the safety of their home and deal with the media maggot at a later time.

Gregor led them across the lobby and into an open elevator. Victor watched Taylor closely as they ascended. She still hadn't said a word, hadn't even looked him in the eye. It was clear she needed time. How much time, he didn't know.

When the elevator doors separated, Kena's angry face was the first thing he saw. Second was his worried-looking brother. They stepped back, giving them room to exit. As soon as Taylor stepped out of the elevator, Lincoln wrapped his arms around her. She seemed so small when she pressed her face to his chest.

"How are you feeling, sis?"

"I'm okay," she responded in a weak whisper.

Lincoln took a step back and looked up at Victor with an expression filled with apprehension. Victor frowned. Normally fierce and powerful, it pained his soul to see his wife that way.

Victor pressed his hand to the small of Taylor's back. "Are you tired, sweetheart?"

"Yes," she replied softly. "I'm gonna go lie down."

"Okay. I'll take—"

"No," she interrupted, placing her hand on his shoulder. "Visit with your brother."

"Babe?"

"*Victor*," she said through a breath. "I'm fine. I know where the bed is."

She didn't have to raise her voice for Victor to know better than to argue. He simply nodded and gestured toward their apartment door.

Victor stared at her back as she walked away. He'd never felt so helpless. When she entered the apartment, Lincoln whispered, "Damn."

Victor's dropped his head. "Yeah, witnessing her commander's death hit her hard. I don't know how to make it better."

"Trust me, bro. There are some things you can't *unsee*. And, I know it sounds cliché, but healing truly does come with time."

After fighting in two wars and participating in countless military operations, Victor was hopeful that Lincoln knew what he was talking about. So, he nodded and turned to Kena.

"What's up?"

"Renee and Vince Hart are waiting in your office."

Victor closed his eyes and exhaled. His publicist and personal attorney in the same room could not mean good news. And when he opened his eyes and noticed Kena's expression, he expected that all hell had broken loose.

Grunting his frustration, Victor entered his apartment and headed to his office. When he entered with Lincoln, Vince and Renee were seated at the small conference table.

Vince stood. He was calm, but Victor could see the tension in his face. Renee, however, had her nose buried in a small pile of paperwork.

"Your campaign manager called," she informed without looking up. "She's on her way up."

Victor took off his jacket off and tossed it on the sofa. "What?" he growled while walking over to his desk.

Vince hesitated as if waiting for Victor to sit.

"What?" Victor repeated as he took his seat. "Get to it, Vince."

Vince shoved his hands in his pockets and steeled himself to deliver bad news. "The Attorney General is investigating you," he blurted, probably thinking that he was landing an unexpected blow.

But the piece of shit reporter had already dropped a hint about the investigation.

Victor flipped open his laptop. He wanted to send Kena an email instructing her to begin a search for a qualified therapist for Taylor.

"What are they looking for?" Lincoln asked.

"Campaign corruption. They're looking into Major Mogul Super PAC."

Victor looked up at Vince with disbelief. "*Jack Storm?* Get the fuck outta here. Are serious?"

Victor couldn't believe what he was hearing. As far as he knew, Jack Storm was the most legit rich man he'd ever come across.

"They're looking at campaign contributions from Jack Storm?"

"Yes," Vince said. "According to some friends on the inside, they're trying to tie his money in with Donati Pharmaceuticals, which is owned by Luca Savelli and cousin, Francis."

"That's fucking ridiculous," Victor scoffed. "Good luck trying to muddy up Storm Enterprises."

There had to be more to it. Why would Renee and Vince get so worried about a bullshit accusation that couldn't possibly be proved? Yeah, Jack and Luca were family, but there was no way they would find a speck of dirt on Jack's money.

"What else?" Victor probed.

Vince cleared his throat and turned to Renee. She reluctantly looked up from her paperwork. Dread was the only way to describe the look in her eyes.

She grabbed a sheet of paper and walked around the table, moving toward him slowly as if walking the plank. After placing the paper on his desk, she muttered, "Tomorrow's headline."

Victor hesitated. Since he'd hired her, he had never seen Renee spooked. She actually tensed when he reached for the paper. He put his readers on, looked down at the paper, and could not believe what he was reading.

"Commander Dies. Did Governor's Wife Drop the Ball?"

UNTITLED

LINCOLN

Victor jumped to his feet and slammed his fists on the desk.

"*What the fuck?*" His rage came out in a roar that shook the walls and scared the hell out of his press secretary. Even Vince startled and took two steps back.

Lincoln placed what he hoped was a reassuring hand on Renee's upper arm. "May we have the room?" he requested.

Renee nodded and hurried out of the office with Vince on her heels. Lincoln closed the door and turned to Victor. Livid couldn't begin to describe his brother's demeanor. He'd seen him angry before, but Victor was almost unrecognizable. As a politician, he'd developed a thick skin. He was accustomed to the media scrutiny. But he may not have been prepared for the media attack on his wife.

However, if Lincoln knew nothing else, he knew Taylor was no shrinking violet. She was tough as nails. With all the shit she'd been through, weak and meek was not an adjective that described his brother's wife.

Lincoln closed the office door and turned to find his brother standing right in front of him.

"Let me pass, Linc." Victor's tone was calm, but he couldn't mask the rage hidden beneath.

Lincoln held out his hand while blocking the door. "Where ya goin'? We need to come up with a strategy."

His normally bright irises instantly went from a vivid green to the darkest jade. "Oh, I have a strategy," he hissed. "I'm gonna go beat the shit out of that little jackoff."

Lincoln placed his hand on Victor's chest to stop his advancement toward the door. There was no way he could let him out of the room. There was no telling what he would do in such an angry state. To most, his brother was the charismatic young governor who solved his problems with diplomacy and charm. However, Lincoln knew his brother better than anyone. If pushed, diplomacy would go straight out the window, and he would have all the charm of the Loch Ness Monster.

"*Victor*, you need to calm down so we can get Renee back in here. Let her do what she's good at. What you pay her for."

"Move, Linc."

"Victor—"

"*Move!*" Victor roared.

Being the eldest brother, Victor was not accustomed to repeating himself. Although they had their squabbles, he was mostly in charge. As children, they'd looked up to him and normally complied when he had a request. But they weren't children anymore.

Lincoln planted his feet, prepared to stop his brother from leaving the room. "What's wrong with you? You're in the middle of a campaign. You can't go beating up some fucking reporter."

"*Fuck* the campaign!" Victor boomed before hurling his fist into the door.

Any other man would've flinched at the sound of the wood splitting beneath his brother's fist, but Lincoln stood his ground. His brother wouldn't do anything to hurt him. At least, he hoped he wouldn't.

"Take a breath, brother. What's more important, expressing your anger or protecting your wife?"

Lincoln pushed him in the chest, just hard enough to move a man as big as Victor. When Victor narrowed his eyes and advanced toward him again, Lincoln held his hands out.

"Come on, Victor." He sighed. "You're not thinking straight. Get Renee to kill that story. Protect Taylor now. Deal with the reporter later."

Victor paused suddenly and looked down at the floor. Lincoln could hear his brother's breathing go from rapid to normal. Hopefully, he was reconsidering a hasty decision made out of anger.

When he finally looked up, his eyes had returned to their normal hue. He walked around his desk and leaned on his palms. Lincoln didn't know whether to walk over to him or hold his position in front of the door.

Victor inhaled a deep breath and exhaled. He picked up his cell and dialed. "Kena, send Renee back in, and get me a meeting with Jack Storm."

Once he was done giving the instruction, he touched the screen to end the call. Victor sat, and Lincoln took tentative steps away from the door. Thankfully, his brother had heeded his advice. The last thing he needed was another scandal.

Lincoln walked over to the liquor cabinet and poured them both a healthy portion of Scotch. He placed a glass in front of Victor and took a seat in front of the desk. Victor retrieved the glass and took a large sip.

"You're right," he admitted. "If anyone could kill or spin a story, it's Renee."

Lincoln nodded his agreement and sipped from his own glass.

"This life is so new to Taylor, Linc. I just worry so much about her."

Although Lincoln had never loved a woman as much as his brother loved Taylor, he fully understood why Victor was so protective. If he'd had a wife, he would have done anything he could to prevent her from experiencing any kind of pain.

"I know you do, but she's strong. She's already proven that."

Victor took another gulp, frowning when he swallowed the

burning liquid. He returned the glass to his desk and sighed. "*She's pregnant, Linc,*" he whispered.

Lincoln sighed, understanding his brother's murderous intentions. It wasn't just concern for his wife, but his unborn child as well.

"That's all the more reason for you to let your team handle the media. This should be a happy time for you and your wife."

Victor nodded. "You're right."

After a soft knock on the door, Renee peered inside.

Victor stood. "Please, come in," he invited, extending his hand, gesturing toward the chair in front of his desk.

She entered and took a seat as suggested.

"I'd like to apologize for my outburst. I'm terribly sorry if you were frightened by my behavior."

Renee shook her head. "Governor, there's no need to apologize. I totally understand. That headline infuriated me as well."

"Thank you, Renee." Victor returned to his seat. "Do we have a plan?"

"We do," Renee replied with confidence. "The copy editor owes me a favor. I'll get him to quash the story."

"A favor?"

"A big one," she confirmed with a smirk and a raised brow.

She seemed sure, and Victor seemed a little less stressed. Feeling as if he no longer needed to restrain his brother, Lincoln stood and excused himself.

He stepped out, closed the door behind him, and headed down the hall. When he arrived in front of Victor and Taylor's bedroom door, he could hear the television. After a brief hesitation, he knocked on the door.

"Come in," she answered softly.

Lincoln cracked the door. "You decent, sis?"

"Yeah. Come on in."

When he stepped inside, he found Taylor seated on the loveseat with the remote in her hand. On the television was a news story about the shooting.

Lincoln walked over to the loveseat and slid the remote out of her hand. He turned off the television and sat next to her. "Wanna talk?"

"Not really," she muttered.

"Taylor, you've been through some serious shit. I know better than anyone that if you leave that shit to fester, it'll rot you from the inside out."

Taylor sighed. "I'm fine, Linc. I *have* been shot before."

Her tone was stern but unconvincing.

Lincoln reached for her hand. "Yes, but you've never witnessed someone murdered in cold blood. That's a traumatic experience for anyone. I've been there and I've had to work through it. Hell, between you and me…I'm still working through it."

Her cheeks flushed and Lincoln could see that she was fighting back tears.

"Yeah?" Her voice was small and timid.

"Yeah. It doesn't matter how strong we are. We're still human, with the capability to feel pain and empathy. You did everything you could to save your boss, including putting your life and your baby's life in danger."

Taylor looked up at him with a surprised look in her tear-filled eyes.

"Yeah," Lincoln confirmed with a smile. "Victor told me the good news. Don't worry, your secret is safe with me."

"We're not ready to announce. Especially now."

"I understand. Congratulations. I'm very happy for you both."

She swiped a tear from her cheek and blessed him with a smile. A weak smile, but a smile nonetheless.

Lincoln draped his arm around her shoulder and pulled her into a hug. As she relaxed against him, he whispered, "I need you to stop worrying and concentrate on growing that little Creed. You understand, little sis?"

She nodded against his chest.

"Promise?"

"Promise."

13

LINCOLN

Lincoln waited patiently in the shadows as a car pulled into the parking garage. When the driver parked, Lincoln pushed off the wall and stalked toward his target. The reporter wasn't hard to find. He had more selfies on social media than any man should. One, stupidly, right in front of his turd colored BMW. A quick phone call to run his license plates revealed where he was laying his head.

Brent Trainer climbed out of his car and grabbed his briefcase from the backseat. Without so much as a sound, Lincoln had made it to within an arm's reach. When he turned around to find Lincoln looking down at him, dressed in all black, his eyes widened with fear. Even before laying one finger on the man, Brent screamed like the pussy Lincoln suspected he was.

Lincoln grabbed the reporter by the throat, silencing him by cutting off his air supply, and looked him square in the eye as he gasped, struggling for air.

To the reporter's credit, he tried to defend himself. He began to swing wildly until his arms went limp from lack of oxygen. Lincoln could smell his fear. He must've thought he was reaching his end. However, Lincoln had no intention of killing the man. He only wanted to get a message across. So, by his throat, he dragged Brent back into the shadows and slammed his body against the concrete wall. The reporter clutched his neck and fell to his knees, coughing and gulping for much needed air.

"I- I know who-who you are," he stuttered, "I'm calling the police!"

When Lincoln grinned, he could see the horror in Brent's eyes when he realized he should've kept his mouth shut.

"Go for it!" Lincoln gritted before slamming his fist against the reporter's jaw.

He tried to stand, but before he could, Lincoln punched him again. He squealed like a little girl when his face slapped the concrete. Lincoln had never heard a man produce such a sound. And yet, he was without pity. This man was coming after his family.

Reporting the news was one thing, but he was using his platform to hurt his brother and his sister-in-law. And for what? Because she rejected his ass. Yeah, it was in Victor's best interest to steer clear of the vindictive asshole, but Lincoln wasn't running for office. He wasn't concerned about voters. Therefore, he absolutely had no problem getting his hands dirty.

He leaned down, gathered a handful of Brent's blonde highlights, and yanked the reporter to his feet. He was bleeding from the mouth and forehead and seemed as if he was fighting to stay conscious as he struggled to stand on wobbly legs.

"Call the police if you want," Lincoln sneered. "According to our United States government, I'm in Afghanistan."

Unwilling to support his dead weight, Lincoln released his hair, allowing him to fall. The reporter hit the ground with a thud and howled out in pain. For good measure, Lincoln pushed his size thirteen boot against his neck.

"You listen to me, you *motherfucker!* If you fuck with my family again, someone is gonna find you rotting somewhere!"

Lincoln was unmoved by the gurgling noises as he pushed his boot to his neck. He kept pushing until he was convinced that the grimy reporter fully understood the consequences of his future actions. Only when satisfied his message had been successfully delivered did he remove his boot from Brent Trainer's neck.

Brent had curled into the fetal position and was wailing like a wounded animal as Lincoln stalked out of the parking garage, avoiding the cameras the same way he had when he entered.

14

DONATELLA

"'And we know that all things work together for good to them that love God, to them who are the called according to his purpose.' Good people, that comes from Romans 8:28."

Donna looked around at the rest of the congregation and wondered if anyone else was bored as all fuck and tired of listening to Bobby Lee's long ass sermon. After sitting on a hard ass bench for at least three hours, she was on the verge of faking a seizure.

Kelly reached over and gave her hand a squeeze. "It's almost over," he whispered in her ear. "It has to be because I'm about ready to blow my fucking brains out."

Donna chuckled softly. "Dude *loves* to hear his own voice."

"No shit. So, I think I may have located the armory."

She turned to see if he was serious. "Yeah?" she asked with raised brows.

Donna felt a rush of excitement. The sooner they got something on the preacher, the sooner she could return to her life.

"Yeah. I think they keep the weapons in that red barn behind the main house. Yesterday, Harry Barber asked me to take a ride to Joliet with him and a few of the fellas."

Harry Barber was Robert Lee Khal's righthand man. The Feds suspected that he was the man in charge of the buying and selling of illegal firearms. So, if he was taking Kelly on a run, that meant he was gaining their trust.

Donna was making progress as well since she'd been living in the main house with the rest of Bobby Lee's future wives. In the commune, everyone had a job to do. Her job was working on the membership committee. With that came sorting and keeping account of charitable donations. She'd also been assigned to help out with the Glory Gala, a formal ball created to court the wealthy. To Bobby Lee, absolutely everything was about money. He made that very clear during one of his sermons where he successfully preached his members into turning over their income for the good of the family. Most of the congregation had outside jobs. They would work eight-hour days just to return to the commune and work more. Some even sold their homes, moved into the commune, and handed the money from the sale right over to the church aka Robert Lee Khal.

The sound of eager applauding alerted Donna that the self-observed, so-called holy man had finally shut the fuck up. When she smiled and started clapping frantically, it wasn't a performance. She was genuinely ecstatic that the service was finally reaching its end.

Joining the rest of the sheep, she stood and shouted praises to the lord. Donna looked around and noticed that although they were verbally praising God, they were actually worshipping Robert Lee Khal.

Kelly grabbed her hand as they moved around the church, engaging in brief conversations with the parishioners. Donna was amazed at how many seemingly educated and successful people allowed themselves to be brainwashed by the false prophet. She was mesmerized listening to one woman speak about how miserable she'd been as a partner in a law firm before she joined The Blood of The Chosen until she was tapped on the shoulder.

"Sister Kateri," a feminine voice came from behind.

Donna smiled when she turned around and saw Clara, a striking, seemingly sweet woman who might have been in her late forties. According to Vera, she had been a member for twenty-five years.

"What's up, Miss Clara?" She shared a smile of her own.

"The prophet would like to see you." Her voice was gentle and soothing. "He'd like for you to meet him by the pond.

"Okay. Thank you, Miss Clara."

She nodded and walked away. Donna turned back to Kelly who was eyeing her curiously. She placed her hand on his shoulder and addressed the small circle of folks who were obviously oblivious to the fact that they were in a cult.

"I've been summoned. I'll see you guys later."

After the goodbyes, Donna stood on her toes and kissed Kelly on the lips. "Sweetheart, I'll be back."

It was important for them to keep up the appearance of being a happy couple. Although a few of the members knew she had been moved to new and better sleeping quarters, and that she'd been chosen to be one of the prophet's many wives, she was still playing the role of a woman reluctant to leave her man.

"Alright, babe. I'll see you at dinner."

Donna nodded and walked away.

"You two make a beautiful couple," she heard a woman say as she walked away. The comment was ridiculous, especially since everyone knew she was set to marry Bobby Lee soon.

She maneuvered through the crowd and walked out into the warm sun. Even though it was late afternoon, it was still hot out.

She walked over rocks and through grass, passing three brick buildings that had been converted to sleeping quarters for the members. Since everyone had attended church services, the compound, which was normally covered with people working the grounds either building or tending the land, was unusually peaceful.

Since joining the Blood of The Chosen, Donna barely had any time to herself. For breakfast, lunch, and dinner, she was always surrounded by other members. She was never alone. So, she walked slow, appreciating every second of serenity.

It was five more minutes before Donna arrived at the pond. Bobby

Lee was standing with his back turned to her, flinging rocks into the water. Yet, somehow, he knew she'd arrived.

"Join me, Kateri," he said without turning around.

He was wearing a white buttoned-down shirt and tan linen pants. His wavy blonde mane was blowing freely in the wind. Donna walked over and stood next to him, and gazed out into the water. Even though it was breezy outside, the water was unusually still.

"I have something for you." He turned and presented her with a rectangular box. When she was hesitant, he grabbed her hand and placed the box inside. "Open it."

Donna opened the box. Inside was a diamond choker with a sapphire cross embedded in the center. The beauty of it took her breath away.

"Oh, my God. This...this is beautiful," she gushed. "But I couldn't possibly accept this."

"Don't worry. It's a loaner. I want you to wear it to the gala Saturday."

"The gala?"

Donna was a little confused. She thought only certain members were allowed to attend the gala. And since her cover was a broke waitress, she had assumed she wasn't invited.

"Kateri, the Glory Gala is the most important day of the year for the church. Recruiting elite members of society is detrimental to the goal of legitimizing our church. And with your beauty, my dear, you will be the prize we'll dangle in front of them. It's what we must do to introduce them to the Lord's light."

Donna continued to play her role and shook her head as if she were unsure. She looked up and stared into his illuminated, hazel eyes, noticing for the first time the tiny specs of olive green. Strangely, she had never been so close to him before. Yet, he was seriously expecting her to marry him.

"We need you to look the part. Clara has chosen a gown for you and some of the ladies will handle your hair and makeup."

Donna nodded and closed the box.

"The Bible says, 'For as the body *without* the spirit is dead, so *faith without* works is dead also.' Kateri, are you a servant of God? Do you have faith?"

"I do," Donna responded eagerly.

Bobby Lee smiled and held her face within his hands. Good looking or not, his touch was cringeworthy and made her long for the feeling of Lincoln's touch.

"Now, sweet child, *your* work begins."

15

LINCOLN

After getting through the rigorous security protocols at the Pentagon, Lincoln entered the elevator. When he arrived at his designated floor, he stepped into the hall and headed to the Situation Room. Leaning on the wall just outside the door was Tahira Raji. She was wearing a cream tailored pantsuit with matching heels, and of course her traditional hijab. The woman was always very well put together.

"As-Salaamu Alaikum," Lincoln greeted as he approached.

"Wa-Alaikum Salaam," she returned with a smile.

"You waiting for me?"

She pushed off the wall and folded her arms. "Don't flatter yourself, handsome. I just didn't want to go in there until I absolutely had to. We're waiting on SECDEF. Although...you *do* look good in that uniform."

Lincoln frowned and moved closer to Tahira. The Secretary of Defense attending a briefing for a routine military operation was a first for him. So, it was pretty safe to conclude that there was nothing routine about what was going down. Something catastrophic must have occurred. Truthfully, he should have realized it the moment Tahira waltzed into the restaurant and summoned him.

"General Gray is inside as well," she informed with a raised brow.

"What? Tahira, what's happened?"

"A plane has been taken. Among the passengers are two US ambassadors, Senator Newman, and one very important CIA operative who's carrying top-secret documents." Tahira sighed and handed him an orange envelope with the word 'CLASSIFIED' stamped on it. Before he could open it, she said, "Colonel, you're on your way to Mosul."

"*Mosul?*" Lincoln asked, perplexed. "Where was the plane taken from?"

"Saudi. Your main objective is to get our operative back, hopefully alive. If you can't, you are to secure those documents and neutralize the insurgents."

Lincoln frowned and glared at Tahira. He couldn't believe what he was hearing. "Main objective? What about the senator and the ambassadors?"

A nonchalant shrug let him know that the survival of the other passengers was inconsequential.

"Who took the plane?" he asked.

"Don't know. No one has taken credit yet. But, know this..." She moved closer, staring him right in the eye. "*The* most important person on that plane is that CIA operative. He has information that—"

When she stopped speaking and looked past his shoulder, Lincoln turned around. Martin Blake, the Secretary of Defense, along with his entourage were headed towards them.

"Colonel Creed," he greeted with his hand out.

Lincoln accepted his hand and shook. "Good morning, Sir."

He smiled. "How's the senator?"

"He's well, Sir. Enjoying retirement. Thank you for asking."

"Good morning, ma'am," he said to Tahira.

"Sir," was her simple response.

Lincoln noticed that he stared at Tahira a little longer than would be considered normal. He also noticed that she wasn't exactly appreciative. She blew out a breath as if irritated and reached for the doorknob.

"Allow me." The senior official attempted to open the door for her.

"I got it," she said curtly as she opened the door, thwarting his attempt to be a gentleman.

Lincoln said nothing as she entered the conference room. The dynamics of their relationship was of no concern to him.

He grabbed the door before it closed and turned to the senior administrator. "After you, Sir," Lincoln offered.

The man grunted something incomprehensible and entered the situation room. Lincoln followed him inside and closed the door behind him. As he made his way to the large conference table, he struggled to keep his composure. Admittedly, his steps faltered when he noticed that Amber Kerry, the White House Chief of Staff was already sitting at the table. Lincoln didn't have to open the envelope to realize that whoever the captured CIA operative was, he or she had some information the United States government did not want to share.

Amber looked up from a piece of paper and noticed that he and Martin had entered the situation room. She placed the paper on the table and cleared her throat.

"Shall we begin, ladies and gentlemen?" she asked, silencing the room.

~

LINCOLN and his team had boots on the ground in Iraq less than twenty-four hours after leaving the Pentagon. The TOC, Tactical Operations Center had been set up just four miles from the small private airstrip connected to Mosul International Airport.

While the soldiers prepped their gear and conducted equipment checks, Lincoln briefed the detachment commanders. The plan was to dispatch two platoons of twelve to breach the aircraft, rescue the

CIA Operative and/or secure the classified documents. Saving the other hostages would be a bonus, but not the objective. It was clear the Pentagon wasn't concerned in the least about preserving the lives onboard or they wouldn't have sent the Rangers.

In light of his meticulous nature, he went over the mission again and again until he felt that his commanders fully understood the objective. Lincoln planned to coordinate from the Command Center. Leading one platoon was combat pilot, Major Keisha Stonebridge, a tough as nails Brooklyn native who behaved as if combat was her calling. The second platoon leader was Major Colby York, a daredevil combat pilot who had previously completed two tours in Iraq. They didn't have much manpower for the mission, but Lincoln was confident in his Rangers.

"Get 'em together, Key," he instructed the Major.

"Yes, sir," she acquiesced before leaving of the room.

Lincoln glanced over at General Gray, the J-SOC—Joint Special Operations Commander. Maybe he wanted the task of briefing the soldiers.

"You got it, Colonel," General Gray deferred in a gruff voice before returning his attention to whatever he was reading.

Lincoln gave the detachment commanders a few minutes to prep the soldiers before entering the area of operation.

"*Attention!*" Major York shouted upon his entry.

The small group of soldiers jumped to their feet and stood at attention.

"At ease," he urged as he made his way to the front of the room.

The soldiers returned to their seats, giving Lincoln their full attention.

"At 0430 hours, the incursion team, led by Major York, is gonna take the lead. His platoon will rope in and get the perimeter on lock, nobody in or out. They'll also provide additional security for the Extraction Team, led by Major Keystone, as they breach the plane."

He scanned the room for his team. His eyes landed on Lieutenant Colonel, LTC Al Wright.

"Relax, Ranger," he told him. "Your team will stay behind and secure the command post."

Lincoln looked out at the men and women chosen for the mission. They seemed laser-focused on the task at hand.

He turned to his commanders and nodded toward the map on the wall. "Take it from here, Major York."

He stood back and listened as Major York went over the mission template. When he was done, the Major turned to Lincoln to see if he had anything to add. He stepped forward, satisfied that the Major had covered the plan thoroughly.

"Swift and stealth, Rangers. We gotta get in, and get out," Lincoln reminded before shouting, *"Rangers lead the way!"*

"All the way!" the Rangers shouted in unison.

"Good luck, Rangers!"

Lincoln nodded at his soldiers and left the Area of Operation or AO. He returned to the Command Center, grabbed his phone from a table, and did what he always did before any mission. Whether he was coordinating from the TOC or fighting with his belly on the ground, before his boots hit dirt or sand, he always called his mom.

∽

At 0410 hours, the soldiers were already loaded into two PR52 stealth helicopters. Since they were technologically designed to avoid detection, they were chosen for the mission. Lincoln left them to it and returned to the TOC. LTC Wright was standing behind a soldier sitting in front of several computers. Lincoln walked over and stood next to him.

The LTC looked over at him and grinned. "What's good, Colonel? How was your leave?"

"Leave?" Lincoln snorted. "Brother, I'll tell you...when I go home to my family, it's never a vacation. Between my brothers and their danger magnet women, there is always some kind of crisis."

Al laughed.

"What's up with you? How are Emma and the girls?"

"Gettin' on my damn nerves," Al jeered playfully. "Man, I tell ya...I am extremely outnumbered."

"A wife and *four* daughters? I would say you are." Lincoln chuckled.

He looked at his watch. It was 0415. He slapped Al on the shoulder and said, "Perform a coms check and get 'em in the air."

"Yes, sir," Al responded, turning back to the computer screens. They would be observing via satellite. Al made some adjustments to the satellite feed and flipped a switch that would ensure all communications were recorded. He raised the volume and spoke into his headset.

"This is Jack 3. Coms check. Over."

Major York's voice broke through radio waves. "Queen Mary 5-1. Over."

"Radio check is loud and clear, Queen Mary 5-1," Al assured.

"Queen Mary 5-2," Major Stonebridge's voice chimed in last.

"Radio check is loud and clear, Queen Mary 5-2."

After conducting a brief equipment check, the pilots were cleared for takeoff. Lincoln folded his arms across his chest and leaned against the table. He listened in silence as both teams prepared to go wheels up.

For thirteen minutes, he heard nothing but flight chatter until a transmission from Queen Mary 5-1 broke through the chatter.

"Queen Mary 5-1 to Jack 3."

"Go, Queen Mary 5-1."

"We have eyes on the target. We are one mike away from doors open. Over."

"Copy that. Over," Al responded.

Lincoln looked at the satellite pictures. All was quiet until Major York's voice broke through the chatter.

"Queen Mary 5-1 to Jack 3!" he called out with urgency. "We're losing power! I repeat...*we are losing power!*"

"Queen Mary 5-1, what's your fix? Over."

Lincoln remained calm. The last thing he wanted was to incite panic.

"We're less than half a click south of the target. Over."

He and the TOC listened in silence while waiting and praying the pilot would be able to get control of the chopper. But listening to the pilot's transmissions, they figured it unlikely.

"We're going down! Prepare for a hard landing! I repeat, we are going down!"

The chatter was chaotic. Lincoln pushed off the table and grabbed a headset. He placed it over his head and positioned the mouthpiece.

"King 6 to Queen Mary 5-1?" he called through the radio.

When there was no response, he repeated his transmission.

"Queen Mary 5-1, do you copy?"

Still no answer.

"Queen Mary 5-2?"

"Queen Mary 5-2."

Lincoln sighed with relief, thankful that at least one of his teams had responded.

"Queen Mary 5-2, we got a bird down, but this mission is still a go. I repeat...mission still a go! How copy? Over."

"Queen Mary 5-2 to King 6. That's a good copy. We're ropes down, hittin' the target in thirty seconds. Over."

"Copy that. King 6, over and out."

Lincoln searched the satellite feed for the crash site. "Keep trying to raise Queen Mary 5-1," he instructed.

"On it, sir."

He walked out of the TOC, into the AO. His team was scattered about, either nodding, reading, or listening to something through earbuds.

"Colonel!" Al called out from the entryway. "I got 'em!"

"Casualties?"

"Three wounded, no dead," he confirmed.

"The medic?"

"In one piece, sir."

Lincoln ran his fingers roughly through his hair as he devised a plan. With such little manpower, he didn't have many options.

"Alright, have the medic and two team members stay with the injured. Send the rest on foot to complete the mission."

Al nodded and returned to the TOC. Lincoln turned to his team.

"Gear up, Kingsmen! We're going on a rescue mission."

16

DONNA

Since Clara had business in Chicago and had asked her to join, they were six and a half hours into a seven-hour trip. The ride was long but pleasant. They talked the whole way, mostly about Clara's upbringing and the family she left behind when she joined BOC. She said the prophet encouraged them to cut their families by quoting John 3:16...

"For God so loved the world, that he gave his only begotten Son, that whosoever believeth in him should not perish, but have everlasting life."

According to Clara, he went on to say, "If the heavenly father could sacrifice his son, surely we, as his servants, can turn away from our families in worship of our Lord."

For the life of her, Donna couldn't understand how a woman so sweet and intelligent could get sucked in by a charlatan. In her former life, she owned and ran a successful party planning business. For the cult, she walked away from the business she had built from the ground up, along with her husband and three children.

As they pulled onto the exit ramp, Clara turned to Donna with a big smile.

"What?"

"I was just thinking. How about, after my meeting, we treat ourselves to a fancy dinner downtown?"

"Really? We can do that?"

Donna wasn't feigning shock. The Blood of the Chosen was all about the cooperative. Everything, every single dollar earned, was deposited into their commune. Clara was one of the most faithful members, and Donna was truly surprised that she would splurge on something as frivolous as a night out on the town.

"I don't see why not. Anybody that can stop us is seven hours away," she said with a chuckle. "The merciful Lord knows that we deserve a treat. At least I do."

"Sounds good to me," Donna said with glee.

She couldn't deny that she was excited. She so desperately wanted something better to eat than the bland survival food served in the commune.

"Alrighty then, I'm gonna get us a room," she said with a beaming smile. "After my meeting with Robert's attorneys, we can decide on a restaurant. We'll just turn this into a little mini-vacation."

∼

Clara used the magnetic key card to open the door. To Donna's utter shock, they'd checked into a suite at the Four Seasons, one of, if not the most expensive hotels in Chicago. When they stepped inside, she did her very best not to gag. The luxurious suite almost took her breath away. It was bathed in gold and warm reds, depictive of the Victorian era.

"Beautiful, yes?"

"Oh, yes," Donna confirmed through a breath.

Clara crossed the room and placed two briefcases on the desk. She took a credit card out of her purse and held it up.

"There's a boutique downstairs. Use this to get something to wear."

"Okay," Donna agreed.

Clara narrowed her eyes, glaring at her. "You understand that you are not to tell anyone about this?"

Donna nodded. "I understand."

Clara smiled. "Good."

When her focus turned to the contents in the briefcase, Donna explored the suite. From ceiling to floor, it was beautiful. She walked over to the large picture window and looked down at the most amazing view of her city. Chicago had to be one of the most beautiful cities in the world. Anytime she was able to view it from a different angle, she discovered something even more beautiful about it. Which made it easy to keep her cover as a woman from a dilapidated area in St. Louis who'd never been to Chicago.

"I gotta go. I'll meet you at RPM Steak. I wrote the address down. Use that card to take a cab."

"Okay," Donna said with a girlish smile. "Have a good meeting."

Clara slipped a few papers from the briefcase into a smaller attaché case and headed toward the door.

"Enjoy the room. Take a hot bath and relax. You know you won't be able to enjoy this when we get back home."

"Facts," Donna agreed through a chuckle.

And it was true. As far as Donna knew, the only bathtub on the whole compound was in Robert's room. It was one the amenities that seemed to excite his wives-to-be. Since she'd been a resident, she realized it was the little things she really missed; a bath, a cheeseburger, privacy, and *whiskey*. Boy, did she miss whiskey.

As soon as Clara walked out and she heard the click of the closing door, Donna walked over to the desk and picked up the credit card.

A fucking Amex Black Card!

While the rest of the members were reduced to eating powdered eggs, these motherfuckers were living like Jay-Z and Bey—sleeping in fancy suites, wearing designer clothes, and eating filet mignon. That was how Robert and the nobles were living.

Donna sat the card back on the desk and jogged over to the door. She flipped on the Do Not Disturb latch, ensuring that Clara couldn't walk in on her if she returned. After hurrying over to the desk, she pulled a tiny camera from her bra and searched through the contents of both briefcases.

Fifteen minutes later, Donna had taken pictures of documents that could put Robert, Clara, and The BOC in IRS hell. Since churches were exempt from having to pay federal, state, and local taxes, they'd flooded their personal holdings into church funds, then used the church funds for private real estate purchases. They were living high off the hog off of charitable donations solicited by members that had been programmed to believe that living by modest means would bring them closer to God. Tax violations were definitely not what the Feds were looking for, but it was start. After all, it was how they got Al Capone.

LUCAS

"I'm gonna grab some dinner," Lucas said into his cellular. "I'll see you tomorrow."

"I thought we were working over."

"It'll keep till tomorrow. Go home to your husband," he said to Quincy, his assistant. "Bella called. She's leaving work early. I'm gonna meet her at Catch 35."

"Cool. Enjoy."

Lucas could hear the relief in Quincy's voice. They'd been working day and night on the acquisition of a smaller, but lucrative cruise line.

"You too. I'm turning my cell off. If you need me...too bad." Lucas chuckled.

"Understood. Later."

"Yep."

Lucas disconnected the call and stuffed the phone into the inside pocket of his jacket. He'd decided to walk from his office, but was suddenly rethinking his decision. It was that part of the late afternoon, early evening when everyone was getting off work. Maneuvering through the crowd of bodies on the sidewalk was like navigating an obstacle course. Right in front of him were two women dressed in business attire. They were both nice-looking women, maybe in their thirties. One had brown eyes, a nice smile, and a wholesome look that was attractive. The other was blonde with blue eyes and big, bouncy tits. The one with the blue eyes grinned mischievously at the other, just before *accidentally* bumping into him.

"I am so sorry, mister," the blonde crooned, looking up at him with flirty eyes.

"It's not a problem," Lucas responded with what he thought was a polite smile.

"*So*, do you w—"

Whatever sentence she had attempted to complete was cut off abruptly when Lucas continued down the street. He was close to the restaurant and the last thing he wanted was for Bella to walk up and think that he was flirting with the blonde.

He looked down the street toward the restaurant. He didn't see Bella, but he did see a replica.

It was Donatella.

She was walking in his direction. But, for some strange reason, she took off in the other direction as soon as she laid eyes on him.

"Donna!" Lucas shouted. Surely, loud enough for her to hear. But she kept going. She even had the nerve to speed up. All was definitely not right. Maybe she was in trouble.

Lucas jogged until he caught up with her. He grabbed her arm, careful not to hurt her, and pulled until she was facing him. She whipped around and glared at him with a look of agitation. Lincoln studied her with a frown.

"Donna, are you okay?"

"Yes!" she said impatiently before yanking her arm out of his grasp. She turned to look behind her, then turned back with pleading eyes.

"What the hell is wrong with you?" Lucas snapped.

He looked past her. There was a handsome, middle-aged woman that seemed intently focused on her. But she definitely didn't appear to be a threat. In fact, she seemed...nice.

"Kateri!" she called out with a smile.

Kateri?

Donna blew out a frustrated breath and narrowed her eyes in warning. She mouthed, "Shut up!" and turned around.

"Hey," she responded in a bubbly tone. "I was just on my way to the restaurant. I got a little turned around."

"Oh." The woman frowned.

"It's okay. This man was nice enough to give me directions."

Clara looked past Donna and smiled. "It was very nice of you to help my friend. Thank you, sir."

Lucas shot Donna a quick glance before returning the woman's smile. "It was my civic duty. Your friend seemed very confused."

Donna let out a nervous laugh and moved toward the woman. She was acting as if she couldn't get away from him fast enough.

"Well, thank you." She turned to the woman and placed her hand on her upper arm. "Let's go," she urged.

"Yes." The woman began to walk away but stopped and looked at Donna. "Kateri, why don't you invite this nice man to the gala?"

"What? Oh, I-I don't think—"

"Of course," the woman beamed. "I'm Clara and this is Kateri. We're from The Blood of the Chosen religious community."

Lucas had suspected, but now he was sure. Bella had told him that Donna was on an undercover assignment. It didn't take a genius to figure out that The Blood of the Chosen was her target.

"We are hosting a gala to end all galas. And you, sir, are invited." She reached in her purse and pulled out an envelope. "We'd love to see you there. Right, Kateri?" She winked as she handed it to him.

Lucas could've been wrong, but it seemed like Clara was pimping Donna out.

"Absolutely," Donna confirmed with a sugary grin that appeared to be more of a threat than an invitation.

"Thank you for the invitation. It was nice to meet you, ladies."

"It was our pleasure," the woman bubbled.

Lucas nodded and decided to give Donna a little peace by getting the hell outta dodge.

17

LINCOLN

Lincoln and his team piled into two Humvees and sped toward to the crash site. He grabbed his radio, ready to contact his downed soldiers when the sound of rapid gunfire rang out in the distance.

"This is Queen Mary 5-1! Jack 3, we're taking heavy fire!" Major York's stressed voice thundered across the airways. "I repeat, we're taking heavy fire!"

"King 6 to Queen Mary 5-1, hold 'em off as best you can. We're about 3 clicks north of your location."

The Humvee swerved violently around a large boulder. The soldiers flew from one side of the vehicle to the other. Lincoln turned to the driver, Sergeant First Class Evan Peters.

"How are we supposed to rescue 1st Platoon if you kill us in this vehicle, son?"

"My bad, boss." The sergeant chuckled nervously. "I can't see nothing but darkness and sand."

"Do better."

"Copy that, sir," he shouted over the roar of the engine.

In a matter of minutes, they'd closed in on Queen Mary 5-1's position. Lincoln clutched his M4 and prepared to bail from the Humvee.

SFC Peters turned a tight corner and found shielding behind a concrete wall. Forgoing the protection of the military vehicle, Lincoln and his team slid on eye protection and jumped out of the Humvee.

"This is Queen Mary 5-2. We're on the ground, ready to make entry."

"Copy that. Proceed, Queen Mary 5-2."

Lincoln waited as the rest of his team exited the second vehicle and moved into the huddle.

"Jake, Rabbit, Ghost, and Bean, you're with me!" Lincoln shouted over a barrage of gunfire. "We're going at 'em straight on! Cam, go west, find high-ground, and get into sniper position! Buster, you go with him. Peaches, find high-ground and take up your position east! Thor, back her up!"

"Copy that!"

"Harp!" Lincoln shouted. "Take Fish, Ike, Veg, and Superstar with you! Triangulate from the right! Tracker, Cole, and Bass, go left and give 'em hell!

Lincoln, along with four of his Rangers, readied their rifles and left the shielding of the concrete wall. They took off southbound on foot while the others moved into their own offensive positions. Fortunately, it wasn't long before they spotted to disabled helicopter. Unfortunately, it was surrounded by armed insurgents.

Lincoln clicked his mic. "Queen Mary 5-1, take cover. We're coming from the north," he warned.

Wouldn't be much of a rescue if they were all taken out by friendly fire.

"Do you copy, Queen Mary 5-1?"

"Copy that, King 6!"

Lincoln and his men ran hard and fast, kicking up a mini-storm of dirt and sand with each stride. Not even the sound of rapid gunfire could drown out the sound of his heart pounding in his ears. Once they were fifty yards from the enemy, Lincoln and his men opened fire. Scores of the large militia were dropping like flies before they realized the rounds were coming from their rear. However, it didn't take long for them to train their weapons in the direction of Lincoln and his men.

The sound of bullets whizzing past Lincoln's head didn't induce fear, but determination. He ran harder and faster, firing at anyone he deemed a threat. Very quickly, they'd shortened the distance to the insurgents. Soon they would be in a close quarter, 15th century, War of the Roses type of battle. All that was missing was the clash of horses and the clank of swords.

"RPG!"

Lincoln had no idea who shouted the warning. But it didn't matter. He banked right and took a dive, taking one of his soldiers with him. Even though the missile missed all of them, its impact was still felt. It rocked the ground beneath them, sending them flying.

Lincoln groaned when his body hit tough sand and sharp rocks with a thud. He opened his eyes, but his vision was obstructed by spots of red. He felt around him, searching the ground blindly for his weapon. The voices and gunfire around him were muffled by the deafening ringing in his ear, and he was fighting his body's growing desire to relax against the warmth of the earth and rest.

He fought the urge, inhaled, and squeezed his lids tight. He allowed himself only one second to recuperate before he rose to all fours. Just as quickly as he'd lost them, his senses returned. After blinking a few times, his vision was restored. And not a minute too soon. A handful of insurgents were practically on top of them.

Lincoln abandoned the search for his rifle and snatched his Glock 19 from the hip holster. He aimed with precision and quickly took out four aggressors. Through his peripheral, he could see that his men were engaged as well. Unfortunately for them all, they were gravely outnumbered.

Soon, more bullets were whizzing past his head. Thankfully, they were coming from his soldiers. Snipers, Cam and Peaches were picking the enemy off one by one with deadly accuracy.

Lincoln located his assault rifle and snatched it from the ground. He scrambled to his feet and created a safer distance between himself and their armed opponents. With Cam and Peaches, the playing field was almost even.

Lincoln holstered his pistol and fired with his rifle. He took a quick look around. His soldiers were bruised, but still standing on their own two feet. It was the momentum he needed. The momentum to kill. That was, until his enemy unexpectedly stood in front of him in the form of a child. The boy couldn't have been more than ten years old, the rifle he was wielding nearly bigger than him.

"It's a kid!" Bean shouted over the noise. "It's a goddamned kid!"

Bean's tone was saturated with indecision. He was hesitant to do what needed to be done. Lincoln, however, was not. He lined his sights and fired right between the little boy's eyes. He turned to Bean and grabbed him by the collar. "He ain't *your* fucking kid! Stay focused!"

Lincoln surveyed his surroundings. Thanks to the extra manpower, he and his men had successfully cleared a path to the downed chopper. Since there was no time to waste, Lincoln took off running.

"*Move! Move! Move!*"

Cam and Peaches maintained their positions as Lincoln and the rest of his men bolted toward the helicopter on a path created by the blood of their enemies. Since they were already so close, it didn't take long to reach the chopper.

Lincoln readied his rifle. "*Go!*"

With his rifle trained, he scanned from the left to the right, covering his soldiers as they assisted the injured out of the helicopter. Once everyone was evacuated safely, Jake and Rabbit began placing C-4 strategically throughout the chopper.

Lincoln noticed movement in the dark. He looked through his sights, discovered a large group running in their direction, and immediately keyed his mic.

"We got action to the East!" he warned. It was a relatively small crowd, but they were still outnumbered.

Lincoln glanced over his shoulder to assess Jake and Rabbit's progress. Thankfully, they'd hopped out of the chopper and were hauling ass toward him. He and his men took off in the dark. Since they were carrying wounded men, they weren't moving as fast as they should have been.

"Blow it!" Lincoln shouted to either Jake or Rabbit. He wasn't sure which one was holding the detonator. Turned out, it was Jake.

Without slowing, Jake pushed a button which set off the explosion that destroyed the chopper. Unfazed by the blast, not one Ranger looked back.

In order to cover his soldiers, Lincoln slowed and fell to the rear. It was only seconds later when a volley of shots rang out in the air. He and his men hooked a right down a narrow street where they used a concrete building as cover while they returned fire.

Lincoln keyed the mic and instructed Peaches and Cam to abandon their positions and return to the Humvees. With any luck, the rest of them wouldn't be too far behind.

He peered around the wall, fired a succession of rounds, then ducked back behind the building. The insurgents were getting closer and just as he was getting ready to grab a handful of Rangers to take up position across the road, he heard the familiar whirl of helicopter blades.

Lincoln peeped around the building just as Major Stonebridge's voice interrupted the silence on the radio.

"Queen Mary 5-2 to King 6."

Lincoln clicked the mic and responded. "This is King 6. Over."

"Queen Mary 5-2 in position for a gun run, but we're flying blind. What's your fix? Over."

"Flare!" Lincoln yelled over his shoulder. "Queen Mary 5-2. We're about a quarter click away from the crowd. Standby. Lighting a flare. Copy?"

"Copy that, King 6."

"Keep your eyes open, Queen Mary 5-2. RPGs in the crowd. Copy?"

"Copy that King 6."

Lincoln rested against the wall while Ghost activated a flare.

"Queen Mary 5-2 to King 6. I got your position. I'm locked onto your target. Gonna lay down a little cover fire. Copy."

"Queen Mary 5-2, that's a good copy. Go ahead and clear the field. Over."

"Copy that, King 6! Queen Mary 5-2, over and out!"

Lincoln clutched his rifle tight and waited. As soon as he heard a barrage of what sounded like mini-cannons, he took off around the building and waved for his men to follow. They ran along the side of the building, cautiously scanning for threats along the way. In order to cover his men, he fell to the rear.

He looked back. To his relief, Queen Mary 5-2 was mowing their enemies down like wild grass. By the time they made it to the Humvees, they were no longer being pursued by armed insurgents.

Queen Mary 5-2 hovered as they loaded their injured into the vehicles. SFC Peters hopped into the driver's seat and started the engine. Lincoln stood by the Humvee and hurried his Rangers.

"Let's go! Let's go! Let's go!"

Once the last man was on board, they took off in the dark and burned rubber to the Command Center.

18

VICTOR

Victor tossed the newspaper on the conference table and pretended to be interested in whatever his campaign staff was debating about. Concern for his wife was dominating his thoughts. Since the shooting, she'd spent the majority of her time either in bed or on the sofa in the bedroom with her eyes glued to the television, watching reality TV. She barely ate, rarely left the room, and refused to see any family and friends. And since she hadn't turned her phone on since the incident, Victor's personal phone had been more active than usual. With all the calls from her friends and their family, his phone could barely keep a charge.

The only people Taylor couldn't avoid were her parents. The Montgomerys were not having it. After the first unanswered call, they'd bullied their way through security until they had eyes on their baby girl.

Renee grabbed the paper from the table and placed it on a smaller table in the corner. "At least they killed the story about Taylor," she pointed out with not a lot of enthusiasm.

Victor had to assume she wasn't at all pleased with the story that had replaced it. Instead of blaming Taylor for her commander's death, the Times focused on the rumors of his pending indictment.

"By the way, how did you kill the story?"

Renee took her seat at the table. "I didn't," she admitted. "I made the call, but my guy at the paper said Trainer decided to go in another direction."

Victor leaned back in his seat. He could feel his brows wrinkle as he glared at his press secretary.

"Why would he do that?"

"Don't know. I was thinking about asking you the same thing," she replied, suspiciously.

"It wasn't me."

The look in her eyes told him that she was skeptical. And, he couldn't blame her. He'd completely lost it when he heard the reporter was planning to write an article so inflammatory and filled with venom about Taylor.

"Renee, I was livid, yes. But believe me when I tell you...it wasn't me. So, I need you to stay on your toes."

Her narrowed eyes softened and turned less accusatory. "Understood."

Victor nodded just as the door was opened. Kena stepped in and escorted his campaign staff inside. Mark Vega, his senior campaign strategist; Nate Williams, the pollster; and Carlotta McGovern, the chief media advisor for the campaign entered, greeting with smiles and handshakes.

"Good news, Governor," Nate Williams announced enthusiastically. "Your numbers are through the roof." He hurried over to the conference table and placed his briefcase in front of him, fished out a file and handed it to Renee. "Your approval rating is in the mid-60s and you're killing it with women."

Nate was like any other poll taker, excited by numbers. But Victor knew all too well that positive polls did not determine the outcome of an election.

"But?" Victor probed, cynical.

Nate glanced at Mark Vega with an unspoken plea in his eyes. He was clearly uncomfortable delivering news that was unfavorable.

"Go on," Victor urged.

"Well, Sir, you lost a lot of conservatives when you bashed the president on national TV and advocated for Planned Parenthood. You are a Republican gubernatorial nightmare to the Republican party."

Victor chuckled. Nate was absolutely right. It was no secret that his beliefs were a stark contrast to the "right-wing" conservatives that had emerged from the proverbial closet with the election of the current president.

"What else?"

When Nate hesitated, Carlotta jumped in.

"Rumors of an investigation into your PAC funds don't help."

"I would think not," Victor muttered.

Mark took a seat at the table and folded his arms. "You're winning this race," Mark ensured. "As Nate said, you have women, you have the non-whites, and you have the Millennials, which is unheard of for a Republican. Now, you have to win the Independents. And a little damage control with your own party wouldn't hurt."

"I assume you have a course of action?"

"Always, sir," he responded with a confident grin.

"Alright, then. Let's go over it quickly. I have an appointment in an hour."

Having been around Victor long enough to know when he set a time limit, he stuck to it, his campaign staff dove right in. In that hour, they covered as much as they could about the trajectory of his campaign. He listened as best he could, but his head wasn't in the game. Besides, they were talking dates, campaign trails, photo ops, debate preps. It was all scheduling; shit they needed to be discussing with Kena. And like clockwork, not one minute after the hour was up, Kena walked in the conference room carrying his briefcase and jacket.

"You got this," he told his campaign staff as he stood and abandoned the table.

Kena handed him his jacket. He slipped it on as they left the conference room.

"Taylor?" he asked, reaching for his briefcase.

"Taylor didn't feel much like going out. I arranged for Dr. Porter to see her at the penthouse."

"Good."

Dr. Jonathon Porter was a well-renowned psychologist that his mother had recommended. Victor had never put much stock into therapy, but the woman he was sleeping with every night was a broken replica of his wife. Maybe she would get better in time, but he wasn't one to waste that time hoping and wishing.

They were joined by Gregor as they bypassed his office on the way to the elevator. Victor glanced over his shoulder, noticing his security detail for the first time. They were so discreet at times Victor often forget they were present.

"Lucas called. He needs your signature on some paperwork. He's sending them to the penthouse by messenger," Kena informed as they stepped into the elevator.

Victor nodded. He'd take the time to review and sign whatever his brother sent over. He knew Lucas was working on the procurement of another cruise line for Brothers Creed, Incorporated. Since Victor began his career in politics, he'd been doing a brilliant job of running BCI on his own.

"Here we go," Kena muttered when the elevator reached the lobby.

Gregor stepped in front and five others formed a protective perimeter around he and Kena. The barrier was created to shield him more so from the media than any physical danger. The story of his impending indictment brought out the sharks.

Gregor, along with the rest of his security detail, ushered them into a waiting SUV. The big man slid into the passenger seat next to Victor's new driver, Naomi. She'd only been with his security detail for a few months, but she was a perfect fit. She was quiet, punctual, and a good driver, not at all afraid to use a little aggression when moving reporters and paparazzi from in front of the automobile.

It didn't take long for them to reach Storm Tower. After pushing through the media, they entered the lobby. Victor felt the warmth of all the eyes on him as he walked to the elevator. When the doors slid open, he stepped inside, not giving one single fuck about any one of them. If the Attorney General was fool enough to come for him using false accusations, they were clearly underestimating his propensity for ruthlessness.

Victor entered the penthouse, anxious to see how Taylor's therapy session had gone. Emma, the new housekeeper, hurried over to him and held her hand out for his briefcase.

"Thank you, Emma," he told her as he handed her the briefcase.

She was polite, respectful, and fifty years old...the total opposite of the flirty housekeeper she'd replaced.

"Taylor?"

"She's in the parlor with Dr. Porter."

Victor began toward the parlor, but Emma placed her hand on his upper arm and stopped him.

"Just a second, Governor."

He frowned at her worried expression. "What is it?"

"Well, sir, Mrs. Creed...well, she's in a mood, sir."

"*Okay?*"

Her blue eyes were awash with apprehension. After a brief hesitation, she said, "She's destroyed the parlor. And...I think she might have struck the doctor."

"*What?*" Victor gasped.

He took off with long, determined strides to the parlor. When he opened the door and stepped inside, the first thing he saw was Taylor slumped down on the sofa looking pissed.

He hurried over and dropped to his knees in front of her. Even without makeup and with her thick, curly locks sprawled across the back of the leather, she was beautiful.

"Taylor, honey, what's going on?" Victor kept his voice soft. She looked as if she could explode at any time. He had never seen her so angry.

"Governor, I—"

Victor threw his hand up, stifling the doctor. He needed to hear from his wife. He'd speak with him after.

"Baby, what's wrong?"

Taylor leaned forward and glared angrily at him. There was fury in her deep, brown eyes.

"When you asked me if I wanted to speak to a therapist, what did I say?" Her tone, on the other hand, was filled with venom.

"Umm..."

"Oh, is that what I said? I said, umm?"

Victor took a deep breath and did his best to ignore her sarcasm. He knew she had gone through enough to make anyone testy, but he needed her to know how concerned he was.

"Taylor," he breathed, ready to explain.

"Don't fucking 'Taylor' me!" she screamed, jumping to her feet. "I am so fucking tired of you treating me like a child! I *said* I didn't want to talk to anyone!"

Victor stood and glared at her. He was searching for the woman he'd married, but he couldn't find her.

The stranger in front of him continued. "I want to be left alone... by everyone," she seethed with narrowed eyes. "Especially *you*."

"Taylor," he implored. She had wounded him, and even he could hear it in his voice.

She attempted to push past him on her way out of the room, but Victor wasn't having it. He grabbed her arm and yanked her around to face him. She looked up at him with rage in her eyes but, at that point, he was unaffected. She had sparked his own impatience.

"Have you lost your *fucking* mind?" he growled.

Her lips parted but he cut her off before any more disrespectful words flew out of her mouth.

"Yes, I think you have. You're going senile. You have to be. Because you clearly forgot who the fuck you were talking to."

She recoiled as if she had the nerve to be insulted and tried, unsuccessfully, to free her arm from his grasp.

Victor leaned in close enough to feel her heavy breath on his face. "You ever speak to me like that again, I will tie you to a chair and leave you there until you learn how to speak to someone that loves you."

He released her arm with enough force to throw her slightly off balance. After securing her footing, she rolled her eyes and stormed out of the room. Victor inhaled a deep breath and released it while looking around the room. Destroyed was an understatement. Judging from the broken furniture and shattered glass, she'd had a complete temper tantrum.

Victor turned to the doctor. He was standing in a corner beside the bar. He didn't appear at all startled by the scene before him. In fact, he seemed to be fascinated, as if he was studying them.

Victor stepped over the glass and crossed the room. "Drink?" he asked as he walked behind the bar.

"Bourbon. If you have it."

He was lucky enough to find a couple of glasses that Taylor hadn't hurled across the room.

"Ice?" he asked the doctor.

"Never." The man chuckled.

Dr. Porter was a tall, black man with a bald head and a salt and pepper beard. He seemed astute and confident, not at all easily intimidated. And because of his prestigious career, impeccable reputation, and a glowing recommendation from his mother, Victor was grateful he'd agreed to see Taylor on such short notice.

"Thanks for coming, Doctor."

"Don't mention it."

Victor poured a nice amount of bourbon in both glasses and handed one to the doctor. He gestured toward a barstool that had been turned over.

"Pull up a chair."

The doctor complied and turned the barstool upright. He took a seat and sipped from his glass. Victor contemplated apologizing for their behavior but thought better of it. The man was a psychologist. It couldn't have been the worst thing he'd ever seen.

Victor raised his glass to his lips and emptied the contents with one gulp. He placed the glass on the bar and refilled it.

"What can I do, Doc? What can I do to make it better?"

"You're doing it."

He looked at the shrink with disbelief. He'd just manhandled, cursed out, and threatened his pregnant wife right in front of him.

"Don't bullshit me, Dr. Porter," Victor warned.

"I wouldn't, Governor Creed. Even though your wife didn't do much talking, judging from what she's been through and her behavior, I can easily deduce that she's suffering from PTSD. That's Post Traumatic—"

"I know what PTSD is, Doctor. And I *deduced* that without a Ph.D. in Clinical Psychology."

The sarcastic comment escaped before he could help himself. Taylor had tested his patience, but he didn't mean to take it out on the doctor.

"I apologize for being rude, Dr. Porter. I'm a bit on edge myself."

"Understandable. No apologies necessary. After everything your wife has been through, Post Traumatic Stress Disorder is the easy diagnosis. But it's also my understanding that your wife is pregnant."

"She is," Victor confirmed before taking a sip.

"Governor, traumatic events, compounded with hormonal changes due to pregnancy, is a powder keg of explosive behavior."

Victor had been so worried about Taylor's state of mind after the shooting that hormonal issues had never even crossed his mind. He'd been ridiculously oblivious to what she was really going through, and he felt like a complete asshole for snapping at her.

"I'm going to hell," Victor muttered.

"Nah." Dr. Porter chuckled. "You got her to calm down."

"Hmph...did I?" Victor scoffed. "She's probably trashing our bedroom as we speak."

"It's better than the alternative," he said through laughter before drinking from his glass.

"The alternative?"

"Yeah. She was about to kick your ass."

TAYLOR

The shining sun through the picture window forced Taylor to roll to her side. She pulled the sheet over her head and tried to go back to sleep. Unfortunately, pregnancy didn't allow for sleeping in. She had to pee. After flinging the sheet off of her head, she forced herself to sit up. She looked behind her and was grateful to discover that Victor had left already. She wasn't prepared to face him after the way she'd behaved the night before. Sure, she was angry he'd set up an appointment with a psychologist after she'd told him not to, but she was embarrassed and appalled by her reaction. Taylor knew she owed him an apology, but she felt like shit and she wasn't ready to face him.

She stood and padded to the bathroom. As she made her way to the toilet, she glanced in the mirror. What a horrifying sight she was. Her big hair was unruly and matted in the back. Her eyes were swollen and red from crying herself to sleep. She had dried tears and dark circles under her eyes. A mess was the best way to describe her appearance.

After doing her business, she flushed the toilet and walked over to the shower. She set the water to her desired temperature and pulled her nightgown over her head. She stepped in the shower and sighed as soon as the hot water sprayed her body.

It was about forty-five minutes later when she emerged from the bathroom wrapped in a towel. She dried her freshly shampooed hair, entered her dressing room, and sat at the vanity.

"Good morning," Victor said from the doorway.

Taylor looked at his reflection in the mirror. She exhaled and turned to face him. Horrible guilt washed over her when she looked in her beautiful husband's eyes.

"I'm so sorry, Victor," she said through a sigh. "I just..."

In two long strides, he was in front of her, lifting her to her feet. He clutched both sides of her face and looked at her with eyes filled with sadness and love. The guilt Taylor was feeling was overwhelming.

"No, sweetheart. I'm sorry. I promise I'll do better."

Taylor couldn't believe what she was hearing. She couldn't understand why he was apologizing to her. She was the one acting a fool.

"What? No. Honey, you have nothing to be sorry for. You were only trying to help me, and I completely lost it."

Victor pulled her against his warm body and held her tight. She melted against him, feeling safer than she'd felt since the shooting. It was the first time she'd actually allowed him to hold her without tensing. She wrapped her arms around his waist and caressed his muscular back. Tears welled in her eyes as she thought about how much she missed being safely cocooned in his arms.

"I love you, sweetheart," he whispered into her thick hair.

"I know you do, and I love you."

Victor took a step back and lifted her chin with his fingers. She warmed under his emerald gaze. With just a look, he was tearing down barriers that had formed the minute that animal killed her commander.

He leaned in, bringing his face close to hers. Shamefully, Taylor recalled the pain and anger in his eyes the last time they were that close.

"Victor, I—"

Victor cut off her words by pushing his soft lips against hers. She moaned against his lips and ignored the slight pain in her shoulder as she snaked her arms around his neck. For whatever reason, her husband's touch, his kiss, made everything all right in the world. At least, for that moment.

When their lips separated, she wanted so desperately for them to reunite. But Victor reached for her hand and led her into their bedroom. He walked her over to the sofa and gently pulled her to sit next to him. He caressed her hand, placing it to his mouth. After a soft kiss, he smiled.

"I'm worried, sweetheart. I don't know how to help."

In his solemn tone, Taylor could hear defeat. It was breaking her heart.

She squeezed his hand, hoping to give him some comfort. "Baby, please don't worry so much. I've heard before, from other cops that have been involved in police shootings, that the way I'm feeling is normal. Now, my behavior," she chuckled, "that shit I can't explain."

"Dr. Porter suggested that hormonal changes are a factor."

"Oh, God." Taylor sighed. "Dr. Porter must think I'm a nutcase."

Victor laughed. "Yeah, probably."

Taylor dropped her head in shame.

"No, babe, I'm kidding. Look, if you don't want to see him anymore, you don't have to."

"No, no. I do. I mean...I think I need to," Taylor admitted.

Victor smiled, and in his eyes, she saw relief. Plus, she was sure that what she was about to tell him would add to his sense of relief.

"Sooo... I've decided to quit my job," she announced.

"What?" he asked with a furrowed brow as if he couldn't believe what she was telling him. "Why are you quitting your job?"

Taylor frowned at the question. His reaction to her news was unexcepted. She, for sure, thought he'd be more pleased.

"I thought you wanted me to stop working?"

Victor straightened and clutched her shoulders. "I do. But I don't want you to quit for me. Honestly, I truly just want you to be happy and safe."

Taylor smiled up at him. He never ceased to amaze. He was so thoughtful that he would put his needs and wants aside just to make her happy.

"This is not about you. It's not even about me witnessing such a traumatic event. I mean...I'm rich. It's just stupid to keep doing a job that could get me killed when I don't even need to work."

Victor studied her for seconds before speaking. "Are you sure?"

"Hell, yeah!" Taylor confirmed. "This police shit is for the birds."

The corners of his eyes crinkled as his smile spread. Victor couldn't hide his happiness if he tried.

"Okay, well, that's great, honey. Now, go and get dressed."

"Get dressed?"

"Yep. We're going out."

For the first time, Taylor noticed his attire. He was wearing jeans and a Nickelback t-shirt. Taylor *loved* him in jeans and a t-shirt. When she looked down at his black boots, she instantly knew where they were going. For the first time since the shooting, she was excited to leave the house.

～

Two and a half hours later, Taylor and Victor were sitting on a rocky bank in Peru, Illinois, fishing for Silver Bass. It was more peaceful than usual. There were no boats disrupting the water, no disruptive jet skiers, and strangely, no other fishermen. Even though it seemed as if they were alone, she knew better. When they left the apartment, she was pleasantly surprised when Victor opened the passenger door for her and hopped in the front seat. She was trying to remember if she'd ever been in a car that Victor was driving.

For the entire ride, it had been just the two of them; no assistants, no driver, no Gregor. Even on the bank, it appeared that they were alone. But there was no way Victor would be out in the open, near a large body of water, without security.

The weather was perfect, the water was still, and the fish were biting. Taylor looked over at her man, loving the way his big body was putting a strain on his t-shirt. A gust of wind pushed his silky, dark hair away from his face, gifting Taylor with an unobstructed view of his beautiful profile. When he grabbed a beer from the cooler, she watched with lustful anticipation as he lifted the bottle and pressed his sexy mouth to the lip of the bottle.

Victor turned, catching her mid ogle. "Stop eye-fucking me, Lady. I am not a piece of meat," he joked with a mischievous glint in his stunning green eyes.

"A big, thick piece of meat," Taylor rebutted through laughter.

"Naaaaw, baby. You know what's big and thick?" he asked, jumping to his feet.

Taylor's gaze roamed his muscular chest, down his lean abs, then to the outline of his package in his jeans.

"What's that, sexy?" she asked in her best, "Gimme that dick" voice.

"This whopper on my hook, *baby!*"

He yanked his pole, winded his reel, and pulled in a giant, fighting Asian carp.

"Shit!" Victor barked.

The disappointed look on his face was hilarious. Taylor almost fell out of her chair laughing at him. He'd done all that celebrating only to catch the worst invasive species. A fish often referred to as pests.

"Throw that shit back in there!" Taylor teased. "You done wasted a damn worm on that water roach!"

"Shut up, woman!"

Taylor was hunched over, roaring with laughter. With the cutest pout, Victor pried the swimming predator off his hook and tossed it toward the trees.

19

DONATELLA

Halfway through a tasteless meal packet of ready-to-eat survival food, Clara approached with a smile.

"Kateri, dear, the prophet would like to see you in the rectory."

Donna trusted Clara even less than she did the so-called prophet. She was always fucking smiling. How could someone like that possibly be trusted? Her sickeningly sweet disposition was nauseating. Yet, Donna played along and sprouted a smile in return.

"Thank you, Clara."

When she walked away, Donna turned to Kelly and rolled her eyes. "She creeps me the fuck out," she whispered before getting up from the cafeteria table.

Being summoned to Bobby Lee's personal living quarters was not unusual. He often sent for his future wives to hold private sermons, preaching about being a good and dutiful wife. But what really surprised her was that in all the times he'd sent for them, he never once tried to get physical. Even though he'd said, several times, that he would wait until after the mass wedding to consummate his marriages, she didn't believe him. She didn't believe a word that came out of the charlatan's mouth.

When she got to the rectory, she greeted the overly happy women who acted as if they were winning some sort of prize by becoming one of his many wives. Again, Donna played along. She smiled and took a seat on the living room floor next to Vera.

All conversations ceased when Bobby Lee entered the room. His golden hair bounced with each step. He was wearing a long, white garb as if he were some sort of medieval friar. She could hear soft gasping coming from the swooning women. By his side was Clara. She was his bottom bitch as far as Donna was concerned.

"*Ephesians!*" he called out dramatically.

He didn't have to do much to have the other women mesmerized. They waited with bated breath for the next round of bullshit to plop out his mouth. It was like they were all puffing on the same batch of Purple Haze.

Donna was tempted to roll her eyes, but she resisted. Instead, she sat with her legs crossed and her chin resting on her fists. She imitated the other ladies and stared up at him with googly eyes.

Bobby Lee smiled, exposing perfect, white teeth and raised the Bible over his head. He was definitely a good-looking man, and he certainly didn't lack charisma.

"The Bible says, 'There is one body, and one Spirit. Even as ye called in one hope of your calling. One lord, one faith, one baptism.'"

He walked over to the fireplace and placed the Bible on the mantel. After scanning the room, he held his hand out to Sonia, a young Hispanic woman who'd arrived around the same time Donna had.

"Join me, please."

Without hesitation, Sonia hopped off the floor and hurried over to Bobby Lee. The excitement in her eyes from being so close to him was… sad. Donna, for the life of her, couldn't understand how he managed to control the minds of people who otherwise seemed perfectly normal.

"*Who can find a virtuous woman? Her price is above rubies.* That's Proverbs 31:10."

Sonia was smiling as if she'd just won the Publisher's Clearing House sweepstakes.

"A virtuous woman," he repeated. "Virtuous."

Get on with it!

Donna totally could've been in the cafeteria finishing her powdered food.

"Beloveds, Sonia is not a virtuous woman. Since she was a child, her body has been bought and used time and time again."

Sonia's smile faded. Her face turned beet red with embarrassment. She folded her arms as if she was trying to put up a protective forcefield.

"Yet, we are not here to judge. Let He who is without sin among you cast the first stone at our beloved Sonia."

Donna was horrified for the young woman. She could not believe the audacity that it took to throw her under a very judgmental and unflattering spotlight.

Clara walked up to Sonia wearing her trademarked creepy smile and placed her hands on her shoulders.

"You will be cleansed, washed, and made clean again, and worthy of our prophet."

When Bobby Lee left the room, Donna looked around to see if any of the other women were as appalled as she was. Nope. The loopy ass women were all smiles.

Clara kept one hand on Sonia's shoulder and turned to the rest of the group. "Ladies, please stand and disrobe."

Donna wasn't sure she'd heard correctly. Maybe she was using disrobe as a metaphor. Surely, this chick wasn't telling them to strip.

"Quickly, please," Clara insisted.

Donna had an inner debate about whether or not she was going to get naked on demand. She'd worked undercover for years, and had to do plenty of strange things to keep her cover. She'd posed as an exotic dancer, a prostitute, hell...even a dominatrix. But she'd never, ever had to get completely naked.

She could refuse and call it quits, but she wasn't squeamish about nudity, and there was no way she was leaving without witnessing

Bobby Lee in cuffs. So, like the rest of them, she took off her clothes and waited for further instructions.

Once they were all naked, Clara walked over to the same door that Bobby Lee went through. "Follow me, ladies."

Like puppies, they did.

They followed her down a hallway with wood paneling until they reached a door. Donna heard gasps coming from the women who entered first. And when she entered, she understood why. Inside the room was a huge indoor swimming pool under a greenroom roof. Donna was amazed at how well Bobby Lee was living in comparison to everyone else.

Bobby Lee, still in his robe, was standing in the shallow end of the pool with his arms raised as if he was John the Baptist.

"'And now why thou tarriest now? Arise and be baptized, and wash away thy sins, calling on the name of the Lord.' Come, wives! Be baptized."

Clara gestured toward the pool steps. One by one, everyone entered the pool. Yes, the baptism was a sham, but at least the water was warm.

Bobby Lee called Sonia over, placed his hand in the small of her back. "I baptize thee in the name of the Lord," he declared as he dipped her into the water.

Surprisingly, it appeared as if he barely noticed her naked body. He seemed focused and, dare Donna say...professional. Maybe he really and truly believed he was the Messiah. Maybe in his mind, the Messiah was supposed to con, steal, deceive, and degrade.

After the fourth baptism, it was finally Donna's turn. She stepped closer and waited for him to dip her in the water. When he didn't, she looked up and found him studying the tattoos that covered most of her torso. His lips parted as if he was about to speak, but he quickly pressed them shut. When he placed his hand at the small of her back, Donna noticed the swollen package beneath his saintly robe. She did her best not to cringe when he pressed his wet fingers to her naked flesh.

"I baptize thee in the name of the Lord."

Donna held her breath as he dipped her in the pool. She came up mad as hell that there were no decent hair products anywhere on the compound.

He pulled her upright and stood her in front of him. "Now, you are clean," he affirmed while pushing her wet hair out of her face.

Donna blinked the water out of her eyes and smiled. She was waiting for him to take his hands off of her, but he was in no hurry. When he finally released her, he said, "Take your place with the rest."

She nodded and shuffled over to the women who had already been baptized.

She watched as he repeated the process with the rest of the women. After yet another small sermon about marriage, sin, and baptism, they were finally dismissed. Clara passed out towels as they climbed out of the pool. Once they were dry, she escorted them back to the living room. There, they dressed in silence.

After they were dismissed, Donna was more determined than ever to rid society of the freak show that was the BOC.

LINCOLN

As soon as the plane landed, Lincoln turned his phone on and checked his voice messages. After clearing his voicemail, he dialed a friend.

"This is Mike," a groggy voice answered.

"Why the fuck do you sound like you're sleeping? It's like one in the afternoon," Lincoln barked into the phone.

"Rough night," Mike grumbled. "What do want?"

"Tahira Raji, I need to find her."

Mike Romello was also CIA. Calling him for information was a longshot, but everyone else Lincoln had called knew exactly jack shit about Tahira.

Lincoln frowned when he heard the rumble of laughter on the other end.

"Linc, you don't find Tahira. She finds you."

That's bullshit," Lincoln spat. "The Central Intelligence Agency doesn't have intelligence on their own operatives."

"Nobody you know, Colonel," he quipped.

Lincoln pushed a button and disconnected the call. Mike was no help and he was beyond pissed. Tahira Raji owed him answers. Because of her intel, he and his soldiers had been sent on a fruitless mission. Thankfully, everyone returned to the TOC in one piece. However, during the debriefing, Lincoln learned that *Lincoln 5-2* had breached an empty plane. Without an explanation, they were dismissed and sent back to the States. It didn't sit right with Lincoln, and he wanted answers.

When the aisle was clear, Lincoln grabbed his bag from the overhead compartment. After a fifteen-hour hopper from Iraq to D.C., he decided to forego a good night's sleep and catch a commercial flight to Chicago.

As soon as he stepped onto the ramp, his phone rang. He answered, not really paying attention to the Caller ID. He just figured it was Mike calling back.

"*What?*" Lincoln barked into the phone.

"Well, now, that is *horrible* phone etiquette."

He recognized his older brother's voice. "What do want, Luc?"

"Well, I don't want shit now, grumpy ass."

"Good. I'll call you back."

He was about to hang up, but Lucas kept talking.

"Okay, fine. Maybe by the time you call me back, I won't have forgotten where Donatella is."

Lincoln clenched the cell phone. "Donatella? Luc, you know—"

Click.

"Hello? Luc?"

You Motherfucker!

20

DONATELLA

Even though there was no full-body mirror in the small dormitory that she shared with Vera, Donna knew she was looking good. Clara had picked out a dress that flattered everything she thought was sexy about her. It was low-cut, slimming, and it accentuated her long legs. Clara was on the mark when it came to dressing her. Actually, she dressed all the women.

Donna was not at all that surprised at her elevated level of taste. After their trip to Chicago, she was able to get a taste of how Clara was accustomed to living. The woman had excellent taste in food, clothes, hotels, and liquor. Donna worked hard but could nowhere near touch Clara's extravagant lifestyle, which was infuriating since the woman was supposed to be living as modestly as the rest of them.

Donna had a feeling Clara would go all out, and she was right. For the Blood of the Chosen, the gala was the event of the year. It was Bobby Lee's chance to lure in wealthy parishioners. And he and Clara had made sure that their young female congregation was able to entice. All of their faces had been done by a crew of talented make-up artists. All of their hair had been professionally done. The goal was to look good and procure members with deep pockets.

Donna glanced over at Vera. The woman was unquestionably gorgeous in her red, formfitting mermaid dress with the surprisingly tasteful peekaboo cutouts. Her normally colorful hair had been dyed back to her natural blonde and was pinned in a messy bun. Her face was beat to perfection. Vera was indeed a beautiful woman, but with the way she behaved, Donna could guess she didn't believe it. For someone so young and so attractive, Vera's self-esteem was shot to hell. She was pretty and kind, but she had no idea what a prize she was. Maybe that was why she was so susceptible to brainwashing.

Vera was a true believer. To her, Robert Lee Khal was the one and only true Messiah. She would, for sure, take a bullet for him.

"Wooooow!" Vera sang. "You look so amazing!"

"You think so?" Donna did a quick spin so that Vera could get the whole effect of the cornflower blue dress Clara had picked out for her. She had her normally straight bob styled with big, wavy curls. The makeup artist had even painted bronzer on her exposed chest and shoulders, enhancing her Native American features.

"You look like a model! That dress was made for you."

"Thanks, V. You look amazing too. That red is gorg! That's your color."

"Thanks. Hopefully, we'll get some new members tonight."

"Surely we will with you looking like that."

Vera did a cute little twerk and walked toward the door. "Okay, well, let's go get this done."

Donna grabbed her silver clutch and followed Vera out of their bedroom. They clacked down the hall in heels. When they stepped out of the building, a car with a driver was waiting to take them to the party. The gala was being held in a ballroom on the compound, but because of the five-inch, open-toed rhinestone covered heels she was wearing, Donna was more than grateful for the ride.

The car drove past the fancy cars pulling up to the entrance of the ballroom to the rear. So, she figured the women who were already members were entering in a different location.

The car came to a stop. Seconds later, the driver was opening the door for them. Vera stepped out and waited as Donna got out. She then grabbed Donna's hand and the walked to the entrance.

"I am excited," Vera beamed.

Donna smiled, pretending to be just as elated to be used, dangled like a carrot in front of a bunch of very rich rabbits.

They entered a back door and joined about twenty other waiting, well-dressed female parishioners in a large conference room. She could hear music and muffled chattered coming from the main hall.

"Okay, ladies!" came from across the room.

She turned in the direction of Clara's chipper voice. Wow, was all Donna thought as she looked at Clara. She was stunning from head to toe in a silver gown covered in sparkling stones. Clara had already been attractive, but as she stood in front of them, she was downright breathtaking. Not only that…she was fucking sexy.

"This is the day the Lord has made; We will rejoice and be glad in it. Amen?"

"Amen!" they all choired.

"Now, just past those doors are the resources we need to champion for the Lord. Soon, we will be able to build the world He intended for us. I want you to smile, bat those lashes, and help them, no, *force* them to join this battle to restore the word and the laws of God."

Donna looked around and saw the glint in everyone's eyes. She wondered exactly how well she was at pretending to be one of the pod people. Thankfully, Clara's pep talk only lasted one minute more. Finally, she was escorting them through a door and into an exquisite ballroom. Nowhere in her wildest dreams would Donna have thought that there would be a place on the compound as magnificent as the room she entered.

As instructed, Donna and the rest of the women spread out amongst the guests. To her surprise, as she looked around, she noticed that there were absolutely no women partygoers. Were none invited? Donna thought this event was all about getting money from rich people. Were there no wealthy women in the world?

Donna smiled and batted her lashes as she weaved her way

through the expensive tuxedos. Her destination, the bar. Not once did Clara forbid them to indulge. So, she'd rather ask for forgiveness than permission.

Unfortunately, by the time she made it to the bar, she had been poked, groped, and grabbed several times by men that gave less than a damn that they were at an event to advance membership in a church. They certainly weren't behaving very religiously. But, somehow, she made it through without getting impregnated by one of the grabby guests.

When she was less than three feet from the bar, she began to experience a great sense of victory. Sadly, it was crushed when Bobby Lee cut her off at the path.

"My God, Kateri." He lustfully looked her up and down. "You are a sight."

He moved uncomfortably close and whispered," I can't wait to make you my wife so that I can have every single inch of you."

Donna took a half step backward and smiled up at him. His golden hair fell perfectly to one side of his handsome face. He was tall and fit in his custom tuxedo, and his golden eyes glimmered like gold. Had he not been a sadistic, manipulating, cunning piece of shit, Bobby Lee would've been totally fuckable.

"Thank you, Bobby Lee. Clara dressed me well."

She lowered her eyes modestly and clutched her borrowed necklace. He seemed, or at least she thought he seemed the type to find shy and weak irresistibly attractive.

"Clara could only make an attempt to enhance what was already near perfection."

Donna laughed softly and raised a brow at him. "Nearly?" she inquired, faking timidity. "Why nearly?"

"Tattoos," he responded dryly.

Donna blinked up at him. She was surprised because when he'd called himself baptizing her, he'd seemed a bit enthralled by her tattoos.

"I see," she replied softly.

He leaned closer and whispered in her ear. "There's one missing."

"One missing?"

"The one of your husband's name, branded on your perfectly round ass. I will have that remedied as soon as you say, 'I do.'"

Wasn't he a fucking charmer? Well, actually, he was.

Donna chuckled out loud at the conversation going on in her head. Bobby Lee was on a roll. He'd dropped his holy man façade and allowed his inner letch to come out and play. As a matter of fact, their prophet wasn't the only letch in the room. Looking around, she noticed extremely uncomfortable women, paired with men who couldn't seem to keep their hands to themselves. It was as if they'd been assigned, or appointed, to a particular man. None of which could've attracted a woman as beautiful as the ones they were groping.

When Bobby Lee placed his hand on her upper arm and squeezed, Donna wondered if she'd been assigned to him.

"How are you enjoying the gala?" she asked in an attempt to make small talk and change the conversation from his name on her ass.

"I am enjoying it as much as I can. I am a very possessive man, Kateri. Every time their eyes roam your body, I get infuriated."

"Well, a lot of us are to be your wives."

He shook his head as if he was truly disturbed. "What we're doing is necessary," he said through a sigh. "We are all soldiers of God, my love, and soldiers go to war. In order to fight a war, we have to use weapons." He placed his other hand on her other arm and looked deep into her eyes. "You, my dear, along with the rest of my flock, are the weapons we must use in this war."

His voice softened. "It kills me inside."

He released her as a waiter, well one of the male members serving as a waiter, passed with a tray of champagne. After grabbing two glasses, he turned and handed one to her. Donna had never been so excited about a drink in her life.

He placed his finger to his lips. "Don't tell Clara," he whispered with a wink.

Donna smiled and happily took the glass. He didn't know it, but it was definitely not going to be her last alcoholic beverage of the evening.

He watched intently as she brought the glass to her lips.

"Though, I have to admit that it wasn't until I saw you tonight that I decided I couldn't let anyone have you, and I simply cannot wait until we're married. I have to have you. And, I have to have you tonight."

What?

"What? But the Bible says—"

"Kateri, listen to me." He reached up and caressed her face. "In the Bible, marriage wasn't about the ceremony. One just took a wife. So, I'll simply take you as my wife. I have been given the authority by God to bless a marital union. That's what I'll do tonight. Tonight, I make you my wife. And tonight, we will consummate our union in *every* way."

Bobby Lee smiled as if granting her greatest wish. As if marrying him would be the pinnacle of her entire existence.

"Wow! Tonight? Really?" Donna gushed.

For her audience, she was putting on the best performance of her life. What she was really trying to do was figure out a way to get out of marrying him without blowing her cover. Getting naked was one thing, but fucking him was out of the question. The Feds could go to hell. She wasn't prostituting herself for them, CPD, or anyone else.

"*Tonight,*" he confirmed with a toothy grin. "Once we're married, I'm gonna do things to—"

"Excuse me, Prophet. There's a problem."

It was Harry Barber dressed in a tuxedo. Apparently, Bobby Lee's righthand man didn't have to dress like a waiter.

"Have Clara handle it," Bobby Lee dismissed.

"She's trying, but we need you," Harry insisted.

Bobby Lee grunted and handed Donna his half-empty glass of champagne.

He turned to Harry. "What is it?" he asked, his irritation evident.

Harry urged him to take a few steps away. They had a hushed conversation that caused Bobby Lee to look over his shoulder. Donna couldn't hear what they were saying, but she did follow their line of sight. It was Vera. She was crying hysterically in front of an angry, overweight man. He was holding his beet red face as if she'd slapped him, and he seemed to be spouting something that didn't seem all that pleasant.

"Fuck!" cursed the preacher.

Since his back was to her, Donna rolled her eyes without the risk of getting caught.

Without a word, Bobby Lee and Harry took off toward the disturbance. While she was being nosy, she took advantage of the prophet's absence and finished his champagne. Then, she finished her own and placed both glasses on a nearby table. She continued to watch until Kelly approached. Since he'd gotten so close to Harry, therefore, close to the prophet, he was also wearing a tux.

"No waiter getup?" she quipped.

"Naw, I guess I'm one of the popular boys. Some of us are here as security, but they want us to blend in." He swiped an imaginary spot of dirt from his shoulder and grinned. "Hence the monkey suit."

"What's happening?" Donna asked, jerking her head toward Vera.

"Apparently, little Miss Vera ain't the loyal, bubblehead they thought she was. You do know what tonight is about, don't you?"

"I do now," Donna scoffed.

She already knew the gala was just a ruse to attract rich men to the cult by using young, attractive women. What she didn't know until she'd arrived was that the fancy ballroom was nothing more than a glorified house of ill repute. They were using the Glory Gala as a way to pimp naive female followers.

"Look, Kelly. This dude just flipped the script. He's planning to marry me tonight. Apparently, he can't wait anymore."

"Daaamn, girl, you're better than I thought," he teased. "You worked him good."

"I'm not fucking that asshole!"

Kelly chuckled. "Calm down, girl. Tell him you're on your period or something."

Donna narrowed her eyes at her partner. He sounded about as naive as the rest of the folks on the compound.

"First of all, Clara knows when we all get our periods. Secondly, when did a fucking period ever stop a pervert from wanting to fuck?"

Kelly blew out a breath. His tone turned serious. "Listen, Detective, nobody expects you to sleep with him or anyone else. Just do the best you can for as long as you can. With the prostitution, the tax shit you found, and the illegal weapons, we're hitting the home stretch."

"What exactly do you have on the weapons?" Donna asked. Since the prophet seemed intent on keeping the men and women separated, she found it hard to get progress updates.

"Oh, man, *so* much. Look." He tilted his head toward her right shoulder.

Donna turned and scanned the crowd of well-dressed men. At first, she saw nothing. But then one stood out. And he stood out for one reason and one reason alone. He was panty-dropping, drive you out of your mind gorgeous in a dangerous, "I'll fuck you and then kill you" sort of way. It was none other than Luca Savelli.

"*Ho-ly shit!*" Donna marveled.

She was wrong. The gala wasn't simply a pussy for money gathering. For good measure, Bobby Lee was working an arms deal. Kelly's dick must've been rock-hard. Feds and local police alike knew Luca Savelli was the head of a Sicilian crime family known for dealing in weapons. So far, he'd been completely untouchable. Now, there he was, less than twenty feet from them at a gala for a bogus religious organization that was currently under investigation for buying and selling illegal weapons.

"We're gonna be wrapping this investigation up a lot sooner than expected."

Donna sighed. "That's good to know."

"And what's even better," Kelly added, "is that the Savelli family isn't the only circus in town. There are others."

"To be honest, Kelly, I'm shocked to see Luca Savelli here in the first place. The Savellis are huge. They sell to countries, not cults."

Kelly shrugged. "He must be here for a reason, and it's my job to find out."

"Well, can you hurry it up before I'm carrying the baby of the Chosen?"

As Kelly walked away laughing, Donna turned to see the outcome of Vera's unexpected outburst. She didn't find Vera, but what she did find made her stumble. Just as she was sure that Luca Savelli was the finest thing in the room, Lincoln Creed stepped into her view.

"Funny meeting you here," he rumbled in the sexiest baritone ever.

She was enthralled by lustrous dark hair, hypnotic green eyes, and the masculinity of his perfectly chiseled jawline. Not to mention his tall, muscular body in a tux that had to be custom made.

Whew! Lord have mercy!

Donna had gotten so caught up in his presence, she'd forgotten she was supposed to be working. She looked around to see if anyone was paying attention to them, then she turned back to him with a frown.

"Lincoln, what are you doing here? You can't be here!"

He smirked with a raised brow. "I can't?"

Donna growled out of frustration. Everything about him was a distraction. She needed to be working her way around the room so that she could conveniently overhear stuff she wasn't supposed to hear.

"This is not a game, Lincoln. This is my job," she gritted angrily. "And, I *asked* you, what are you doing here?"

Lincoln's smile fell as he moved closer. "I'm here for you, Donatella. Lucas gave me his invitation."

"I'm not Donatella here!" she snapped in a hushed tone.

"I know that...Kateri."

Donna's brows furrowed as she tried to figure out how he knew her covert identity. His resourcefulness wasn't enough of an enigma for her to forget that he was on the verge of blowing her cover.

"Lincoln, you-cannot-be-here."

"And yet, I am," he quipped, sipping from a glass filled with brown liquid.

Donna's eyes flashed to the glass. She had a fleeting moment of jealousy before snapping back to her senses. She opened her mouth to speak, but he cut her off by snaking his arm around her waist and yanking her body to his. He leaned down and pressed his soft lips to her ear.

"I'm not a fucking idiot, Donatella," Lincoln whispered. "By the way, I hear you're getting married tonight."

"Linc—" Donna grunted while trying to pull out of his arms. But Lincoln held on tighter.

"You'll find that you'll need me. And once you do... *Kateri*, it's gonna cost you dearly."

Lincoln released her and took a step back. With a lopsided grin, he looked her up and down. "Magnificent," he remarked with a wicked gaze in his eyes before walking away, leaving her to stare at his broad back.

21

LINCOLN

There he was, at a pseudo-religious gathering, staring at the devil in a blue dress. Not wanting to freak Donatella out any more than she already was, Lincoln stood close to the bar on the opposite side of the ballroom. He knew he shouldn't have been there. She had a job to do and he didn't want to do anything that would place her in harm's way.

From the moment he'd pulled into the compound, he'd been fighting a battle within—stay or go? Even when he'd entered the surprisingly opulent ballroom, he'd been tempted to turn around and leave. It wasn't until his eyes landed on Donatella did he realize that he couldn't leave, even if he wanted to. She was a vision, like a pleasant dream in an elegant blue dress. To him, she had always been beautiful, but he'd never seen her in formal wear. She was mesmerizing.

Lincoln watched from afar as she charmed man after man with the fakest smile she could muster. He knew it was fake because he'd been present to witness her smile brighten a room.

"Are you enjoying yourself, Colonel Creed?" Lincoln frowned when the feminine voice interrupted his thoughts and dragged his attention from Donatella. He turned to the woman and took a page from Donna's book. With a smile, he said, "I am."

"I'm Clara, and I'm here to facilitate all of your needs."

Her voice was low and raspy. She was flirting, and he was interested. Not in her, but she knew his name. After all, it wasn't he who was invited. It was Lucas. Now, he knew they looked alike, but not that much alike.

"It's so nice to meet you, Clara. Please, call me Lincoln."

She nodded and locked her fingers just under her bosom. It was a trick that women used to draw attention to their tits. His fake grin turned genuine. Clara was attractive, but she had no way of knowing that he was there for one woman, and one woman alone.

"Well, then, Lincoln it is. I'd like to introduce you to our prophet. He's very excited to meet you."

Lincoln looked around for their so-called prophet. If he was so excited to meet him, where the hell was he? Clara, presumably reading his mind, chuckled softly.

"He's right over there, Lincoln."

She held out her hand toward a nearby table as if she expected him to scurry over to greet their holy man. Lincoln glared down at the woman.

"I'll be right here," he told her pointedly before raising his glass to his lips.

Lincoln knew exactly what The Blood of the Chosen was really about. Besides, Clara and their prophet knew that people like him knew exactly what The Blood of the Chosen was. Therefore, he was not about to entertain Bobby Khal's need to be worshipped.

"Very well, Lincoln. I will fetch the Prophet."

Lincoln nodded and took another sip. He was grateful when she walked away so that he could return his attention to the reason he was there in the first place. He scanned the room for Donatella, and what he saw when he found her made him tense. She was talking to John Holloway, millionaire CEO of Gorga Pharmaceuticals. At least, that was who he was during the night. When the moon rose, he became "Big John," fat piece of shit with a penchant for underage girls...*and* boys.

He was holding Donatella's wrist and refused to let go when she tried to pull away. It took every ounce of discipline that Lincoln could muster to keep from racing across the room and choke-holding his ass to sleep. But Donatella didn't seem to be in distress. The fake smile was still plastered on her face. Lincoln prayed that John didn't do anything with his hands that would make him think, *Fuck her job!* and blow her cover by beating the shit out of him until he was thin again.

"Are you okay, Colonel?"

Lincoln heard the voice, but he ignored it. He was engaged in something much more important.

"Colonel?"

Had he been a woman, he'd have rolled his eyes. Instead, he turned to see who was talking to him. He couldn't promise that his aggravation would not show.

"*Yes?*" He could hear the irritation in his own voice.

"Is everything okay, Colonel?" Khal repeated.

"It's fine."

The preacher nervously cleared his throat. He was accustomed to being revered by weaker people. Clearly, not at all accustomed to Lincoln's brashness.

"It's a pleasure to meet you, Colonel. I'm a big fan of your brother. I voted for him."

Lincoln knitted his brows and glared at the preacher. "Is it a pleasure to meet me because you voted for my brother?"

He cleared his throat again. "No...ugh...well, I'd like to thank you for your service."

Lincoln nodded and looked past him to check on Donatella. Thankfully, she'd moved on from Holloway and was in conversation with a woman. The tension in his shoulders instantly relaxed. He decided to give Khal the attention he so desperately needed.

"I appreciate your hospitality seeing as how I'm an uninvited guest."

Khal smirked as if he had regained his superiority. "The Bible says, 'And he said unto them, go ye into all the world, and *preach* the gospel to every creature.' All are welcome, Colonel."

Lincoln frowned at the nerve it took for him to speak to him through scripture while pimping out his female flock. He decided to test the preacher to see how long he could stay in character.

"Membership drive, huh?" Lincoln asked, rubbing his beard.

"Yes, sir. Come one, come all to the Lord!" he exclaimed.

"Hmm? What does your church have to offer that the others don't?"

"Why, the true Word of God, Colonel Creed."

"The Bible is the Word of God. Don't need a church for that," Lincoln pointed out, shaking his head.

"Ahh, but...not every church is blessed with someone that can interpret and *teach* the true word."

"And, that's you?"

"Yes, it is, praise God," Khal declared.

Enough of this shit!

Lincoln scanned the room with a squint until his eyes landed on Donatella.

"You have some beautiful women here. Are they all members?"

"Yes, sir, they are," Khal boasted with a proud smile.

"And... are all these men members?"

The preacher hesitated before answering. He was carefully choosing his response. "No, not all of them. Most of them are like you, influential men of power."

"I have no power," Lincoln scoffed.

"Oh, but you're wrong, Colonel. You're a Creed. Your father is a retired senator and your brother is a governor."

"That means *they're* powerful," Lincoln mused.

Khal laughed. His shady brown eyes lit up with glee. "Colonel, if I were a betting man, I'd say you were on the fast track to being promoted."

Even though both his dad and his brother were politicians who led very public lives, it never ceased to irritate him how much strangers thought they knew about his life.

"If that were true, how would that help you and your church?"

"The more influential members we have, the easier it is to spread the word. The battle is near, Colonel. We need an army, an army of powerful soldiers."

"Alright, Khal. Let's cut to the chase. Is any of this for me?" Lincoln asked, nodding his head toward one of the women walking by.

Khal turned around to see what he was referring to. When he turned back, he was smiling.

"Of course, brother. *All* that we have to offer is yours."

"In exchange for?"

"Your allegiance and a monthly monetary donation to our church."

"A donation of what sort?"

"100."

"100?" Lincoln snorted.

Surely, the preacher didn't just say what he thought he heard. From ballroom chatter, he knew the going rate was ten thousand. He guessed he was getting the special, "You're a Creed" rate.

"Done," Lincoln agreed. "I want that one." He pointed to Donatella.

"Which one?" Khal asked as he turned around.

"The black lady in the blue dress."

Khal turned back to him. The look on his face was priceless, like Lincoln was trying to take his favorite toy.

He stood silent, seconds before shaking his head. "She's off limits."

"Hmph. I thought *all* that you had to offer was mine. Is it not?"

The preacher smiled, but he was clearly uneasy. "All, except her. She and I are getting married."

"So are you and all the rest," Lincoln sneered.

"Pick any other woman. She and I are to be married."

"Not tonight," was Lincoln's blunt response.

A scowl marred Khal's face. He shook his head vehemently. "I'm sorry, Colonel. She's mine."

Lincoln glared down at the slightly shorter man and looked him right in the eye. "Not if you want my 100 thou," he hissed at the conman.

DONATELLA

Donatella was trying to subtly ease closer to Luca Savelli when she was halted by a hand grabbing her wrist. She froze and turned around to see who grabbed her, and was looking up into a pair of beady blue eyes that belonged to another well-dressed fat man.

She forced a smile. "Hello."

"So, I hear that you're off limits."

"Oh?"

"Yeah, and it's a damn shame. I would've changed your life."

Donna attempted to pull her wrist from his grasp, but he was holding on tight. She stared at the sausage-like fingers wrapped around her wrist and contemplated breaking one. Instead, she placed her hand over his and smiled up at him.

"I could have sworn you were already smitten with a special young lady."

If she was going to be assaulted by pudgy digits and the smell of sweat, she might as well get some information out of his greasy ass.

"Oh, that one," he grimaced, exposing multiple chins.

Donna tilted her head as if extremely interested. "Oh, my. What happened, Mr..."

His fat fingers crept up to her forearm. "Call me, Big John, darlin'."

Go figure. The fat "John" was actually called Big John. He was ogling her as if he was starving and she was a Hungry Man dinner.

Donna was utterly disgusted. The rotten, corrupt, fake house of God was nothing more than a place for men who couldn't get laid unless they paid for it. There was no way in hell she believed a woman would ride Big John without coercion or incentive. And it wasn't because he was a big man, but because he was a pig and smelled like one. Donna did her best not to wrinkle her nose and his offensive odor.

"Well, Big John, I don't like being anyone's second choice anyway," she said with the bat of her lashes.

He smiled and made a rumbling noise. She guessed it was laughter. It came from his gut like Santa Claus.

"Darlin', you could never be anybody's second choice. You caught my eye soon as you walked in, but we were quickly told that you belong to that...*prophet*."

His smile turned into a frown when he said the word.

"We're to be married," Donna goaded, knowing that her words would prompt him to spew out more information.

"So was that other lil' gal," he scoffed. "But they said I could have her."

Donna looked around, pretending to be looking for Vera. When, of course, she didn't see her, she looked back at Big John.

"Well, shouldn't you be wooing her?"

"Wooing? Huh! Not hardly. I didn't come here to woo. I made a pledge."

"Oh, I see," Donna said with a nod.

"But that lil' thang don't know how to act. She refused me," he fussed.

"*Nooo*."

"Sure did. But don't you worry your pretty lil' head. My man, Harry, is gonna handle that."

Donna was preparing to respond when Luca Savelli walked by.

She continued to look up at Big John while struggling to watch the mobster from her peripheral. He was tall and intimidating. She wondered if he ever smiled. And, if so, for who or what? He was having a conversation with a well-dressed giant of a man with crazy blue eyes. She guessed they weren't talking about cotton candy and puppies because neither looked very happy.

"So, what do you think about that?"

Donna blinked, realizing she'd totally blocked out the bullshit coming out of Big John's mouth.

"I think that's something," she improvised.

Donna had no clue what he was talking about it, nor did she care. She needed to get closer to Savelli.

She reached up and pried his fingers from her flesh. "It was a pleasure, Big John. But I think the prophet might be looking for me."

"Well, I—"

Donna walked away, not interested in one more word flying from his trap. Thankfully, one of the ladies was standing alone about three feet from Luca Savelli. She did her best to remember the woman's name as she made her way over to her.

She couldn't.

"Hey, pretty."

The woman turned to Donna with a smile filled with relief. She seemed just as disgusted by the event as Donna was, but she knew better to express that out loud.

"Hi. Kateri, right?"

"Yep, that's me."

"My name is Hope," she announced in a sweet voice.

Hope was a young black woman with a soft, natural afro that complemented her smooth onyx complexion. She dressed sexy and sophisticated, but everything about her screamed innocent.

"So, how's your night going?" Donna probed.

Hope checked her surroundings before answering. "I don't know, Kateri," she whispered. "These *men*...they don't act like their looking for a church."

Duh!

"I mean, seriously. I have been touched in places where no man of God should touch an unmarried woman."

Looking in her big brown eyes, there was no way for Donna not to feel sorry for her. The members of the Blood of the Chosen were complete believers. To them, theirs was the one true religion, and Bobby Lee was the one true messiah. Knowing that everything Hope believed in was a sham, and it would soon be exposed, was tragic. However, as sorry as Donna felt for her, she still had a job to do. She'd pity her later. At that very moment, listening in on Savelli's discussion with blue-eyed Goliath was her immediate priority.

So, while she managed a conversation with Hope, she did her best to eavesdrop on the mobster. Unfortunately, Harry Barber approached sporting a stupid looking grin and the confab ended. Before Harry could speak, Savelli raised his hand.

"Don't come over here," he warned with a scowl in the sexiest of accents. "You people disgust me."

After scolding Harry with that deep, masculine voice, Savelli and his guy stalked away. Donna's eyes followed them until they cleared the exit of the ballroom. Donna could've been wrong, but she suspected that Savelli was totally fine with the sale of weapons, but disgusted by the sale of women, which left her totally surprised. A criminal with morals. Who knew?

Donna searched the room for Kelly. She needed to let him know that Savelli wasn't going to be the bonus he thought he would. When she spotted him across the room, she turned back to Hope.

"Sweetie, I'll be right back. Keep your head down. Try not to make eye contact with anyone."

Hope smiled solemnly and nodded. Donna felt bad when she walked away, leaving her standing alone. When she got close, Kelly shook his head subtly and tilted his head toward Bobby Lee and Harry, who were headed his way. They didn't look pleased. Donna stopped, turned on her heel, and ran right into Clara.

"Kateri, honey, I need you to come with me."

It never failed. Like a ninja in the shadows, Clara was always nearby.

Donna planted another fictitious smile on her face and longed for the days when all she had to do was pretend to be either a crackhead or a dope boy's bitch.

"What's wrong? Is everything okay?" she asked in a concerned tone that almost made her sick.

As usual, Clara smiled. She placed a gentle hand on her shoulder. Donna looked at her perfectly manicured nails and wondered why she was being so affectionate. Smiling was one thing, but Clara wasn't very touchy feely.

"Everything is perfect, child. But we all must do our part for the Lord. It's your turn."

"My turn? What do you mean?"

"The Bible says, 'Preserve me, O *God*: for in thee do I put my *trust*'. Do you trust God, Kateri?"

"Of course," Donna declared through a breath.

"Do you trust God's prophet?"

"I do. You know that, Miss Clara."

Donna was afraid she'd barf if Clara put forth one more phony ass biblical inquiry.

"Well, now it's time to prove your love for the Lord, and your love for the prophet. There are things we need for our church, for our family, if we are to succeed in preparing this world for the Lord. In order to get the things we need, you'll have to prove your loyalty to the prophet, *and* your love for God. You'll preserve your immortal soul by sacrificing your body."

"My body?" Donna played dumb. She was going force Clara to spell it out.

"Yes, my love. Come with me."

Clara extended her hand and waited for Donna to take it. Of course, she did. Then, she allowed her to escort her across the ballroom and out of the rear exit. Just beyond the door, a car waited. Together, she and Clara walked to the car. Another member, who was posing as a chauffeur, held the door to the backseat open for them. Donna slid into the backseat and waited for Clara to get in. Soon after, the driver hopped in and drove off.

"Where are we going?"

Clara didn't answer. She just reached over and placed her hand over Donna's.

Donna looked out of the window. They were passing the main dormitory where she slept every night. Just a few feet from her living quarters, they pulled in front of one of the few modern buildings on the property. During many of her exploratory walks, she would often walk past the large building. Yet, she'd never been inside.

Once the car stopped, Clara opened the door without waiting for the driver. Without being told, Donna climbed out behind her.

"Come," Clara urged.

They walked a short walkway to the front door. Clara pulled a set of keys from her handbag and unlocked the door. When they stepped inside, Donna was floored. They were standing in a foyer that could rival the interior of the Governor's Mansion.

"Oh, my God," Donna marveled through a gasp.

Clara sighed. "It's beautiful, yes?"

"Oh, *yes*."

"I designed it myself," she bragged. "It's where we entertain. Well, it's where you'll entertain."

Donna was tempted to jam one of her acrylic nails into Clara's back. She couldn't wait until the day Clara would have to answer for her crimes. To her, she was worse than the so-called prophet. She was a woman who had a major role in the sexual exploitation of other women. She was nothing more than Bobby Lee's bottom bitch.

"Come with me."

Clara led her up a winding staircase and down a long, lantern-lit hall with French-inspired décor. Near the end of the hall, she opened a door. It was a bedroom, but not an average bedroom. It was exquisite. The walls, furnishings, and linen were well-placed splashes of rich creams and gleaming golds. The giant poster bed was covered by a sheer cream canopy with gold, woven tassels.

"Enjoy, my darling. You have all night to bask in this luxuriousness."

Donna whipped around just as Clara was walking out of the room.

"*Wait!* Where are you going?"

She gave no reply as she closed the door.

"Clara!" Donna called out as she hurried to the door. She turned the knob and yanked at the door, but it was locked from the outside. Out of frustration, she kicked the door. As if everything else going on in the cult wasn't bad enough, she'd just been taken prisoner.

"Unbelievable!" she fumed.

She pushed off the door and moved further into the bedroom. She'd allowed herself to be backed into a corner, like a trapped rat, and time was something she definitely didn't have. Any minute, Bobby Lee was going to come in, sprinkle holy water of something on her, and declare himself her husband so he could get his rocks off. But Donna had absolutely no plans on being his human pin cushion. She was sure if she turned him down, he would try to force himself on her. But, if he wanted her that bad, he would have to fuck her dead, rotten corpse.

She ran over to a door across the room and flung the double-doors open. It was an empty closet. There was no clothing, no hangers. Nothing she could use as a weapon. She slammed the doors and ran around the bed to another door. She'd assumed it was a bathroom, and she was right.

She hurried over to the sink and opened the medicine cabinet. Nothing. The drawers and other cabinets were empty too. There weren't even any towels or soap. So, when she got done whoring herself, what was she supposed to clean herself with?

Donna ran back into the bedroom and searched for anything she could use to defend herself. She took an inventory of every potential weapon in the room. She looked down at her feet. Her stilettos were a weapon. So, no matter how bad her feet hurt, she kept them on.

She ran over to the bed and yanked down a couple of the tassels. She stuffed one under the pillow and the other in her bra. If push came to shove, she would strangle his ass.

Before she could find anything else that would be useful, she heard the creak of footsteps on the other side of the door. The knob turned and the door crept open. Donna took a deep breath and prepared to go to battle. But to her utter shock, it wasn't Bobby Lee Khal entering the room. It was Lincoln.

Donna exhaled loudly. She was so relieved that she almost collapsed to her knees. She watched him close, thankful that no one was coming in behind him. Everything in her made her want to run into his arms, but she couldn't get her legs to move. Thankfully, he took long-legged strides to her and covered her with his embrace. His fresh, masculine scent gave her sweet memories of the last time they were together.

Sadly, Donna knew she couldn't hold on forever. She raised her head so that she could see his handsome face and tell him exactly how happy she was to see him. But, as soon as she opened her mouth to speak, Lincoln pushed his lips to hers. He kissed her, and she kissed him with a passion that told the story of two people who desperately missed each other. She clung to him and fed on him like he was the oxygen that she needed to endure.

Lincoln clutched her face. She whimpered from the loss of him pulling his lips from hers.

"Linc—"

He cut her off by placing a finger to her lips.

"Shhhh. Cameras," he whispered.

Lincoln stepped back and surveyed the room. His focus went to an empty picture frame on the dresser. He went over, picked it up, and flipped it over.

"I will not be recorded," he said into the frame.

He pulled a device no bigger than a nickel from the back of the picture frame and snapped the tiny cord that was attached. He dropped the device to the floor and stomped on it.

After tossing the frame on the dresser, he searched every corner of the bedroom, closet, and the bathroom. A thorough search produced another camera and two listening devices. Lincoln destroyed the surveillance equipment and walked over to the closet. Since there weren't any hangers, he hung his tuxedo jacket on the top of the door. He moved to sit on a settee and patted a space next to him.

"Sit with me."

She acquiesced and took a seat next to him. "These fucking people." Donna chuckled.

Lincoln shook his head. "Yeah, they'll sell you a woman, film it, and blackmail you for the rest of your life."

"And, what kind of gala doesn't have food?" Donna pointed out.

"Oh no, they fed us before you guys got there. We had lobster and filet."

Donna's eyes flew open. "Get the fuck outta here!"

The deep rumbling of his laughter made Donna smile. She couldn't believe that she was actually sitting with him, the one bright spot in the darkness of working such a horrible undercover mission.

"How long are you gonna be under?"

"Not sure, but I believe we're wrapping it up soon."

Lincoln nodded but sighed as if he was troubled. "What?"

"These *people*, Donatella. They're dangerous," he warned.

"I know, Lincoln. That's why I'm here."

"That fucking *prophet*." He said the word as if it made him physically ill. "That motherfucker went from telling me that you were off limits to wrapping you up in a bow."

"I'm not surprised. What did it cost you?"

"100k."

"*What?*" Donatella clutched her chest. "You paid a hundred thousand dollars for pussy you done had already?"

Lincoln frowned. "Fuck no! I *pledged* one hundred thousand. But, I would...for you."

Donna could not believe what she was hearing. She couldn't believe that Bobby Lee would trust a pledge. Then, she understood.

"The video," she realized aloud.

Lincoln nodded. "Yep. Every man invited has something to lose if they're discovered paying for church pussy."

Donna laughed. Lincoln had the greatest sense of humor. Even though they hadn't spent a whole lot of time together, the little time they had was spent laughing.

"I'm gonna kill your brother," she teased.

He turned to her with a raised brow. "Why? If it wasn't for me, you'd be the first lady by now, Kateri Khal," he joked.

"*Shee-iid*! The lies you tell!" She pulled the corded tassel from her bra and tossed it on the floor. "I was gonna choke his ass out, send him to meet the real Messiah."

Donna watched Lincoln while he laughed quietly. He had perfect, white teeth and a beautiful smile. She'd never been a big fan of men with beards, but Lincoln's made him the picture of masculinity. It was perfectly trimmed and accentuated his rugged good looks. She narrowed her eyes, remembered that there was something she wanted to ask him. He was truly a distraction. She couldn't think straight when Lincoln was around.

"How did you know about the wedding? I found out minutes before you mentioned it."

"Some guy named Harry. He talks a lot. Apparently, Khal has Indian girl fetish and he's gets turned on by your tattoos."

"How did you know about the girls?"

"Sweetheart, I'm exactly what they're looking for—a rich, white man. I've been invited before."

Donna narrowed her eyes at him. "You've been here before?"

"No. But, I know men who have. They talk."

"Wow."

Lincoln reached over and grabbed her hand. He brought it to his lips and kissed her sweetly. "Why do you disappear every time we sleep together. Is the sex that bad?"

He donned a smirk that said he knew better. He knew exactly what he did to her by her body's reaction.

"As far as me disappearing, this job keeps me in the wind. And, as far as the sex being bad, I don't remember. It's been a while," she joked with a cheeky grin.

"I see."

He stood, pulling her up with him. He gripped her waist and

turned her around. When he pressed his palm to her belly and pulled her close, she could feel his hard body against her back.

He lowered himself enough to whisper into her ear. "I'm going try to remind you how good we are together."

When his tongue grazed her ear, her belly fluttered. With his other hand, he reached up and caressed her throat. He placed sensual kisses along her neck. Donna's breathing became intense. Her head fell weakly against him. She'd been in relationships with both men and women, but his lips on her skin and his hands on her body were like no other. She melted under his touch.

Donna felt instantly cold when Lincoln took a step back. He clasped her zipper and slowly eased it down. He peeled the dress from her body and allowed it to fall to the floor. Without moving, she stood there in a black, lace strapless bra and a tiny lace thong. Even the undergarments Clara had picked out said she was for sale. Or, at least, for rent.

She could feel Lincoln fumbling with the clasp of the necklace Bobby Lee gave her. When he got it off, he walked around until he was in front of her and held the necklace up.

"Khal?" he asked.

She nodded. "It's a loaner."

He inspected the glittery piece of jewelry for a few seconds. "Gawdy," he muttered under his breath before tossing it on the settee.

Donna chuckled and stepped out of her dress that had pooled on the floor. She walked across the room and stood at the foot of the bed. Lincoln moved to stand in front of her. His eyes roamed her semi-nakedness with appreciation.

"My, God, you are stunning," he praised in a deep, breathy voice. "Absolutely beautiful."

"Thank you, Lincoln. Now, can you do all that complimenting without all those clothes?"

He grinned, and it was oh so sexy. The look he gave her as he loosened his tie was a promise. Intent on ensuring that he kept that promise, Donna reached back, worked the clasp of her bra, and dropped it to the floor. Cool air tapped budded nipples that were already erect and calling him out.

After freeing himself from his tie, he worked on the buttons of his shirt. The striptease was alluring, but Donna didn't have a clue how much time she'd have with him. So, she stepped to him and ripped the possibly very expensive shirt open until buttons flew about the room. He laughed at her eagerness as he peeled the shirt off and pulled his t-shirt over his head.

Now, Lincoln had always been easy on the eyes, but Lincoln without a shirt was blindingly erotic. Their other encounters had been so rushed, she had never had time to savor his deliciousness. His tan skin and military tattoos stretched under the rippled muscles of his chest and arms. He obviously spent a considerable amount of time in a gym. She reached out to touch the smooth hairs on his chest, but with a gentle shove, her butt bounced on the bed.

He lowered to his knees, grabbed her hips, and pulled her to the edge of the mattress. He pushed her legs apart and toyed with the lace thong.

"As long as you're here," he started with a grimace. "You'll never need these again."

One large finger looped the thin material and tore it from her body. He gathered the lace into a ball and stuffed it in his pocket.

He pushed his face between her thighs and moaned when his tongue contacted her eager clit. Donna pushed her fingers through his thick hair and cried out when he sucked her into his warm, wet mouth. She squirmed under his expertise, but he tightened his grip on her hips and held her still.

"Mmmm!"

Under *the* most pleasurable assault on her throbbing clit, Donna fell limply to the bed. She clawed at the satin bedding as he mouth-fucked her with vigorous enthusiasm. He moaned against her pussy and slurped her pleasure until she could take no more. As she neared her end, her legs stiffened and her entire body convulsed.

"Lincoln, I'm...*aghh. Fuck!*"

"Mm-mm," he mumbled confidently over her exploding clit as she shattered to pieces.

Donna was a sweaty, quivering mess as her body melted against the bed. Yet, Lincoln was not done.

She jerked violently as he continued to lick the electrified bundle of nerves between her thighs. The unadulterated pleasure was nearing unbearable. She reached down and attempted to push his head, but he grabbed her hand and pinned it to her side. Without allowing her to come down, he took her even higher, licking fast then slow, sucking hard then soft until she was having another earth-shattering orgasm.

"Got-damn it!" she blurted through heavy breaths.

As Lincoln worked his way out of his pants, Donna did her best to control her trembling legs. She tried to push herself up to the top of the bed, but he grabbed her ankle and slid her back to the edge.

"Be still," he ordered with a stern voice and narrowed eyes.

She watched with amazement as he rolled protection over his hard-on. Thick veins vined an almost intimidatingly large dick.

When he was done, he leaned over her, lowering himself enough to reach her lips. Donna caressed his face and raised up until their lips met. She opened enough to accept his tongue and to offer her own. The taste of her own pleasure filled her mouth as she kissed him with brazen hunger. Just as well as he'd made love to her clit, he was making love to her mouth. The passion in his kiss was like an electrical current, shooting directly to her sex. Without severing their connection, he guided himself into her wet opening. Her breath hitched when he buried his enormous dick deep inside.

"Mmm." She moaned from the sheer pleasure of his invasion.

She'd missed him. If only to herself, she could admit it. She'd missed his smile, his laughter, his kiss, his touch, and damn did she miss his big, thick dick.

After allowing only seconds to adjust to his size, he pulled out almost completely before pushing into her with a force that pushed her upward. He rested on one forearm and slid his other hand under her ass. He lifted her so she would have no other choice but to take every inch of dick he was giving.

Her hands flew to his wide back. She dug her fingers into his moist skin and held on for dear life while he fucked her with the clear mission of driving her insane.

"Oh, baby," he groaned. "So, fucking tight...ugh! You're gonna make me cum."

Although his strokes slowed, they were just as deep, just as powerful. Donna's moaning and groaning bounced off the walls of the borrowed room. If anyone was listening, surely, they'd be envious.

Lincoln was fucking her life, her entire past away. Right then and there, he'd erased every sexual encountered she'd ever experienced. There were none before him, and there would be none after him. The way he was occupying her insides, no one could follow.

He continued to fuck her but lowered his head enough to roughly suck her nipple into his mouth. He flicked his tongue over it and gnawed on it with just enough force to make her scream. Sucking her nipples while rocking in and out of her pussy pushed her completely over the edge.

"*Ughhh! Fuuuuuuuck!!*" she cried out, not giving a damn who heard.

Donna had never heard such a sound escape her throat. It sounded as if he was performing an exorcism. Still, Lincoln offered no reprieve. He stood straight, placed her legs on his shoulders, and pounded her senseless. Donna went mute, no longer able to speak, or even cry out. Breathing was all she could muster, and her breath was loud, labored and heavy.

"You keep running from me!" he gritted between strokes. "*Aghh!* Stop. Fucking. Running from me, Donatella!"

His fingers tightened around her hips, pressing into her flesh. Her toes curled as he rode her hard and deep. Sweat dripped from his head to her stomach as his strokes frenzied.

"Fuck!" he cursed, thrusting into her with one last powerful stroke.

Donna's inner walls clenched involuntarily around his throbbing dick as he pulsated his hot seed into the thin sheath. He blew out a harsh breath and collapsed over her, catching himself with his forearms. He cupped the back her head and kissed her forehead.

"Shit, Donna!" he gasped against her skin.

Donna struggled with her own breathing as she willed her body through the trembles. As they lay there in post-coital exhaustion, the sweet, masculine scent of his sweat mixed with hers.

"Oh my God, Lincoln. You are—"

"Yours," he interrupted. "I'm yours. And, now you're mine."

He slipped his arm under her body and pulled her to the top of the bed. He pulled the sheet and blanket from the corner and lifted her until she was lying on the fitted sheet. He slid inside and tucked in next to her. After covering both of their bodies, he cozied in next to her.

"Sleep," he told her, kissing the side of her face. Without debate, because she was spent, she did as told. As soon as she relaxed on the pillow and in his arms, she slumbered.

22

DONATELLA

A loud knock on the door made Donna startle. She gasped. When her eyelids fluttered open, the brightness of the shining sun through a window was almost intolerable. She'd actually forgotten where she was and had allowed herself to get too comfortable.

In an attempt to soothe, Lincoln caressed her face. He placed a finger on her lips and shushed her.

"Good morning, beautiful," he greeted softly with a gleam in his vivid green eyes.

Donna smiled. She couldn't help it. The thought of waking up next to him made her.

"Good morning, Colonel."

Another bang on the door made Lincoln frown.

"Play sleep," he whispered.

Donna nodded. He cupped the back of her head and kissed her softly on the lips. After granting her one of his disarming smiles, he flipped the comforter off of his glorious naked body and got out of bed. Without covering himself, he walked over to the door and flung it open.

"What?" he barked rudely.

The person clearing their throat in the doorway sounded like it might have been Clara.

"Good morning, Colonel Creed."

It was for sure Clara. Her greeting came out husky and breathy. Even with her back turned, pretending to be asleep, Donna could hear the woman's arousal.

"I trust your night went well."

"Very well, thank you. What can I do for you?"

Clara cleared her throat again. Lincoln's gorgeous naked body and massive, even when flaccid, dick had to have been driving the woman crazy. If she weren't playing sleep, she might have chuckled. She wanted to turn around so badly. She'd do anything to see Clara's face.

"I'm here for Kateri. Prayer service is in an hour. I have some fresh clothing and toiletries for her."

Donna heard footsteps. Clara had entered the room. She could hear her fumbling with something across the room, but she wasn't exactly sure what it was.

"What is this?"

"Well, it looks like a picture frame," Lincoln responded sarcastically.

"You've destroyed our property."

"Sue me," Lincoln scoffed. "You were trying to record me. You people got a lot of fucking nerve!"

"Colonel Creed, I have no idea what you're talking about. I assure you that we would never—"

"Get the fuck out!"

Donna wanted to cheer him on, but for the sake of what she was trying to do, she held her tongue. She could hear Clara's footsteps as she hurried to the door.

"Kateri?"

"When I'm done with her, I'll send her out."

Donna turned around and sat up when she heard the door slam. "I think I'm in love," she crooned.

Lincoln sat on the bed and grinned. "All part of my plan, little lady."

Donna chuckled and flipped the linen off of her own naked body. When she looked as if she was about to get out of bed, Lincoln tackled her to the mattress.

"Where do think you're going?" he growled against her neck.

Donna giggled while playfully wrestling her way out of his hold. "I have a prayer meeting in an hour," she told him while trying to keep a straight face.

"Come on, babe. You got time for another round."

He made the cutest pouty face that made her wanna climb back into the bed. But she had a job to do. Thankfully, he'd run interference the night before, but she had to get back to the mission.

"Oh, how I wish. But we are so close to wrapping this up. And, I am *so* ready to go home."

Lincoln bowed his head in compliance and got out of bed. She admired his delicious physique as he gathered his things.

"They got nothing to hold you to your pledge. The Prophet is gonna have a fit," Donna pointed out.

"Your prophet can go fuck himself!" Lincoln blustered.

Donna walked over to the dresser and grabbed the bag Clara left behind. While he dressed, she went through the contents. Clara had included everything she needed to get dressed. However, everything in the bag was Donna's, which meant she'd had no problem whatsoever going through her personal effects.

She grumbled quietly and snatched the bag. Lincoln was buttoning his shirt when she walked over to him and grabbed his face. She pulled him down and kissed his lips.

"I'll see you soon," she promised.

Lincoln snaked an arm around her waist and pulled her close. "I have two questions."

"Shoot," she said with a raised brow.

"One, I know your job keeps you away a lot. But when you're not working undercover, will you consider spending time with me? Giving us a chance?"

With a smile, Donna nodded emphatically.

"Good." He rewarded her with a peck on the lips.

"And, two..." he waved his hand over his nose. "Is there a toothbrush in that bag?"

Donna smacked him on the arm when he burst into laughter. She pushed him off and headed to the bathroom.

"Get out! I gotta go wash my snatch so I can go and praise the Lord."

∽

DONNA HURRIED down the hall and pushed through her bedroom door. Since they weren't allowed to have locks on their door, there was nothing to stop her from surprising Vera. She was wrapped in a towel, wet as if she'd just gotten out of the shower. Whereas Vera may have been a little startled, Donna was out-and-out shocked. Her entire back was covered in bruises. In fact, as she stared, dumbfounded with her mouth wide open, she realized they were actual whips. She'd been whipped.

When she noticed Donna staring, she raised the towel and tried to cover them up.

"Oh my God!" Donna gasped. She ran over to Vera and gently grabbed her by the shoulders. "Vera, who did this to you?"

She shook her head and tried to pull out of her grasp, but Donna refused to let go until she got an answer.

"Who did this to you?" she asked again.

Tears fell from Vera's eyes and trickled down her pretty face. Since Donna had arrived, it was the first time she'd ever seen Vera unhappy.

She sniffed and blinked excess moisture from her eyes. After swiping a tear from her cheek, she looked up at Donna. "Did you do it last night?" she asked quietly as if she was afraid that someone might hear.

Donna knew exactly what she was referring to, and she'd been through enough. So, she wasn't about to blow smoke up her ass by playing dumb.

"I did," she admitted.

Vera's head dropped from shame. "I should've just done it."

"Fuck that!" Donna blurted.

Vera's head flew up. She looked around the room as if they weren't alone.

"Don't use that language!" she admonished in a hushed tone.

Even after everything, she was still a believer. Donna couldn't remember ever feeling sorrier for anyone in her life. Vera was completely lost, and when the walls around them came crumbling down, she was worried that she wouldn't survive the fallout.

Donna guided Vera to her bed. She sat, pulling her to sit with her. She looked her in the eye and tried to be as plain as possible.

"I went with that man because I wanted to. I mean...did you see him? He was totally gorgeous. That man they tried to force on you was repulsive."

Vera was utterly distraught. She shook her head and grabbed Donna's hand.

"I-I'm so ashamed. I couldn't even show my loyalty to the Prophet. I'm just grateful they're not making me leave."

Donna could not believe what she was hearing. "Vera, you listen to me, and you listen to me good. Your body is not for sale. I know I may look like a hypocrite, but you did the right thing by refusing to sleep with that slob. He was rude, disrespectful, and disgusting. I don't blame you not one bit. That pig couldn't have touched me with a ten-foot pole."

Vera grunted her frustration and swiped another tear from her cheek.

"How did they punish you?" Donna inquired "What did they whip you with?"

"A b-belt," Vera sobbed. "A big belt."

Donna was enraged. Not only were they brainwashing women into believing in their shitty cult, but they were also physically abusing them when they weren't cooperative in their prostitution racket.

"Who whipped you? Was it the Prophet?"

Vera nodded. "Clara tied me down and the Prophet punished me."

"*Ugh!*" Donna grunted out of rage.

Vera's eye widened with panic. "Shhh! Kateri, I'll be fine. Please don't make a fuss."

Donna couldn't take it anymore. Vera was way too sweet and trusting. She didn't deserve anything that was happening to her.

She grabbed her by the face and forced her to look in her eye. "Leave this place," Donna implored. "Just get all your stuff, right now, and leave."

Vera began to cry. Her head fell on Donna's shoulder, so she held her as she sobbed. She rubbed her shoulder, careful not to agitate her wounds.

"Vera, leave now," Donna implored.

"I can't. This is my home," she whimpered. "Where am I going to go?"

"Sweetie, this is not your home. This is not your family. Family wouldn't hurt you like this."

"Maybe not your family," Vera quipped.

There it was. Vera was accustomed to abuse from people who were supposed to look after her. Her seemingly broken home life had prepared her to fall prey for people like Clara and Robert Lee Khal.

She grabbed the front of her bath towel and hopped up from the bed. "We gotta get ready," she pressed with her chin in the air. Vera was doing her very best to feign strength and resilience. What she had no way of knowing was that she was, in fact, a very strong woman. She'd clearly survived familial abuse. Donna was no shrink, but that was quite evident. Vera was simply a woman that needed something to believe in. Had she not been working undercover, Donna would have totally introduced her to her Mom and Dad. They'd for sure show her a better, safer way to worship God.

"Okay. Let's get ready," Donna relented.

23

TAYLOR

"Well, since you're pregnant and you can't take anything to help you sleep, try this. When you lie down at night, make sure it's totally silent. Listen to your breathing and count every time you exhale."

Taylor nodded. "Will do, Dr. Porter. At this point, I'm willing to try anything."

"Try telling your husband," the doctor quipped.

Since the shooting, sleep did not come easy. Because she didn't want to worry Victor, almost every night, she pretended to be asleep. She'd wait until he fell asleep and sneak out of bed.

"With the election and this stupid investigation, he's got enough to worry about."

Dr. Porter uncrossed his leg and leaned back in the chair. "Taylor, I suspect that you're more important to him than any of that."

"I am," she assured with a chuckle. "That's exactly why I don't want to bother him. He'll drop every damn thing, probably try to rock me to sleep every night."

The doctor laughed as he stood. "Talk to your husband," he urged.

Taylor stood when he grabbed his briefcase from the table. "What I gotta talk to him for? I got you for that."

"Mm-hm, okay. I'll see you in a few days."

Taylor walked him out of the den and down the hall. "Do you really think it's necessary for us to meet twice a week?"

"Yep," he affirmed. "For now, at least."

Taylor said nothing as she walked him to the door. Maybe he was right. Maybe she did need to see him twice a week. So far, she'd only had two sessions. The first session, she'd behaved like a complete nutjob. The second one, she did her best to prove to him that she wasn't a complete nutjob.

After they said their goodbyes, Taylor closed the door and headed to the kitchen. Emma was wiping down the sink. When she turned and noticed that Taylor had entered the room, she smiled.

"Can I fix you some lunch?"

"No, ma'am. Thank you. I just came to get some juice." Taylor walked over to the fridge. She opened the door and searched for orange juice.

"We're out."

Taylor peeped around the refrigerator door. "Out of what?"

"We're out of orange juice, only got apple and cranberry. I'll pick some up from the market later."

Emma was super sweet. At some point during every day, she did or said something to make Taylor smile.

"You're a mind reader, Emma."

"Don't take a mind reader to know you like orange juice. The fact that it's all gone is a clue."

"Makes sense." Taylor chuckled.

"How was your session with the doc?"

"Pretty good. I'm just glad he came back after I acted a whole fool."

"A whole fool," Emma teased.

Taylor laughed and grabbed an apple juice. She closed the fridge and threw a hand on her hip. "You gotta rub it in?"

"I'm just sayin'. I think the Governor was ready to bend you over his knee."

Taylor laughed, but Emma moved closer. The serious look on her face was anything but funny.

"Your husband has been so worried about you."

A feeling of guilt washed over her. With Dr. Porter's help, she understood that she was experiencing some post-traumatic stress. It was the reason she was having trouble sleeping. She'd lost her appetite for food, social events, and even sex. Even though she was positive that she was driving Victor crazy, he had been nothing but supportive and understanding. It wasn't until she lost her shit that he showed the slightest bit of impatience.

"I know," Taylor admitted with a sigh.

"You haven't left the apartment, except to go fishing. You stay in your room most day, and you won't let your friends visit. After the horrible things you must've witnessed, a little anxiety is expected. Just try not to shut out the people who can help you get through it."

Taylor exhaled and opened her apple juice.

"You listening to me?"

"Yes, Dr. Emma. I'm listening," Taylor grumbled.

Emma turned and resumed the task of cleaning the counters, done kitchen shrinking her.

Taylor understood. Emma lived under their room. Of course, she knew what went on behind their closed door. Admittedly, she was surprised Emma had spoken to her about it. But she wasn't mad, and Emma was right.

"You sure you don't want any lunch?" Emma asked without turning around.

"Nah. But, thanks. I'm going out to lunch."

Taylor finished her juice and tossed the bottle in the trash can. As she hurried from the kitchen to her bedroom, she went over what she was going to wear in her head.

VICTOR

"It's only a few points. You still have a slight lead," Nate Williams, his campaign pollster justified. "This fucking investigation is a menace. But, to be honest, it's nowhere near a nail in the coffin."

"Governor, your constituents love you," Mark Vega, Victor's chief media strategist added. "I truly believe they couldn't give less than two shits where your campaign funds come from. Keeping it real, because of Taylor, the black vote is yours. You're a millennial favorite. You are the semi-liberal Republican that this presidency created. This administration has gone beyond right wing to all-out racist. Your party is still behind you."

"And..." Carlotta McGovern, his chief media advisor, interjected. "You're hot. No offense, Governor, but you're freakin' hot. You're locking votes based on that. They could find the Lindbergh baby in your trunk, and women would still vote for you."

Victor chuckled. Carlotta was amusing. She had a funny way of putting things. She was extremely likable, and had an awesome sense of humor. If they were out, having a beer, he'd definitely enjoy hanging out with her. However, Victor was facing an investigation into his campaign funds. Though he was sure that he was clean, the perception of corruption could cost him the election.

He was just about to tell her that when his office door was opened. He'd given Kena strict instructions that he wasn't to be disturbed while he was consulting with his campaign staff. So, whatever it was that caused her to defy his request had to have been important.

To Victor's surprise, it wasn't Kena that entered his office. It was Taylor. He had been leaning, half sitting on his desk but stood as soon as she stepped inside.

"Sweetheart, is everything okay?"

He was in utter shock to see her in his office. She hadn't left the apartment on her own since the shooting. Not to mention, not one person from her security detail had called to inform him that she was out and about. She must've forced them into silence. Taylor could be a bit of a bully with the security personnel.

"Everything's fine, Governor. May I have a minute?"

Her words were formal, but her demeanor seemed relaxed. Even with a small crowd in the room, her beauty dominated the space. She'd pinned her naturally curly hair up in the back, and left the curls in front to fall in her face. Uncharacteristically for Taylor, she was wearing a Burberry raincoat, makeup, and tall high-heels—a huge contrast to the SIU t-shirt and shorts she'd been wearing around the house.

She smiled and stepped further inside, leaving the door open. "I need the room," she announced sternly as she stared him right in the eye.

Without one single word of protest, the team of campaigners hurried out of the office. She closed the door behind the last person and turned to him.

"What's up, babe?"

She sauntered closer to him with a mischievous glint in her eyes. Victor was more than curious as to what had finally gotten Taylor out of the house, and why she was looking so damn good.

"I just came to bring you lunch. Even the Governor has to eat, right?" Her voice was filled with seduction.

Victor eyed Taylor from head to toe. All she had was a tiny purse which couldn't have possibly held any sort of lunch inside.

He returned to his half-seated position at the front of his desk and crossed his arms. "What's for lunch, sweetheart?" he asked with a raised brow.

When she reached for the very first button on her raincoat, Victor's cock stirred. By the time she reached the last button, he was rock-hard. And when she opened the coat, revealing a lace, cream-colored bra and panty set that flattered her smooth, dark skin, he nearly came in his boxers. He'd been missing her beautiful body so bad, he thought he would explode.

"Lunch is served," she declared seductively.

24

DONATELLA

After Bible study, Donna avoided Clara and Bobby Lee. Although she was a professional, she was still human. After seeing what they'd done to Vera, to all of them, she was struggling to maintain her cover. What she wanted to do was pistol whip Bobby Lee Khal and beat the shit out of Clara. Smiling in either one of their faces would be a challenge. She certainly had a few questions for Clara, questions that were essential to their investigation. For example, where were all the children? Donna had never been to a church that had no children. Finding out why was important to their investigation, but Donna needed a minute. Just a bit of time to get back into character because she was truly ready to hurt someone.

Donna headed toward the chapel exit, which was in the complete opposite direction of where Clara and Bobby Lee were communing with several other members. She smiled and exchanged forced pleasantries with other members on her way out. She was mere seconds from the door when Kelly grabbed her by the arm.

"Where ya going?"

"Outta here before I hurt somebody. Do you know they beat the shit outta Vera because she wouldn't fuck that blob?"

"What?"

"Yes," Donna confirmed through gritted teeth.

"Well, it's a good thing you won't have to deal with it anymore. We're outta here."

She glared at him with a furrowed brow, hoping she'd heard him correctly. "When?"

"Now. Go get your stuff and meet me at the gate north of the pond."

"Are you serious?"

"Dead ass. We're done. We have everything we need to put Khal, Clara, Harry, and a few more away for a long time."

"Yes!" she blurted in hushed celebration.

Kelly grinned and walked out of the door. Donna was right on his heels.

She hurried across the lawn, to her dormitory. She didn't speak to anyone when she entered and hurried to her room.

She walked inside and searched the small room for Vera. Thankfully, she wasn't there.

Donna hurried over to her bed and got on all fours. She grabbed her backpack from under the bed and darted around the room, collecting her things. She hadn't taken much with her, so it didn't take long to pack.

She tossed the bag over her shoulder and turned to walk out but stopped short of the door. She turned back, walked over to the dresser, and picked up the small box containing the diamond and sapphire necklace.

"He won't be getting this back," Donna mumbled under her breath.

Without an ounce of guilt, she stuffed the box in her bag and got the hell out of dodge. With his fake ass, it probably wasn't real anyway.

LINCOLN

"Man, lil bro, you sure have been in town a lot more than usual," Lucas teased. "Don't get me wrong, I'm happy to see you and all. But, what's the deal?"

Lincoln shrugged. "What can I say? Between you and the shit-magnets you guys have for women, I feel like here is where I'm needed."

"Linc is so full of shit. It's that other Devereaux that keeps him here," Jaysen, the youngest Creed, argued.

"Watch your mouth, boy!"

Lincoln look up to find their dad standing in front of their table. On the count of their celebrity brother, they'd rented out a private room at *Next*, Lucas' favorite restaurant.

"Dad!" Lincoln called out as he stood from his seat. As customary, he shook his father's hand before going in for a hug.

"It's good to see you in one-piece, son," Victor Creed Sr. greeted as they hugged. He cupped the back of Lincoln's head and kissed him on the cheek.

"It's good to be seen, sir."

Lucas cleared his throat, loudly interrupting their father, son display of affection. "Hey, Dad. We're here too."

Their father chuckled as he exchanged handshakes and embraced his other sons. "You fellas didn't just get back from a war zone," the older Victor pointed out.

"You don't know where he's been," Jaysen remarked.

"Don't be silly, son. I always know," his dad assured.

After they were done with their greetings, Victor Sr. took a seat at the table. "Where's Victor?" he asked.

"He's on his way," Lincoln offered. "Campaign stuff."

"And Xander?"

"He had a meeting run late," Lucas responded.

Victor Sr. nodded. "It's not easy to start a new business."

Lucas took a good gulp of brown liquid from his glass and shook his head. He wasn't disagreeing with his dad. Starting a business wasn't easy, but he believed Xander was brilliant, and he had a good head on his shoulders. If anyone could handle it, his little brother could.

"Yeah, Dad, but Xander's not new to this. He's been running everything tech for CBI since it began."

"Yes, but now he's running tech for CBI and building XCREED Technologies. That's no easy feat."

"You're right, Dad, but I got this," Alexander chimed as he and Victor walked up to the table.

"Finally." Lucas scoffed, taking another sip from his glass.

It wasn't unusual for the Creed men to meet for dinner. Certainly, since they were all so busy, it wasn't easy to meet as often as they'd like, but they still managed to either have dinner or cocktails at least every other month. Sometimes minus Lincoln, of course. However, when he was able to make it to one of their stag gatherings, he enjoyed them immensely.

As Victor and Xander took seats at the table, two servers arrived. Since it was Lucas' favorite eating spot, he knew them both.

"Why is it that we don't get this kind of service until he shows up?" Lincoln fussed, pointing at Victor Jr.

"Not true," Joselyn, the waitress rebutted. "You get amazing service when the Governor is not around. Well…it's only because you're his brother, but you still get it."

She chuckled, winking at Victor Jr.

He winked in return and asked for a Scotch neat with a water chaser. Lincoln checked his phone while the others placed their drink orders.

"Looking for a call from a certain little Indian girl?" Lucas asked facetiously.

Lincoln looked from his phone to his older brother. "That is so politically incorrect," he scolded with a scowl. "I'm telling your girlfriend."

Lucas raised his hands in defense. "How is that politically incorrect? She's Native American!"

"Little Indian Girl?" Xander mocked. "That's why *your* little Indian girl is never gonna marry you."

Lucas frowned and sipped from his drink. "That's not why," he muttered under his breath.

"Yeah, it's because she doesn't trust her 'gaydar' anymore." Jaysen chirped with laughter. "Maybe you're not manly enough for her. I mean…you do have the most excellent taste in clothes. Like a fashion-ist-o," he teased with a grin.

"Shut up!" Lucas blurted. "Who's says I wanna get married anyway?"

"Helen Keller. She saw and heard it," Jaysen joked.

"Talk about politically incorrect," Lincoln muttered under his breath.

"Victor, you're awfully quiet," their dad interjected. "What's up?"

Victor sighed. "Just thinking about this investigation. It all seems so timed."

"Of course, it is," Victor Sr. assured. "What's your plan?"

"After dinner, I'm going over to the Storms to meet Jack for drinks. We need to discuss PAC."

"A fucking headache!" Victor Sr. blustered.

Lincoln and the rest immediately turned to their dad. It was very rare for him to use profanity, at least in their presence. Politics was the one thing that could provoke their dad to curse, which was why Lincoln was so shocked he'd encouraged and cultivated Victor's political ambitions.

"Watch your mouth, young man," Victor Jr. joked.

"Yeah, yeah. Let's get the announcements out of the way. First, after the election, your mother and I will be spending the winter in Tuscany."

"I don't know..." Victor doubted, raising a brow at his dad.

"What are you talking about? It's been decided."

"Taylor is pregnant," the junior Victor broadcasted to his family.

Even though Lincoln and Lucas already knew, they celebrated with the rest as if it was their first time hearing the news. None of his brothers did well with being left out of the loop, especially Jaysen.

His dad's green eyes beamed like stage lighting. "Congratulations, son! That's great news!"

"It is. Thank you."

While the others were congratulating Victor, the waitress approached. She handed Lincoln an envelope that had his name written on it. He looked up at her with confusion, but she shrugged and said, "It was left on my tray."

"Thank you."

She nodded and walked away. Lincoln inspected the envelope before deciding to open it. Inside was a piece of paper that read, *"I hear you're looking for me. Stop!"*

Lincoln crushed the paper into a ball and tossed it on the table in front of him.

"What's that about?" Victor inquired.

Lincoln was sure that his face was etched with irritation when he looked over at his older brother. "That was about *my* business, and you minding yours, Governor."

"Who are you talking to, boy? Are you talking to me?" Victor's question was laced with a threat. He sounded just like their father.

Lincoln ignored him and blew out a harsh breath. He still hadn't gotten the answers he was looking for. He and his men had been sent on a blank mission. None of the intel had added up to what they actually found in Mosul. As a soldier, he understood that his job was to take orders that trickled down the chain of command, but something about this mission didn't sit well. From the time Tahira approached him while he was dining with Lucas, it didn't feel right. He couldn't explain why, but for some reason, it felt personal.

Lincoln looked at his dad. He'd always been able to reach out to old acquaintances. Maybe he could get the answers Lincoln wanted.

"How was your weekend, Linc?" Lucas asked with a mischief that furthered his irritation.

"It was fine."

"Dad, Linc went to the Blood of the Chosen's Glory Gala."

Lincoln wanted to get up and slap the shit out of his older brother, but he could feel his dad's eyes lasering in on him.

"Lincoln Creed, have you lost your complete mind? You were not raised to patronize places like that."

"Dad, I can assure you that I am not a patron. I was there for another reason."

"What other reason?"

Lucas laughed, but not even he would expose Donatella's covert assignment.

"I'll have to explain it to you later."

"That so-called church is a haven for deviant behavior," Victor Sr. spat with a look of abhorrence.

"Agreed," Lincoln concurred, looking over at Lucas. In his eyes was the threat of bodily harm, but if his older brother was fazed by his ire, he certainly didn't show it.

Lucas smirked and lifted his glass to his lips. He couldn't have had any idea how close he was to getting choked out.

25

VICTOR

After a boisterous dinner, Victor and his brothers had a small argument about who was going to pay the bill. Victor slipped the waitress a credit card as Linc, Luc, and Xander fought for the tab. When she came back for his signature, they went silent and looked at him as if he'd committed some nefarious act of treachery behind their backs. Victor sighed, overwhelmed by the overdose of testosterone. He couldn't wait to get home to his wife. Unfortunately, he had other business.

He dialed Kena's number. "Tell Naomi that I'm ready," he said into the phone when she answered.

When she agreed, he disconnected the call.

"How worried are you about this investigation into your PAC funds?" his dad asked.

"I'm not very worried about the outcome of the investigation, but I have to admit, I'm concerned about its effect on my campaign."

Victor Sr. slapped him on the back. "I can make some calls, son."

"No, Dad. Let me handle it."

"Okay, son," he agreed with a nod. "If I need to step in, you let me know."

No matter how old or powerful Victor became, his father had a way of making him feel like a little boy again.

"If I need your help, Dad, I'll definitely let you know."

"Be sure." Victor Sr. reached to shake his hand.

"Yes, sir," Victor assured, shaking his father's hand.

When he turned to his brothers for a proper goodbye, Lincoln whisked their father away. The two of them were huddled in conversation. After the way he snapped at him before, Victor wouldn't dare to inquire about the topic.

Lincoln was in a mood for sure. He didn't know why, but what he did know was that he was ready to snatch him by the collar and drag his ass across the restaurant. He made a mental note to have a conversation with his little brother later when he'd calmed down. He suspected that his rotten disposition had something to do with his latest mission, but he wasn't sure.

After more goodbyes, Victor hugged his father and kissed his cheek before following Gregor out of the restaurant to their awaiting vehicle. After about thirty minutes, his small caravan was pulling into a short driveway that led to a tall iron gate with a large iron "S" fashioned in the metal. The first car in his security detail stopped just before the gate and had words with a guard that emerged from a guard shack.

"The Storms have more security than I do," Victor chortled.

"Not quite," Gregor refuted dryly.

"What's with everybody and their shitty attitudes? I'm the one about to be indicted."

"Yeah, sure," Gregor scoffed. "I got a better chance of winning American Idol."

Victor laughed. It was rare for Gregor to joke. So, when he did, it didn't necessarily have to be funny to make him laugh. The stern giant's attempt at humor was funny in itself.

When the gate opened, they moved forward down a long road lined with plants and trees. About a half-mile down the road, they curved right. The curved path ran alongside a perfectly manicured lawn.

They rounded the curve and pulled up in front of the Storms' magnificent estate.

"Please, Governor, stay here," Gregor insisted.

Victor remained inside. Not too long ago, he'd made a promise to Gregor, and Taylor, to let him do his job, which was to protect him.

Gregor dispatched his security detail to various points on the property, and less than a minute later, Gregor returned and opened the door for him.

He stepped out and followed his bodyguard up the marble walkway and steps. The front door was already open, but it wasn't Jack that awaited. It was an elderly Caucasian woman with frowning, bright red lips. In her arms was a tiny Jack lookalike with slightly darker skin.

Victor smiled. A vision of what his son or daughter would look like flashed in his mind.

When the woman's gaze switched from Rory, a member of his security detail, to him, her blue eyes lit up and her frown instantly shifted.

"You're...hello," she greeted in a husky voice meant to allure.

Victor smiled. He thought it was cute, a woman of her maturity openly flirting.

"Good evening, ma'am. Victor Creed to see Jack Storm."

"Of course. Come in. Come in, Governor."

She stepped back, allowing him entry. When Victor crossed the threshold, he could swear that she was smelling him.

He stepped into the large foyer and created a few feet of distance between them.

"You're even more handsome in person," the older lady crooned.

"Thank you, ma'am."

Thankfully, Jack came jogging down a curved stairwell. "Governor, it's good to see you," he greeted as he approached with his hand extended.

"Jack, thanks for the invite." Victor looked around the spacious, elegantly decorated foyer. "What an extraordinary home you have."

"Thank you, but you know I would have come to you. With the campaign underway, this must be a busy time for you."

"Yeah, well, I needed some air."

Jack walked over to the older lady and cupped his son's head. A warm, paternal feeling washed over Victor as he watched him kiss his sleeping son. He couldn't wait to hold his son or daughter in his arms.

"Thank you, Mrs. O'Malley. Why don't you go put him down?"

She hesitated as if she didn't want to leave, but the look on Jack's face left her no choice.

She pursed her bright red lips and headed up the stairs.

"Nanny?"

"Nah. Mrs. O'Malley is a friend of the family. She comes over and helps us with the kids because she doesn't trust anyone." Jack laughed softly. "I mean...*nobody*."

"Sounds like you," he said, turning to Gregor. "We're good here. Give us a minute."

Gregor nodded at Rory and backed against the wall. Rory did the same against the opposite wall.

"How about a drink?" Jack offered.

"A drink sounds good."

"Follow me."

It was a short walk down the hall to the parlor. When they entered, Victor nodded acknowledgment to the other men in the room.

"Victor, you remember my cousins, Gianni and Luca."

"I do...gentlemen," he greeted. "It's nice to see you again."

"What's your poison, Governor?" Gianni asked from behind the bar.

"Scotch, neat. Please, call me Victor."

Jack held out his hand, gesturing for him to take a seat. Victor chose a barstool next to Luca Savelli.

"Jack tells me that you have a legal issue," he began, wasting no time.

"Possibly. The source of certain PAC funds is being investigated by the Attorney General's office."

"PAC funds?" the Sicilian asked with a furrowed brow.

"He's talking about money donated to his political campaign," Jack explained.

"What does this have to do with our family?" Luca questioned.

"The Major Mogul Super PAC is the focus of the investigation."

"What?" Jack asked with a puzzled look on his face. "Why would they investigate my contribution?"

Gianni finally slid his drink across the bar.

"It's being alleged that the money, your money, is actually a payoff from the Savellis. They're trying to link their money to yours."

"Wait a second," Luca intervened. "Why would a Savelli need to pay off a state governor? What does the Attorney General know of the Savellis?"

"I don't know, but I can guess they assume you're linked to some sort of organized crime."

Victor sipped his drink as Luca glared at him with narrowed eyes.

"Why would that be your guess?" he asked in a tone that would normally induce fear.

But Victor feared no man.

He finished the liquid in his glass and slid it back over to Gianni for a refill. He turned directly into Luca's glare. "I guessed that, Don Savelli, because I am an educated man. I do not know, nor do I care to know the specifics of your business dealings. What I *do* need to know, is if it's going to affect me."

A soft laugh came from Gianni Storm as he handed Victor another glass of Scotch.

"You got balls, Governor," Gianni quipped before sipping from his own glass.

"Two of 'em," Victor affirmed.

Jack laughed and joined Gianni behind the bar. He poured himself some cognac and rested his forearms on the marble top.

"Victor, my money is as clean as whistle, and I know you know that. Now, I don't know who you pissed off in the Attorney General's office, but investigating you by investigating me, is a colossal fuck up on their part. It offends my delicate sense of power." He poured himself another round. "So, drink up, Governor. Enjoy a night with the fellas. Then, go home, spend time with your beautiful wife. Rest assured that when you wake, you will have no more issues with the Attorney General's office."

Jack raised his glass and emptied the contents.

"Yeah, well, that's that," Gianni muttered, sipping from his own glass.

Jack was known to be a man of his word. If he felt as if he could handle the situation, Victor had no reason to doubt him. Like the Creeds, the Storms had a vast amount of power in many arenas. And since Victor, apparently, had none in the State Attorney General's office, he'd did as suggested and enjoyed a night with the fellas.

Around midnight, Jack was walking him to the door. Gregor and Rory were exactly where they'd left them. Gregor opened the front door and surveyed the surroundings.

"Thanks for your time, Jack."

"No thanks necessary, Governor. It's an honor to have you in our home."

After they shook, Victor followed Gregor outside. Rory was right behind him. They descended the few steps that led to the walkway and made their way to the SUV, but it was empty. Naomi was nowhere to be found.

Victor looked around the long circular driveway and spotted her cozying up to who he assumed was another driver because the man was leaned up against a black Cadillac SUV as if waiting for his passenger. He was tall with a darker, olive complexion. Victor guessed he was of southern Italian descent; most likely Sicilian. He could have been Luca Savelli's driver, or bodyguard, or both.

"Unacceptable!" Gregor growled.

He turned to Rory and nodded his head in Naomi's direction, gesturing for him to go and get her. She was twirling her hair around her finger and giggling at something that probably wasn't all that funny. Victor was quickly becoming annoyed. He had a good buzz going and wanted to get home so he could climb between his wife's thick thighs. Collier, his former driver, may have been a psychopath, but at least he always had the car ready.

As Rory hustled Naomi to their vehicle, Gregor opened the back door of the SUV. When Victor slid in and relaxed against the soft leather, the rest of his detail loaded into the other cars.

"My apologies, sir," Naomi expressed as she hopped into the driver's seat. Rory took the passenger seat, and Gregor slid in next to him.

"Go!" Gregor ordered in impatiently.

As they rounded the circular driveway and drove toward the gate, all Victor could think about was the way Taylor had shown up at his office with her sexy body half covered in skimpy underwear. The way she'd dropped to her knees in front of him and took him deep in her mouth. The way he'd licked her sweet, wet pussy while she was spread eagle on his desk. And how he'd ridden her hard with her legs on his shoulders.

His dick swelled, almost to the point of pain. And, it stayed that way the entire ride home.

Naomi pulled around to the back of the building and stopped at the private entrance. When Gregor and Rory got out, Victor sat in the backseat and waited for them to clear the area. He didn't make a move until Gregor opened his door and gave the go ahead.

Rory stayed behind as Gregor escorted him through the entrance to a waiting elevator. Inside, there was yet another member of his security detail. Victor entered the elevator and held his hand out to stop Gregor.

"Go home and don't come in tomorrow."

"Excuse me?"

"Take tomorrow off and spend some time with your boys. I think I can manage to stay alive for one day."

The man had a family. Yet, he was always right by his side. Gregor's work ethic was impeccable, but he was a single parent. Surely, he was needed at home.

"Okay," he agreed easily, to Victor's surprise.

However, as soon as he stepped further in the elevator, Gregor entered as well. He smirked and pushed the button for Victor's floor.

"I'll go home after you're inside the apartment. And... I appreciate the day off. Thank you."

Victor chuckled, shaking his head. "Fine," he relented.

After a quick ride up, they were entering the apartment. While Gregor did a quick safety check, Victor crossed the foyer and made his way over to the bar. Since his small buzz had disappeared, he poured himself a Scotch, neat. He adjusted his hard-on and took a sip.

"All clear," Gregor announced on his way out.

Victor finished off his drink and left the glass on the bar. On his way to his room, Victor contemplated what position he would have his wife in first. Unfortunately, when he opened the door and stepped into darkness, the sound of Taylor's soft breathing told him that she was sleeping peacefully. Damned, if he didn't want to slip some hard cock into her, but she hadn't been sleeping since the shooting. There was nothing that could convince him to wake her up, not even his carnal need.

He slipped out of his shoes and crept quietly to the bathroom, making sure to close the door before turning the light on.

Victor pressed his head to the door and sighed. He gripped his aching dick and squeezed, hoping it would calm his need to be inside his wife's snug pussy. But calm did not come. So, he walked over to the shower and turned it on.

After stripping out of his clothes, he stepped into the cool water. He adjusted the temperature and he grabbed a bar of soap. His plan was to lather up, rinse off, and get out. However, when his soapy hand landed on his throbbing dick, the plan changed.

He wrapped his fingers around the shaft and squeezed his lids closed. His imagination took him to Taylor, bent over in the shower while he pushed his hard dick into her from behind. As he stroked his dick, he pictured her ass bouncing as he fucked her behind. He stroked harder when he imagined her pussy clenching his cock. And, before he knew it, he was growling through a much-needed orgasm, blowing a huge load on the shower floor.

26

DONATELLA

Less than a week after she and Kelly fled the BOC, Donna found herself just outside the property. An intense feeling of glee washed over her as she spied the scene from a distance. Bobby Lee, Clara, Harry Barber, and a handful of other cult members were handcuffed and ushered into the back of local squad cars. They were being taken to the police station in Springfield and from there, they'd be transported to the Sangamon County Jail.

The satisfaction she gained from putting away drug dealers was no comparison to the satisfaction of taking down the religious cult, or at least its leaders.

Donna knew that drug dealers played on the weak and addicted. But for the life of her, she still didn't know how Bobby Lee Khal had conned hundreds of seemingly intelligent people into relinquishing their free will. He preyed on those that so desperately needed some sort of purpose in life. Something, or someone, to believe in. His followers would do anything for him, even allowing the cult leaders to enslave their children.

Donna often wondered why there were no kids in the BOC, and she had plans on finding out before their mission ended. She'd inquired about the children with several members, but she had yet to get a straight answer from any of them.

When she did find out why she never saw any children running around the grounds, she was sick to her stomach. During the raid on the compound, agents discovered an unoccupied building to the far south end of the compound. After further inspection, they realized the building wasn't unoccupied at all. Once they breached a door that led to a basement, they discover where the children were being held.

It was dark, damp, and filthy. Essentially, a dungeon. There were sewing machines in the middle of the room and dirty pillows and blankets surrounded them. It appeared that the child laborers had been constructing work uniforms for several major grocery and department stores. They would work during the day and sleep on the filthy blankets at night.

Donna watched with binoculars as dirty, malnourished children were led out of the building. With their tiny hands, the children shielded their eyes from the sun. They'd obviously been denied fresh air and sunshine.

After a final head count, the Department of Children and Family Services confirmed that there was a total of seventy-five children. It was safe to assume that some, if not all, of the parents would be charged down the line.

Donna had had enough of the scene. She'd face the monsters in court, and she couldn't wait. In the meantime, she needed a distraction.

She raised the window and grabbed her phone from the center console. A smile formed when she found the number she was scrolling for. Now that her part of the investigation was over, she was ready to put the BOC in her rearview mirror.

Are you in the states?

She sent the text and waited eagerly for Lincoln to respond.

Chicago. How are you?

Done. Mission over.

Great! Dinner tonight?

You read my mind. Pick me up at 8?

Address?

You found me in Springfield. Use your resources.

I know where to find you. I was just trying not to be creepy. See you tonight.

27

VICTOR

Renee pushed a button to end a phone call. She opened her mouth, but nothing came out. Her stunned expression was startling.

"What?"

"That was Vince Hart. The Attorney General's investigation into PAC funds has been quashed."

"You don't say," Victor murmured.

"How did you do it?" Renee asked, astounded.

"I did nothing. I had a conversation with Jack Storm. He said he'd handle it. Good shit. I guess he did, huh?"

Victor had no clue how he did, but true to his word, Jack made his legal problem disappear.

"What do you mean?" Renee asked with furrowed brows. "How could Jack Storm influence the State Attorney General's office?"

Not willing to be interrogated by his press secretary, he simply shrugged. Victor had no illusions about the amount of influence Jack held. He didn't know the specifics, and he didn't care. The night before, Jack had assured him that his every dime was legit and that he would handle the Attorney General. With everything he knew about Jack Storm, he had no reason to doubt his sincerity. So, after his jerk-off session in the shower, he went to bed without worrying about a pending indictment.

"You got anything else?"

Renee paused in response to his dismissiveness. When she didn't answer, he did something that he never liked to do and repeated himself.

"Is there anything else, Renee?"

She sighed and placed a folder in his hand. "Just set a date for the gubernatorial debate."

Victor's eyes snapped from the folder to Renee. "How did you pull that off?"

Now, Victor was surprised. Bill Thornton, his opponent, had been avoiding a debate like the plague. Anytime Victor's team mentioned a debate, the democrat acted as if they were discussing the apocalypse. But he really couldn't blame the man. With his stuttering indecisiveness, Victor could understand why he didn't want to face off in front of millions.

"What's the date?"

"October 29th in the Rosemont Park Hall."

"Really, Renee, how did you get him to agree to that?"

"Governor, I can be very persuasive when need be. And…you're ahead in the polls. Your support base is secure. If he doesn't debate, this election is over him."

"And me?" Victor asked. "What do I need to stay ahead?"

"Win the debate and…" She smirked with a raised brow. "Try not to get indicted."

Victor laughed. He walked over to Renee and placed his hand on her shoulder "I can do that," he assured with a grin.

"Good."

"And, rest assured, once I *am* reelected, we can concentrate on the White House. You, me, and Kena are gonna go all the way. You ready for that?"

Renee smiled. "Damn right, I am. We're gonna run the free world and fix what's broken in the White House.

When she raised her hand for a high five, Victor slapped his hand against hers.

"Team Creed," she called in a bubbly tone, their fingers locked. "Team Creed."

Renee twisted her fingers out of his and grabbed the folder from his desk. "First, we gotta kill the debate," she pointed out.

"Consider it done, Ms. Griffin. I got this debate on lock."

"On lock, huh?" Renee mocked playfully. "Your wife done rubbed off on you."

"Yeah, probably," Victor admitted with soft chuckle.

"Okay then, *homeboy*. Your team is in the conference room. They're ready to conduct a mock debate."

He went to follow Renee out of his office but paused when his cell phone vibrated in his pocket. He fished it out and saw that it was Jack calling him.

"I'll meet you there," he told Renee as he pushed to answer. "Jack, what's up?"

"All should be well for now."

Victor smiled. "Yes. I've gotten word. Thanks for your help."

He walked over to the window and looked down at the busy downtown street.

"That's the thing, Governor. It wasn't me. When I put in a call, I was told the situation had already been handled."

Something much more sinister was going on.

"What do you make of this whole thing?" Jack asked, breaking the silence.

"I don't know, but I think it's time for me to put in a call of my own. Thanks for your help, Jack."

"No problem. Good luck to you."

Victor disconnected the call, deciding it was time to call in the big dog. He tapped the screen to place the call and waited for an answer.

"Good morning," came from a gruff voice on the other end of the line.

"Dad, I need your help."

28

DONATELLA

Donna was trying to figure out where Lincoln was taking her. But he made a left on 18th Drive, and she was even more clueless than before. The only thing that far down on 18th Drive was the Shedd Aquarium. It was well past 8 o'clock. Surely, they were closed. When they turned down a dark service road, she was certain that they weren't open for business.

"Are you taking me back here to kill me?"

"Yep," he quipped with a devilish smirk and a raised brow.

"Oh, well," Donna said through a sigh. "Gotta go sometime."

He chuckled softly and pulled over behind the building. "Here we are."

He shifted into park and turned off the ignition. After he climbed out of the passenger seat Donna looked around. She'd never been to this part of the aquarium before. It was dark and secluded, but she was far from afraid. She felt safe with Lincoln. When he opened her door, she stepped out on black, five-inch pumps. Since she had anticipated a normal restaurant, she was wearing a simple black cocktail dress. For the Shedd Aquarium, she was definitely overdressed.

Lincoln tucked her arm in his and escorted her to the building.

Her curiosity was getting the better of her. "What is this, Lincoln?"

Without responding, he led her to a small door and knocked twice. Seconds later, the door was opened. Waiting on the other side was a short, older man wearing a crisp, black suit.

"Good evening, Ma'am," he greeted with a polite nod. "Colonel Creed...welcome."

"Good evening, Mr. York. Thank you."

"If you'll please follow me?"

The man may have been short, but he had a big voice.

They followed him up an iron staircase and through a metal door. They walked down a long glass corridor filled with every type of sea creature one could imagine. Before long, they'd turned a corner which took them to a huge, round aquarium. It wasn't until they were halfway around the tank that she noticed the two huge sharks gliding in the water.

"Wow," Donna marveled with a whisper.

She hadn't been to the Shedd Aquarium since she was a child. And as an adult, she never had a desire to go. But standing in front of the giant tank staring wide-eyed at the predators made her feel like a little girl again.

"They are extraordinary creatures. Don't you think?" York commented.

"I do."

"This way, please," he insisted, gesturing for them to follow.

He led them further around the tank until they arrived at a table covered with crisp, white linen. It was elegantly set for two with exquisite gold and rose-colored china, and what looked like very expensive crystal drinkware. The champagne and candlelight was setting a very romantic scene.

Lincoln pulled out a chair for Donna to sit. She took her seat and looked up at him with a smile.

"You are full of surprises, Colonel."

"You have no idea, Detective," he muttered, gifting her with a sexy grin.

He took the seat opposite her and placed his napkin in his lap. A young woman in all black approached, introducing herself as Jackie. She uncorked the champagne and recited the menu as she poured. Donna thought it funny, but they were sitting in an environment solely for the display and preservation of marine life and everything on the menu was seafood.

After placing their order, the conversation veered to her undercover investigation into the BOC. Normally, she would never discuss a pending case with anyone who wasn't working it. However, Lincoln inserted himself into her case when he showed up at the Glory Gala.

"The adrenaline of working undercover must be so intoxicating," he noted while forking a sautéed scallop.

Donna couldn't keep her eyes off of him when he slipped it between his sexy lips.

"Umm...no, sir. Intoxicating was running into you while undercover. You were lookin' really good in that tux, Colonel."

Lincoln chuckled while chewing. He swallowed and pointed his fork at her. "You certainly didn't seem that intoxicated when you first saw me."

"That's because I thought you were gonna blow my cover."

He scratched at the masculine stubble on his jaw and frowned as if confused.

"*What?*" he asked, jokingly puzzled. "I did blow you under the cover. Didn't I?"

Donna cringed inside when she giggled like a school girl. Lincoln was smart, charming, funny, and gorgeous as all hell. He had a way of bulldozing through a protective wall that had taken years to build. Although she'd had a few breakups, she'd never experienced a broken heart. After watching her sister suffer through a failed marriage, Donna was determined to never allow herself such vulnerabilities. Not that it was even a possibility with Lincoln. He didn't even live in the same state. And even if he did, his military duties kept him on the move.

Not to mention her career. Sometimes working undercover kept her away for an unreasonable amount of time. No man would put up with that.

With those unrealistic thoughts out of the way, Donna allowed herself to just enjoy a wonderful dinner with a ridiculously hot man.

LINCOLN

Lincoln tapped the key fob and opened the passenger door. His eyes roamed Donna's curves as she folded herself into his brother's Range Rover. Though the dinner conversation was stimulating, he couldn't wait to get her alone and naked.

He closed the door and plotted the rest of their evening as he walked around the back of the SUV. She hadn't invited him back to her place, and he didn't want to risk taking her to Victor's just so she could wind up engaged in girl talk with Taylor all night. By the time he slid into the driver's seat, he'd made up his mind. He started the engine and took off.

It only took twenty minutes to get to her house in Mount Greenwood. When he'd picked her up, he was surprised that she lived in one the most segregated neighborhoods in Chicago. The neighborhood was 87% white, 11% Hispanic, Asian, and other, and only 2% black. The area was known as the home of the Southside Irish.

Lincoln parked in her driveway and turned to face her. "I meant to ask. Why do you live in this all-white neighborhood?"

A low rumble of laughter escaped her throat.

"*Seriously*. Why? How do you get along with your neighbors?"

"I barely see my neighbors, but they're cool. Everybody around here are either cops or firemen. We have great block parties though."

"Really?"

He wasn't sure if she was being serious, or facetious.

"Really," she chortled. "I know this neighborhood has a reputation for being racist, but that hasn't been my experience."

"Good to know. I'd hate to have to drop a bomb on your neighborhood," Lincoln joked.

"Me too. Here's the thing, Lincoln. I work undercover narcotics in the most segregated city in America. And let's face it, they ain't sending me to buy and sell dope in Mount Greenwood. Which means I'm safe here. I can rest well knowing that I ain't living next door to somebody I done locked up."

Lincoln nodded. "Makes sense," he muttered.

The glaring streetlights invaded the window, illuminating her beautiful, copper skin. He was jealous of the straight, black hair kissing her delicate bare shoulders. He leaned closer, determined to taste her warm flesh.

"Why are you looking at me like that? What are you thinking?" she rasped in a voice that revealed her own arousal.

"I was timing in my mind how long it's going to take for me to tear you out of those panties."

Lincoln heard the need in his own deep voice.

Donna reached behind her and pulled something from her seat. She lifted her hand and twirled a pair of satin blue panties around her finger.

"You mean these panties?" she asked with a wicked grin.

Lincoln, not even bothering to try and figure out when she found time to rid herself of the tiny undergarment, reached over and grabbed her arm. He used a thoughtful amount of force to pull her over the middle console, and on his lap.

"You *are* ready for me, Donatella."

He lowered his fingers down her body, grazing the material of her dress. He rang a single finger teasingly slow up the naked skin of her inner thigh. When he reached her point of pleasure, she threw her head back and moaned. She was indeed ready for him as he massaged circles against her slippery clit. He'd go slow, then fast until she was squirming in his lap.

Thankful for the tinted windows, Lincoln pulled the top of her dress down, exposing her braless tits. Her body jerked when he pinched her puckered nipple between his lips and sucked it into his mouth.

"Ah, fuck this!" she blurted before falling back on the steering wheel.

Without difficulty, she reached down and unfastened his belt. She dipped her hand in his boxers and wrapped her small fingers around his erection. She secured a good grip and began to stroke him into delirium.

"Damn!" he gasped.

His head fell against the back of the seat while she handled him with raunchy proficiency. When his toes curled involuntarily in his shoes, he made the only choice he could. He gripped Donna's hips and guided her on his dick. She stiffened when he penetrated her tight, saturated channel without protection. He could sense she was hesitant, ready to pull away. The thought of stopping also danced around in his brain, but once his dick was enveloped in the warmth of her insides, pulling out was no longer an option. Truthfully, in that very moment, Lincoln knew Donatella was to be his, and his alone.

He wrapped his arms around her waist, hugging her tight, and propelled into her deep enough to make her breath hitch. She raised and lowered her snug pussy on his dick, rolling her hips, and riding him like a trained steed.

"Shit!"

Lincoln tried to concentrate on their immediate surroundings, Donna's shallow breathing, hell, even the moon. Anything besides the way she was milking his cock of all its glory. If not, he'd be coming way before he wanted.

He pressed his hand to the small of her back and pulled her close. Their lips collided, their tongues connected, and their mouths mimicked their lovemaking.

Lincoln was overwhelmed by the passion of their coupling. The foreign and unfamiliar feeling robbed him of every single solitary ounce of his self-control. His stomach clenched, his thighs stiffened, and his balls constricted. To his dismay, he was about to cum, and there was nothing he could do to stop it. As Donna bounced up and down, riding his dick like she owned it, he couldn't come up with one rational way to prevent himself from ejaculating prematurely.

"Goddamn it, Donna! Fuck!"

As if an unspoken prayer had been answered, within the first pulse of his orgasm, Donna snaked her arms around his neck and held on tight. Her pussy convulsed around his dick and her body quivered in his arms. To Lincoln's enormous relief, she was coming with him.

"Oh my God!" she cried out and collapsed on top of him in.

As she tried to regulate her breathing, Lincoln rubbed her back. In his entire life, he'd never been more grateful for a woman's orgasm.

29

VICTOR

When they pulled close to the curb in front of Lucas' Gold Coast high-rise, Gregor hopped out of the SUV, vacating his seat for his younger brother.

"What's up, Linc? I can't believe you're still in town."

"I got business here."

"I'm sure," Victor jibed. "The Devereaux kind."

"Hmph."

Lincoln had an irritating way of avoiding inquiries thrown in his direction. Even though their father was still with them, and he had two older brothers, Lincoln appointed himself the family's protector. Which was no surprise to Victor. Even when they were little boys, Lincoln was the first to throw a punch if someone so much as mean mugged one of his brothers.

"So, you're staying at Luc's now?"

"Yeah. Thanks for letting me crash, but you guys have a lot going on. And Luc's always at Bella's. It's kinda like having my own place."

Victor nodded. After all, he couldn't blame him. It wasn't like he was lying. There was Union Station-like traffic running through his place on a daily basis. For Taylor's sake, win or lose, he'd be glad when it was all over. He vowed that within a week of the polls closing, he was taking her away.

"Where are we going?" Lincoln asked, interrupting Victor's thoughts.

"We're going to meet Dad for dinner at Lou Malnati's."

Lincoln looked over with a furrowed brow. "Dad's here? Why? Where's Mom?"

"Shopping with Taylor and Bella."

Victor couldn't help the smile that grew on his face. He was pleased that Taylor was finally starting to re-engage in normal activity. And the look on Lincoln's face told him that he understood. If anyone knew what witnessing a traumatic event could do to a person, it was his brother. Victor had never allowed himself to imagine the things that Lincoln had seen, or maybe even done.

"That's great, bro," he said with a sincere smile.

"And, then, she and her friends are going to have a ladies' night."

"Wow! I'm proud of her. Hell, I'm proud of you too. You're actually gonna let her out of your sight?"

"Hell, no!" Victor blurted with a chuckle. "Gregor has appointed himself her official bodyguard."

"And she didn't argue?" Lincoln asked, skeptically.

"She tried."

Lincoln laughed. "Sounds like business as usual."

"Yeah. If it weren't election season, things would almost seem normal."

"And, how's that going?" he asked in an impassive tone. "I see you're looking good in the polls."

"Yeah, but you know we can't bank on the polls. Everything falls on the voters. With this bullshit indictment—"

Victor paused when he realized Lincoln was showing zero interest in what he was saying. He was staring straight ahead, and even though he was halfway engaging in the conversation, he could tell his focus was elsewhere.

"Linc?"

He seemed to have zoned out.

"*Linc?*" Victor called again, slightly raising his voice.

Startled out of his trance, Lincoln blinked over at him. "Hmm...what?"

"What is it, Linc?"

He opened his mouth to speak but stopped when they pulled to the curb in front of the popular pizza place. His security detail scrambled to secure his entry inside. Probably to Lincoln, his routine may have been a distraction. But for Victor, it was simply his way of life.

The back door of the SUV was opened, but Victor remained still. Lincoln hadn't answered his question.

"Linc?" Victor prompted. He blew out a frustrated breath and nudged him with an elbow.

"It's nothing. I was just thinking about something Donatella said." Lincoln waved his hand toward the street.

"You plan on getting out?"

Victor narrowed his eyes at his brother. His behavior was evasive. But, since there were a handful of armed, attention-grabbing men and women standing just outside the door, he let it go and climbed out of the SUV. "We *will* finish this conversation," he warned when Lincoln joined him.

Lincoln shrugged and walked ahead of him into the pizzeria. A hostess led them to a small area for private parties. Victor Sr. stood at their entry and smiled. Victor smiled in return, noting that his dad was standing as tall as he and Lincoln. He still had a good head of their signature thick, dark hair, and his green eyes were still as luminous as they'd been in his youth.

Lincoln made it to their father first. As usual, they shook before hugging. Senior managed to be formal and affectionate at the same time.

"Good to see you, son."

"You too, Dad."

He kissed Lincoln's cheek before releasing him. When Victor walked over to him, he was given the same greeting. Victor unfastened the button on his suit coat and took a seat at the table. Lincoln seemed comfortable, casually dressed in jeans, a t-shirt, and boots.

"So, what'd you come up with?" Victor asked his dad, eager to get to the bottom of the bogus investigation.

Lincoln looked from Victor to Victor with confusion. "What are you talking about?"

"I asked Dad to looked into my so-called pending indictment."

"Oh." Lincoln frowned. "Have you talked to Storm?"

"Of course, I have. He put in some calls, and the indictment was suspended the next day. But, here's the thing. He says he had nothing to do with it. The investigation concluded before he even made the first phone call."

"And he didn't know why?"

"Nope," Victor responded, shaking his head.

"And, neither do I," Victor Sr. admitted. "I've used every connection that I have to find out what initiated this investigation. Whatever it is, it's bigger than me."

Since his dad was a retired United States senator with endless connections, that was really saying something. Of course, Victor could just be grateful that the witch hunt had ended, but that wasn't who he was. If someone was out to get him, he wanted to know exactly who it was.

LINCOLN

Lincoln excused himself from the table and headed toward the bathroom. But instead of going into the men's room, he walked into the ladies. He locked the door and waited. He was waiting, less than patiently, for the woman that had entered to come out of the stall. And as soon as she did, Lincoln rushed her.

He grabbed her by both shoulders and slammed her against the wall. She startled and opened her mouth as if she were planning to scream. He placed his hand over her mouth even though he knew she wouldn't. She wasn't the screaming type.

"What the *fuck* is going on?" Lincoln snarled.

Only rage could overcome the shock of seeing Tahira Raji, CIA Operative, in the driver's seat of his brother's car. Even with a wig and dark glasses, he recognized her as soon as he slid in the backseat. During dinner, he'd inquired about her as if he was interested romantically. He learned that she was going by the name Naomi, and she'd been driving him around for months before she approached him and Lucas in the restaurant.

"Get. Your. Goddamned. Hands. Off. Of. Me!" she spat with fire in her eyes.

She tried to pull away, but Lincoln shoved her against the wall. Manhandling a woman wasn't something he had been raised to do, but Tahira was no normal woman. There was no doubt in his mind that had he released her, she wouldn't hesitate to cut his throat.

"I'll ask one more time. What the fuck is going on?"

He worked at making his tone more threatening, but she was unfazed. In fact, she got the drop on him with the age-old knee to the balls. When he jerked in pain and reached instinctively for his junk, her sharp elbow contacted the side of his face. Because she thought he was incapacitated, she tried to run around him.

She didn't get far.

Lincoln gathered himself quick enough to swing his arm and clothesline her ass to the filthy bathroom floor. When she hit the marble with a violent thud, he wrapped his fingers around her throat and balled his other hand into a fist.

"Don't fuck with me, Lady!" Lincoln warned through gritted teeth. "I will punch through your soul!"

She reached up and clawed at his fingers. Once she realized she couldn't pry his thick fingers from her neck, she relaxed against the floor. She mouthed the word, "Okay" and held her hands up in surrender.

Lincoln didn't trust her, but he wouldn't get answers if he choked her out.

He picked her up like a rag doll and slammed her to her feet. When he released her, she clutched her neck and gasped for air. He watched her struggle to breathe without one ounce of guilt. She was fucking with his family, and he had a sneaking suspicion that it was somehow connected to the fruitless mission in Mosul.

Lincoln stepped back but kept his guard. If looks could kill, he would have dropped dead immediately.

"You're an asshole," she sneered, massaging her neck.

Lincoln narrowed his eyes and closed the already tiny distance between them. She was going to be sorry if he had to repeat himself.

"I'm working Luca Savelli," she blurted.

Lincoln squinted, trying to connect the dots. "What the hell does that have to do with my brother?"

When she hesitated and looked away, Lincoln grabbed her face and made her look him in the eye. The distress she was trying so hard to display disappeared immediately when she brandished a sly grin.

"You are so damn sexy," she rasped in a hoarse whisper.

Her face twisted in agony when Lincoln squeezed her small jaw between his fingers.

"What does my brother have to do with Luca Savelli?"

"Let me go and I'll tell you," she bargained.

Because he was probably crushing her jaw, her words came out distorted. He loosened his grip on her face and waited for her to speak.

"Now, you know I'm trained to resist invasive interrogation tactics. But...since you have a level 3 clearance, I'll share. Mosul was about weapons, and the Savelli family deals in weapons. The agency got a hold of some intel about a mass weapons deal that was to take place in Mosul. Supposedly, the plane was a drop. We needed to find out who the recipients were. We suspected the Russians, but it could be North Korea."

"There was nothing on that plane," Lincoln pointed out.

"We were wrong," she admitted with a casual shrug. Her nonchalant attitude was pissing him off.

"Again...what the fuck does that have to do with my brother?" Lincoln growled. He was tempted to snap her neck when she blew out a harsh breath as if frustrated.

"You can blame The Times for involving your brother. That article about him consorting with Luca Savelli is what put him in the Agency's sights. For years, the Savellis have been practically untouchable, with very few ties, if any, in America. Jack Storm happens to be one of them. Problem is...Jack Storm is a boy scout."

"So is Victor!" Lincoln snapped.

"Oh, please!" she scoffed, rolling of her eyes. "He's a fucking politician for God's sake!"

Tahira was pushing every last one of his buttons. She couldn't know how badly he wanted to put her body through that bathroom wall. But she was talking, and no longer fighting, so there was no justification in putting the smaller person down.

"Tahira!" he gritted in warning.

"Okay!" she relented. "I needed to create a problem that would get Luca Savelli in the room. Storm was my only way in, and your brother was my only way to Jack."

Because Lincoln's level of rage was nearing explosive, he took a much-needed step back. He ran his fingers roughly through his hair.

"So, you risked ruining my brother's campaign when you could've just shaken your ass in front of Jack Storm or that gangster? Why aren't you driving for any of them?"

"Well, believe or not, Colonel, I can't pass for Sicilian. And, surprisingly, the Storms are not very trusting. They don't hire new people."

"Un-be-lievable!" Lincoln blustered.

"Hey! Once I got in, I killed the investigation!"

She didn't seem to have a clue, or she really couldn't care less about the people she trampled to get what she wanted.

"But the damage is done, Tahira! What about his reputation? His campaign?"

"Lincoln, you and I both know that Bill Thornton doesn't stand a chance in this election. The governor could go jerk off on Michigan Avenue and still win by a landslide. Besides...we *need* to know where those weapons are going."

"*What fucking weapons*? The plane was empty! Your fucking intel sucks! You put my soldiers at risk and you played Russian Roulette with my brother's career!"

She exhaled, pretending like she was capable of remorse. "Linc—"

"Shut up!" Lincoln barked, shoving her against the wall. He didn't like roughing up a woman, but for the CIA Operative, he'd make an exception.

"Stay the fuck away from my family!" he cautioned.

Not knowing how long he could continue to resist inflicting bodily harm, Lincoln turned and kicked the bathroom door open.

"I'm done! I got what I needed!" she cackled as he walked out.

Bitch!

30

TAYLOR

"Babe, all the other girls are riding on the party bus."

"And you can too, sweetness."

Taylor blew out a frustrated breath. "Don't you 'sweetness' me. Don't nobody else have to bring a bodyguard."

Victor folded his arms and glared at her with a raised brow. "You know damn well Victoria Storm doesn't go anywhere without security. Besides, you're the First Lady of Illinois. It's time you came to terms with that."

"I have!"

"Nope," Victor retorted. "No, you haven't."

"Victor!"

He threw his hand up, dismissing any further discussion. "Don't wanna hear it. Have fun with the girls."

Taylor growled at his back when he walked out of their bedroom. She was debating whether or not to follow him when he stuck his head in the doorway.

"By the way...you look beautiful, my love."

He said it with the same sexy grin and deep, masculine baritone that always rendered her submissive.

"I can't stand you," she muttered with narrowed eyes.

"I know, babe, but I love you."

"Get out, Victor!"

"Yep. Okay," he quipped before dipping out of the doorway.

Taylor walked in her closet and looked in the mirror. She was already on the thick side, but the new baby weight made her damn near Amazonian. Victor seemed to love the extra inches, but her jeans didn't. So, she settled for a black jumpsuit. It was wide-legged and loose-fitting, but the haltered top made it sexy. Hopefully, her full cleavage would take away from her growing waistline.

The night before, she'd twisted her hair into Bantu knots. After getting dressed, she took them down and used a pick to stretch her natural curls. To Victor, big natural curls, a jumpsuit, and curves, equaled Pam Grier. His ultimate obsession.

Taylor checked her lipstick, grabbed her purse from the mirrored vanity, and left the closet. She walked out of her room and down the hall, bypassing Victor's office. As she walked past the door, she heard several voices.

She sighed.

Not even at home did he have a moment to himself. And had he not practically forced her out of the house, she would have kicked everyone out and picked out a movie on Netflix. But she fully understood that he was trying to ease her into normalcy. However, governing the state, running for reelection, and worrying about her was wearing on him.

Before reaching the end of the hall, Taylor froze. She'd just made a sudden decision she wasn't sure Victor would appreciate. Nonetheless, she fished her phone out of her purse and turned to go back to their room.

She sat on the edge of the bed and made the necessary phone calls. Once she was done, she took off the dressy jumpsuit and hung it in the closet. She grabbed a pair of sweats and pulled her SIU t-shirt out of a drawer. After stepping into a pair of UGGs, she was ready. They were comfortable as hell but ugly as shit.

Taylor left her room and headed to Victor's office. She took a deep breath before walking inside. The work continued. No one seemed to notice her presence, so she cleared her throat to get their attention. Victor looked away from his computer. His brow contracted with confusion when he noticed her appearance. He got up from his desk and hurried over to her.

"What happened, honey? Why'd you change your mind about going out?"

The anxiety in his voice made Taylor sad. She must have been a constant source of worry to him. She smiled to reassure him and caressed his handsome face.

"Nothing happened, sweetheart. I came up with a better plan."

He smiled, but his furrowed brow revealed confusion. "What better plan?"

Taylor grinned and glanced around his broad shoulder. "They gotta go."

"Hmm?"

She stepped around him and moved to the middle of his office. His campaign staff was hard at work, barely noticing her presence.

"Excuse me, everyone! May I have your attention, please?"

With reluctance, his team tore themselves away from the tasks they were performing and afforded her their undivided attention.

"Thank you. Now, forgive me for being rude, but I need you all to leave."

The looks on their faces were priceless, akin to a deer in headlights. She'd apparently rendered them speechless, but none of them moved to leave.

"What are you doing, Taylor?" Victor asked in a hushed tone.

"My job," she said over her shoulder. "Now, please. Y'all can pick up where you left off tomorrow."

Carlotta McGovern, his Chief Media Advisor, was the first to move. She gave Taylor a knowing smile and collected her things. Her compliance prompted the rest of his team to do the same.

Victor stood by the door, seemingly still confused by her actions. She offered goodbyes to each of them as they departed. But when Kena approached to say goodbye, Taylor grabbed her wrist and pulled her close.

"We need to get you into some comfortable clothes," she told her.

"Huh?"

"Some sweats and a t-shirt or something like that. Can you change and come back?"

"*Sss-ure*," she replied with obvious bewilderment.

"Great! See you soon."

Kena's perplexed expression remained as she left the office. Once they were alone, Victor turned to Taylor with a raised brow.

"What are you up to?"

Taylor grabbed his hand and pulled him toward the door. "I'll explain while you get dressed. Come on."

∽

Within a couple of hours, the noise in their apartment had converted from campaign chatter to Frankie Beverly. Taylor was pleasantly surprised that their friends and family were willing to come when called on such notice.

"What's going on here?" she asked Victor, referring to Donatella and Lincoln huddled together, giggling and whispering.

"I think they're a thing."

"Whaaat? Get outta here!"

"Yeah. I'm not sure, but I believe they've been seeing each other for a while."

It wasn't hard to believe when looking at them. They seemed very comfortable with each other. Taylor wanted to get the details, but a knock at the door prohibited her from going over there to be nosy.

She went for the door, but Victor stopped her.

"I'll get it. Can you pour me a Scotch?"

"Sure thing, honey." Taylor walked over to the bar where Victoria was acting as bartender. "So, you actually remember how to perform manual labor?" she teased.

"Girl, please," Bella scoffed. "The only thing she's poured since she's been back there was Jack Daniels for herself."

Victoria rolled her eyes at Bella. "Would you *really* trust a drink I made for you?"

"I thought they buried the hatchet," Maria muttered.

"In each other's backs maybe," Donna quipped as she walked up.

"*Heeeey, Donna.* You lookin' good, girl," Victoria crooned in an obvious effort to irritate Bella.

It worked. Bella blew out a frustrated breath and walked away. Taylor didn't even believe that they still disliked each other. Bickering just came natural to them. It was simply the nature of their relationship.

"Hey, Vic." Donna chuckled. "Stop fucking with my sister."

"Pissing your sister off is just too much fun."

"Hmm... if I didn't know any better, I'd suspect you had a little thing for her."

Victoria's laughter was wicked. "Nah, I suspect the only thing y'all got in common is your face. And I'm willing to bet hers is nowhere near as comfortable to sit on as yours."

"*Damn!*" Taylor exclaimed.

"Wait! What?!" Maria questioned, clearly unaware that they'd had a *thing* at one time.

Donna chuckled and leaned over the bar. She brought her face close to Victoria's and looked at her through narrowed eyes. "Fix me a drink," she demanded in a soft, but domineering tone.

Victoria grinned and grabbed a glass from the overhead glass holder. "Jameson, right?"

VICTOR

For the third time in the last hour, there was a knock at the door.

"I'll get it!"

Victor hurried to the door before another knock interrupted the fun Taylor seemed to be having with her friends. It had been too long since he'd seen her laugh. Even though she'd put the evening together for his peace of mind, his true peace surfaced when he saw glimpses of the old Taylor.

As soon as his hand touched the knob, there was another knock.

"Hold on!"

When he opened the door, Gregor was on the other side carrying two cases of Heineken. Next to him was Emma balancing five pizza boxes.

"She got you too, hmm?" Victor chuckled.

Since he thought Taylor was going out, he'd given Emma the night off. And Gregor had been sent home to his sons after they left the office. Of course, he wouldn't leave until he was tucked safely in the penthouse. Now there he was, standing in the doorway, wearing a Collin Kaepernick jersey and blue jeans.

"We come with provisions," Gregor announced with a grin.

"I see that. Well, come on in. And thank you."

"Not a problem," Emma said. "We didn't come to work. We came to hang. So, while we put these away, I'm gonna need you to fix me a drink."

Victor laughed and nodded. "What'll it be, Miss Emma?"

"I'll take a Screwdriver."

"Yes, ma'am. Coming right up. Gregor?"

"Nothing for me. I'm gonna grab one of these beers."

"Alright."

When Gregor and Emma headed toward the kitchen, he closed the door and scanned the room for Taylor. She and Bella were laughing, competing in what looked like a Running Man contest. Victor folded his arms and found himself staring. Taylor's smile could lighten the darkness. Her glee traveled through him like electricity and comforted him like a warm blanket.

"You are really far gone," Lincoln teased.

Victor hadn't even noticed him standing next to him. "Yup, and it looks like you're on your way too," he rebutted.

"Nah. Donna and I have to keep things casual. Neither one of us is ever in one place for long."

Victor turned to Lincoln and grinned. "Things like that have a way of working themselves out."

"Maybe, but what's more important...who's the blonde with Xander? Her nose has been in the air since they arrived. She's all like, 'Governor who?'"

The twisted face Lincoln was making made Victor laugh. Xander's date was a bit uptight, maybe even bit snobbish.

"They were already on a date when Taylor called," Victor told him.

"Well, I hope she got a chance to eat. She's like 98 pounds. soaking wet," Lincoln snickered.

"That's not nice, little brother."

Lincoln shrugged. "I don't like the way she's looking at our womenfolk. Like *they* don't belong."

Victor chuckled and nudged Lincoln with his elbow. "Forget how she's looking at our womenfolk. Look how Xander is looking at NiYah Reed."

"Oh, shit!" Lincoln breathed. "Who is she? I've seen her before, but we've never met."

"Dr. NiYah Reed is Bella's friend. She's the Cook County Medical Examiner."

"She's a looker."

"That she is," Victor agreed.

Which was more than likely the reason Alexander couldn't keep his eyes off her. She had a much lighter complexion than her friends, light-brown, hazel-colored eyes, and long reddish-brown African locs. She was on the short side, about 5'5. However, her slim waist, generous hips, and sizeable breasts gave her an hourglass figure.

"Maybe you should get over there and remind him who his date is."

"Not my business," Victor muttered.

"And? When has that ever stopped you?" Lincoln asked through a chuckle.

"Ugh," Victor grumbled under his breath when Jeffrey Morgan, his sister-in-law's fiancé approached. What Nicole saw in the bootlicker, he would never know.

"You don't like that guy, huh?"

"I don't trust him."

When Jeffrey walked up, he was sporting the same cheesy ambition-filled smile he always had. "Governor, thanks for the invite," he beamed like a woman who'd received a marriage proposal.

"Thank Taylor. She put this little shindig together."

"Cool! How's the campaign going? You're a shoe in. Thornton doesn't stand a chance."

"Not necessarily. The current administration has made it very hard to be Republican in these times."

Victor looked past him and noticed that Taylor was no longer competing in the amateur dance contest.

"I know exactly what you mean, Governor. I—"

"Excuse me," Victor rudely interrupted before stepping around him.

He walked away, not in the least interested in anything Jeffrey had to say. During all of their past conversations, he never had anything of substance to contribute. His entire role was to suck up to anyone who could possibly advance his career.

With Jeffrey in his rearview, he made his way over to his smiling wife. He wrapped an arm around her waist and pulled her close.

"You are strong, beautiful, thoughtful, and sexy as can be."

Taylor snaked her arms around his neck and kissed his chin. "Yeah? You think so?"

"Absolutely. Are you having a good time?"

"Oh, yes," Taylor sighed. "But tonight, is about you, baby, not me."

Victor caressed her head, pressing it against his chest. "Thank you for knowing what I needed even when I didn't know."

"Well, that's my job," she said, pulling slightly away.

She looked up at him with a smile that made his heart skip a beat.

"Now...let's tell these folks about the new Creed."

"Really?" Victor grinned, laughing inside, thinking that it was now *he* who was beaming like a woman who'd just received a marriage proposal.

Taylor took her phone out of her pocket and paused the music. Victor grabbed her hand and led her to the tall arch that separated the foyer and the living room.

"Friends, family, may we have your attention!" Victor called out.

When he had everyone's attention, he looked around to see if everyone was present. Of course, everyone wasn't. Lincoln and Donatella were missing. Since Lincoln already knew, he didn't bother looking for him. He was eager to let his loved ones know just how happy Taylor had made him.

DONATELLA

"Yesss!" Donna cried out from the immense feeling of pleasure she derived from Lincoln's thick dick stretching her with every invasion. She dug her fingers in his back and thrust her pelvis to meet his rhythmic strokes. She was so aroused, the wet noises of their coupling resounded throughout the room. Before she knew it, her core was throbbing in orgasmic ecstasy.

Lincoln rocked her through an explosive orgasm until the climactic waves calmed, leaving her a trembling mess

"Oh, God, baby!" she gasped through heavy breaths.

Her body melted into the plush mattress while she reveled in postcoital bliss. However, Lincoln hadn't reached his ending. And apparently, he fully intended to.

He flipped her on all fours and pressed his hand to the small of her back, pushing her face to the mattress. Donna groaned as he reentered her well-worked pussy. As big as his dick was, taking it from behind was a job meant for a pro, but she was going to do her best to accommodate his size.

"*Lincoln!*" She gasped, squirming as he pushed against her cervix.

He gripped her hips and pumped into her from behind. After a while, taking all of him had become a little easier. And with each stroke, his balls smacked her clit, bringing her close to another orgasm.

"Goddamn, Donna!" he blurted through heavy breaths. "Pussy soooo gooood."

His erotic word fueled her carnal desire. But, just was climbing toward another happy ending, he stopped suddenly.

"Linc!" she cried out in desperation.

When he pulled out and climbed off the bed, she was ready to scream and beg for a merciful return.

Donna turned and looked over her shoulder in enough time to see him slipping into his boxer briefs. "What the fuck, Lincoln?"

"Hold on," he told her right before she heard a loud thud.

When a male voice cried out in pain, she fumbled to turn on a lamp. What she saw made her mouth fly open. Feeling instantly disgusted and exposed, she snatched the duvet and covered her naked body.

Nicole's grimy fiancé was crouched in a corner with his pants and boxers draped around his ankles. He scrambled to his feet, but Lincoln punched him so hard that his head bounced against the wall and cracked the drywall. He looked like he was going to pass out, like he *wanted* to pass out. However, Lincoln wouldn't allow it.

He stomped him in the ribs, prompting Jeffrey to squeal like a wounded pig. He snatched him by his collar and forced him on his knees. Lincoln flung the door open and dragged him out of the guestroom.

"Lincoln! Wait!" Donna called after him. But the fact that he was dragging a bloody Jeffrey through his brother's penthouse, with a house full of people, in his drawers seemed inconsequential to him.

Donna quickly slipped into her t-shirt and jeans and ran down the hall. She arrived in the living room just in time to see Lincoln dragging Jeffrey's limp body through the living room.

"What the fuck!" blurted a few people at the sight of Jeffrey's bloody face and exposed genitals. Not to mention, Lincoln in socks and drawers.

"What are you doing?" Nicole screeched, running over to him.

She first tried to pull Jeffrey away from Lincoln's grasp, but when she couldn't, she converted to punching Lincoln in the back.

Donna ran across the room. She understood that Nicole was Taylor's sister, but she needed to keep her fucking hands off of Lincoln. However, before she could reach Nicole, Taylor cut off her path.

"Um-mm," she said with a firm stiff arm. "I'll get my sister."

Out of respect, Donna remained where she was standing, hoping that Taylor would handle her sister because if she didn't, they were gonna fall out.

Taylor hurried over to Nicole and grabbed her from behind, pulling her away from Lincoln. Victor jogged over to the door and opened it, clearing the way for Lincoln to toss Jeffery violently through the door. When he slammed the door, Taylor released Nicole.

"*Why would you do that to him?*" she screamed at Lincoln.

Before he could answer, Donna heard, "*Good God-damn!*" come from by the bar. She turned to find Taylor's friend, Maria Mendez, practically salivating while staring at Lincoln. And she wasn't the only one. Bella's friend, NiYah, couldn't seem to take her eyes of off him either. He seemed oblivious to the extra attention as Donna walked over to him.

She looked up at him with narrowed eyes. "*Go put some clothes on!*" she growled through gritted teeth.

31

DONATELLA

Donatella walked up the steps to the Federal Courthouse where Kelly was waiting for her. It had been months since the raid on the BOC compound. They were there to testify against Bobby Lee and the other ringleaders, who were out on bail.

"Good of you to join us," Kelly quipped facetiously when she reached the top of the stairs.

She was only six minutes late. She would've been much later had she not fled from Lincoln, who was determined to go another round in the sack.

"Yeah. Yeah. Yeah. You probably just got here."

His smirk told her she was right. Donna laughed as they entered the building, flashing their badges to bypass security.

"We got time to grab a coffee?" Donna asked.

"Yeah. You know they tell you to be here at 9, but court never starts until about 10:30."

"If you're lucky," she scoffed.

After checking in with the court sergeant, they went to the cafeteria. Donna got coffee and a blueberry muffin and sat at a table in the corner. Kelly walked over carrying orange juice and a dry piece of toast. He joined her at the table and stuffed the crunchy bread in his mouth.

"That looks tasty," she remarked sarcastically.

"What? You think I keep this sexy body by eating... *muffins*?"

"I manage," Donna said through a giggle before stuffing a big chunk of muffin in her mouth.

"Oh, my God! Kateri, Cameron, I never thought I'd see you again!"

When Donna looked up, Vera was standing over them. She grabbed a chair from another table and joined them without an invitation.

"Can you believe what they're doing to us?" She sighed and looked at them with sad eyes.

"Vera, what are you doing here?" Donna asked with a frown.

"Same thing you're doing here. I'm here to show my support for the Messiah."

"Are you fucking serious? This is the same church, and I use that term loosely and with disdain, but it's the same church, with the same people that whipped you like a slave because you wouldn't allow yourself to be pimped out."

"No!" she shouted, slamming her palm on the table. "That's our family!"

"Are you off your fucking meds? You let that cult leader in your head and he scrubbed away what little brain you had to begin with. You need to wake up. He's a goddamned con-artist."

Vera's face twisted with rage. "*He's my husband!*"

Donna shook her head with a chortle. The woman was unbelievable.

She looked around, realizing that everyone in the cafeteria was staring at them. Not willing to provide any more entertainment, Donna grabbed her coffee and muffin and stood to leave.

"He married *me*!" she spat as if she'd won a prize.

"Well, if it's legal, I'm sure it was so you couldn't testify against his crooked ass."

She felt Kelly's hand on her back.

"Donna, let's go."

Vera glared at her with a furrowed brow. "*Donna?*"

Vera looked her up and down with narrowed eyes and gasped when her eyes landed on the badge attached to her belt buckle.

"W-who are you?" she questioned. Her voice cracked as she breathed the words in a labored whisper.

"Let's go. We're gonna be late," Kelly urged, grabbing her arm and pulling her toward the exit.

"*Who are you?*" she screamed at their backs. "Cameron! Kateri! *Who are you?*"

∽

DONNA WALKED into the 2nd-floor outer office of the Organized Crime building starving, wishing she'd stopped to grab a bite after she left the courthouse. They were there for an hour, getting prepped by the State's Attorney only for the trial to be postponed due to a request for a continuance by Bobby Lee's attorneys. To keep postponing the case until they either ran out of witnesses or lost interest was an age-old strategy used by defense attorneys.

She mumbled greetings over her growling stomach as she walked into the roll call room.

"Welcome back, Lady," her partner, Joe Preston, said with a smile. "How was your big FBI assignment?"

"It was cool. Glad to be back, though."

"Roll Call!" Bruce Riley, her team sergeant called out as he entered the room. He walked to the small podium and opened his binder. After a few announcements, he scanned the room.

"Welcome back, Devereaux."

"Thank you, Sergeant."

"It's good to have you back, and your timing is perfect."

"Why is that?" she asked suspiciously.

"We're going up on a new spot. Need you to make a buy."

"Huh?" Donna couldn't believe what she was hearing. She hadn't even been back a full fifteen minutes and they were tossing her right on the street. She looked around at any number of people that could've made the buy. In particular, Bonnie Sanders.

"I know what you're thinking but we've set up surveillance on Washington and Leavitt. Bonnie won't fit it. They'll make her as soon as she hits the block."

"*Really?*"

That was complete bullshit. Her sergeant was insinuating that Bonnie couldn't buy in that area because she was white. Since white girls often traveled to the hood for dope, his reasoning was flawed. Besides, Bonnie had been in Narcotics for six years. If she couldn't buy, why was she there?

"You and Joe hang back while we set up surveillance."

Donna leaned back in her chair and blew out an aggravated breath.

"Go get ready," the sergeant said, closing the matter to further discussion.

Donna rolled her eyes. She was sick and tired of the double standards. Officers like Bonnie were privileged enough to be assigned to specialized units, but they didn't have to perform the same duties as the rest of them. It seemed most prevalent with women. Unfortunately, undercover units such as Vice and Narcotics mostly operated in neighborhoods inhabited by black folks. So, the common excuse was that they needed a black undercover officer. Truthfully, white women bought dope in black neighborhoods on a regular basis. In fact, it was common.

"This is some bullshit," Joe muttered as their team filed out of the roll call room.

"Yeah, but I'm used to it at this point."

"Well, gon' and get crackheaded out," he said through a chuckle.

"Washington and Leavitt is a heroin spot," Donna pointed out.

"Is that gonna make a difference in how you dress?" he asked sarcastically.

"It actually does," she informed with a grin. "Dope fiends and crackheads have an entirely different look."

"How so?"

"Heroin users tend to appear a bit more functional. If they're not high, some of 'em can fool you. But crackheads look like crackheads 24/7."

"Yeah! Yeah!" Joe blurted. "Go get ready. I'll be downstairs."

Donna giggled and hopped out of her seat. "You know I know what I'm talk'n about," she said over her shoulder as she walked out.

She went down the hall to the lady's locker room. Since there were, of course, more men than women assigned to any unit in the Organized Crime division, it didn't surprise her that the locker room was empty. She entered a combination to open her locker and pulled out a large duffle bag. Inside was everything she needed to ugly herself enough to pass for a drug addict.

She changed into tattered leggings, a dingy t-shirt, and a pair of beauty supply flip-flops. In other words, the "hood-rat" uniform. She grabbed a cheap red purse, and filled it with deodorant, a bunch of miscellaneous pieces of paper, a broken cellular phone, and a roll of tissue. It was what they usually found in an addict's purse when searched. The big, red bag was loud and noticeable, a helpful visual identifier for her surveillance team.

Donna grabbed a smaller bag and walked over to the sink. She pulled a few items from the bag and placed them on the sink. She looked in the mirror at her straight, chin-length bob-cut hair and frowned. She'd just got it done, and it wasn't like the police department was going to reimburse her for the fresh shampoo she was about to ruin.

She grunted and dipped her finger into a jar of petroleum jelly and rubbed the greasy substance between her palms. After a deep breath, she massaged it into her freshly washed hair. She used just enough to make it look oily and dirty, then she combed it into a stringy bun at the top of her head. A dark eyeliner smudge only on the bottom lid gave her that zombie dope-fiend appeal. And a little petroleum jelly mixed on her lips with a light coat of powder on top added the crusty lip effect.

Donna gathered the items, returned them to the bag, and went back to her locker. She tossed it inside, slammed the locker shut, and headed out. As promised, Joe was parked just outside the door in a covert vehicle—a 2010 Honda Accord.

It only took ten minutes for them to reach the targeted location. Joe grabbed the radio and alerted the surveillance team of their arrival. He pulled into a gas station a block and half from the targeted location and handed her what appeared to be a cellular phone. But, in actuality, it wasn't a cell phone. It was a COH, or consensual overhear device. The device would provide a little extra protection by allowing her team to hear everything she heard.

She turned it on and tucked it into her bra. "How do you copy?" she queried.

The sergeant's voice came through the radio. "Loud and clear."

Then Marco came through. "We got eyes on about seven; four lookouts, 1 on the northwest corner, 1 southwest, 1 northeast, and 1 southeast. And, surprise surprise, they're all wearing a white t-shirt, blue jeans."

"Lee, what does the spot look like?" the sergeant asked over the air. Lee, her teammate, had the dope boy look. He was usually the undercover that made the bigger buys. Donna understood why she was making the buy instead of him. Lee buying a dime bag wouldn't fly. Which is the reason he was tucked in somewhere, secretly conducting surveillance.

"Alright, we got two on security, and one on the pack. Security on the porch is wearing, get this," he chuckled, "a blue t-shirt and jeans."

Donna got the joke. Sadly, the description of suspects was usually male, black, white t-shirt, blue jeans.

"Security at the fence is a male, black, long locs, white t-shirt, grey sweats."

"What about the seller?" Joe asked.

Lee responded. "Male, black, light complexion, anorexic motherfucker wearing all black."

"Okay. She's getting out," Joe announced.

Donna hopped out of the car and walked into the gas station where she bought a bag of hot Cheetos and a dollar juice. That was the ghetto breakfast, lunch, and dinner. When she walked out of the gas station, Joe was gone. She opened the bag of chips and began her flipflop journey to the target location.

It didn't take long to make it to the block. She ignored the lookout, and he ignored her as she turned the corner. She popped Cheetos in her mouth and gulped juice until she reached the fence that surrounded the dope house. She leaned on the fence and looked up at the dealer on the porch.

"Wassup, Shorty? Whatchu want?"

"Gimme two," Donna told him, popping another Cheeto in her mouth. She made a hissing sound with her tongue because the shit was hot. As she stood there trying to buy dope, she wondered to herself why people eat bullshit that burned their tongue. She shook her head and gulped a large portion of the way too sweet blue juice.

"Two what?" the dealer asked suspiciously.

Donna narrowed her eyes at the skinny, barely grown boy on the porch. He needed security, she thought as she took another drink.

"Stop playin' with me. My motherfuck'n mouf burnin'. Can you give me two so I can go?"

"Bitch, who you talkin' to?" he blurted with his chest puffed out.

"Ughhh!" she grunted as if frustrated. "Come on, bae," she whined. "I'm just trying to get you to hit me two times."

The dealer relaxed and leaned back in the filthy, raggedy ass La-Z-Boy that had no business on a front porch and nodded at his security, who immediately held his hand out for payment. Donna reached in her bra and pulled out a twenty. She handed it to security and waited while he handed it to the dealer. In turn, the dealer slipped a tiny package in his hands. The guy on security walked over to the fence and handed her two, tiny foil-wrapped packets.

"Thanks," Donna said as she stuffed them in her bra. She went to walk away, but the dealer called out for her to stop. She turned and looked back at him.

"If you need some more, I take other forms of payment," he said with a horny, sinister look in his eye.

"Okay. I'll let them other bitches know," Donna retorted as she walked away.

She made it to the end of the block. Once she passed the lookout, she turned the corner and kept walking.

"I'm headed back to the gas station," she announced to all who were listening on the COH.

When she arrived at the gas station, she walked inside and watched from the window. She waited to make sure she hadn't been followed. When Joe pulled up in front of the door and signaled for her to get in, she knew that surveillance had given him the go ahead.

She left the gas station and hopped in the car. "They get it?"

"Yep. Photos, video, everything they needed."

Since the plan was to survey, make frequent buys, and gather intel on the supplier, there were no arrests to be made. At least, for a while. As Joe drove them back to their office to inventory the dope, Donna sat back in her seat. She relaxed and thanked God for another successful undercover experience. And, by successful, she didn't mean buying the dope. She meant not getting a bullet to the brain.

32

LINCOLN

"How was your flight?" Donatella smiled. "Pretty cool, thanks to you. Had my nose in the air with all the rest of the folks flying first class," she joked.

Lincoln chuckled softly. "You got your snob on?"

"Yep. I frowned at everybody walking to the back of the plane."

Lincoln laughed and put on his seatbelt. Donatella Devereaux could be very silly, but she put on no airs. She was who she was, and he'd never met a woman like her. She could drink him under a table, and she ate more than any woman he'd ever fed. She wasn't shy about sharing her opinions, but she was still very open-minded. Donatella was fun, intelligent, and ridiculously beautiful.

Since he had to return to Fort Benning, he was only able to see her on weekends. Usually, he flew to Chicago. But, for the first time, she volunteered to visit him in Fort Benning.

"So, what have you got planned for me this weekend?" There was something about her voice and the suggestive way she asked the question that sent waves of desire straight to his manhood. Since she was sitting right next to him, he avoided adjusting his package.

"Dinner tonight and tomorrow, a surprise."

"I don't like surprises."

"Don't care, young lady. I said it's a surprise, and you're *gonna* like it."

He could feel Donna glare as he rounded a sharp curve that led to the road to his house. When they drove down the tree-lined path and through the open gate, she looked out of her window.

"I thought you lived on base. What's all this?"

Lincoln could hear the confusion in her inquiry. "I have a house here as well. Just up ahead."

Just as she turned to look ahead, his house came into view.

"Wow!" she gasped. "This beautiful."

"Thank you. I'm glad you like it."

"Like it? It's amazing!"

His home was no mansion. In fact, it wasn't very big at all. It was a comfortable, two-story, four-bedroom house made from logs. There was a pool and a lake, so they shouldn't have a problem finding things to do around the house. Not that Lincoln wanted to do anything that required them leaving his bedroom.

He pushed a button on the rearview mirror of his Jaguar F-Type and opened the garage. He pulled in next to his pickup truck and killed the engine.

"We're home," he announced with a grin.

"Home, huh?" Donatella quipped, grabbing the door handle.

Lincoln frowned. "Hold on." He got out and walked around to the passenger side. After opening her door, he said, "I do that."

"I can open my own door," she scoffed.

"I do that," he reiterated with his hand out.

She placed her hand in his and allowed him to help her out of the car. He closed the car door and escorted her to the door that led inside. After unlocking the door, he pushed a button on the wall to close the garage door.

"Come on in so I can fix you a drink. I'll get your bags in a minute."

She nodded and took the step up to enter the mudroom. Lincoln stepped inside and closed the door behind him. He eased past her to lead her further inside where they stepped into the hall.

Lincoln grabbed her hand and led her to the living room. As she looked around, he was praying she liked the place. Because if she liked it, she'd more likely visit again.

She walked over to the large picture window and stared out at the land.

"Make yourself at home. I'll get you a drink."

Donatella turned around and nearly blinded him with a heart-stopping smile. Unable to resist, he walked over and joined her at the window. He cupped her face in his hands and kissed her, reveling in a feeling of passion and contentment he'd never felt before. When the kiss ended, he stared into her beautiful brown eyes, surely long enough for her to peg him as a weirdo.

"You got Jameson?" she whispered with a smirk.

"Of course." He chuckled. "I'll be back."

He allowed his hand to fall to his sides. It took effort. He wanted to have her right there, right in front of the window. He decided that at some point during the weekend, he would. After all, his land was vast, and he didn't have a neighbor for miles.

DONATELLA

"So much for dinner," Donna purred. Hungry or not, she was more than okay being tucked in the nook of Lincoln's arm. She rubbed the soft hair on his chest and looked into his hypnotic emerald gaze, marveling at his incredible talent for fucking her stupid.

"Our reservation isn't for an hour. We have time," Lincoln assured.

He kissed her forehead before flipping the sheet back and climbing out of bed. Even under the dim candlelight, Donna could see the muscular work of art that was his body. Even flaccid, his dick was hanging generously down his thigh.

"I have told you, young lady, I am not a piece of meat," he teased through soft laughter.

How he knew she was ogling him in the dark, she didn't know. Maybe he could feel the burn from the desire in her eyes.

He grabbed his still wet dick and stroked the shaft from base to head, putting on a very erotic production.

"Like I said, so much for dinner." Donna crawled over and reached for him, but he stepped just out of her reach.

"No, no. I have every intention of feeding you tonight. You go get cleaned up. I'm gonna get your bag."

When he turned to leave, she tore her eyes away from his tight ass and sat up in the bed.

"Lincoln?"

He stopped and turned around. "Yes?"

"Is that a real moose over the fireplace?"

Lincoln looked up at the moose head and grinned. "Sure is. Bagged it myself," he affirmed proudly.

When he left the room, Donna stopped staring into the marble eyes of the stuffed animal and fell back in the soft bed. Dead animals in a bedroom was definitely a white person thing. Black folks just weren't down for sleeping in the same room with dead shit.

Donna's stomach growled. She was most certainly hungry, but she didn't feel like getting out of bed.

Lincoln walked in and placed her bag on a chair by the bed. He grabbed her arm and dragged her out of bed.

"Bathroom! Now!" he ordered in what was supposed to be a serious voice.

She sat up with a huff. "What you *ain't* gon' do is walk in here with your dick bouncing and bark orders at me."

Lincoln recoiled as if he wasn't accustomed to anyone disobeying his orders. He leaned over and pulled her out of bed. He picked her up, threw her over his broad shoulder, and smacked her ass.

"What you *ain't* gonna do is talk back." He carried her into the en suite bathroom. He didn't put her down until they were in the shower.

"Now, I promised to take you out for a nice dinner, and that's what I'm going to do. You're gonna get pretty and say things that'll keep my dick hard all night. And when we get home, if we make it home, I'm gonna lick your sweet pussy until a tear falls from your eye, until you beg me to stop, and until your twin screams out in ecstasy 900 miles away."

"Damn," Donna rasped through a heavy breath. "That's sexy, baby. Well, everything except making my sister scream."

"Eh, maybe." Lincoln chuckled and grabbed a bar of soap. "Come here. Let me wash you."

He pulled her to the back of the shower and turned the knob. After adjusting and testing the temperature, he pulled her in front of him before she could stop him.

"*Lincoln!*" Donna screamed as the water sprayed over her head.

She pushed at his chest and slid past him. She scurried to the furthest end of the shower and pushed her wet hair out of her face.

"What? Baby, what did I do?"

Donna wiped her face and squeezed lids to expel the excess water. When she finally looked at him, the horrible look on his face made her feel guilty.

He stepped closer and grabbed her shoulders. "What happened? What did I do?" he asked with furrowed brows.

Donna shook her head and forced a smile. "It's okay. Don't worry about it."

Lincoln wrapped an arm around her waist and pulled her against his wet torso. "Donatella, tell me what's wrong. Please...tell me what I did."

Donna exhaled and snaked her arms around his neck. "My hair," she responded.

He reached up and ran his fingers through her wet hair, squinting while he checked it out.

"Oh, wow," he marveled. "It got curly. *Pretty.*"

Donna looked up at him with disbelief. He couldn't have been that dense when it came to black women and their hair. Now, she loved her natural curls, but she'd had a whole look planned for the night.

"Lincoln, honey, I need you to get out of this shower and get my toiletry bag." She tried to keep her tone as relaxed as possible.

"Okay, babe. I can do that."

He kissed her forehead, gave her butt a little squeeze, and stepped out of the shower. Donna grabbed the bar of soap he left behind. She took one whiff of the soap. The clean masculine aroma made confirmed that she definitely needed her bag.

Donna gave herself a once over in the mirror. For the evening, she'd chosen a slimming wintergreen, knee-length bodycon dress that perfectly matched Lincoln's beautiful eyes. The plunging square neckline and "trick-a-fella" pushup bra gave her cleavage that she didn't normally have. Before leaving the bathroom, she finger-styled her curly hair one last time. Since there wasn't enough time for her to dry and straighten her hair, she was rocking her natural curls. So, she used pins to create a cute updo, pinning the back and leaving soft curls to bounce in her face.

She padded on bare feet out of the bathroom, taking shorter steps because her dress was a little tight around her knees. After grabbing her purse from the nightstand, she left the bedroom and went into the kitchen. When she walked over to the freezer, the sound of Lincoln's voice made her turn around.

"There you are. Oh, wow. Donatella, you look... you're...breathtaking."

She would've said thank you, but the sight of him standing in the kitchen wearing a perfectly fitted black suit with a charcoal dress shirt underneath was paralyzing. From head to toe, he was perfection, even down to his black leather dress shoes. She would bet a finger they were made by some fancy designer she couldn't afford.

Donna couldn't ignore the butterflies in her stomach as he stood there with his gaze locked intently on her, probably not realizing exactly how drop-dead beautiful he was. His thick, ink black hair was pushed back from his face, enhancing the beauty of his striking green eyes, a masculine jaw that was somewhat covered by a soft, neatly trimmed beard, and his perfect jaw-dropping smile.

"Thank you." She finally managed, although her words came out breathless and awkward.

She turned quickly and opened the freezer. After grabbing her shoes, she walked over to the island.

"You clean up well, Colonel," she told him.

She spread a towel over the island and placed her black, stilettos on top of it.

"Ummm... thanks."

He joined her at the island and sat on a stool across from her. "Donatella?"

"Hmm?"

"Why were your shoes in the freezer?"

"Oh," she chuckled, "they're new."

"Oooo-kay?"

She looked up at him and grinned. His confused expression was too cute for her to bear.

"So, when women get new shoes, they can be torturous before they're broken in. And, for people like me who don't wear dress shoes all the time, it could take years to break them in. Since I don't have years, I have learned a trick." Donna reached inside her shoe and wiggled out a sandwich bag with a block of solid ice. "See? First, you get two Ziploc bags, or really, any kind of storage bags. Second, you fill them with water until they're completely full. Third, you place the bags inside your shoes. Then, you stick the shoes in the freezer. You wait a while. You see, water expands when frozen. Then, after all that, you take the bags out of your shoes. And, voila! You've stretched your shoes."

Donna pulled the bag out of her other shoe and tossed it in the sink. "See?" she asked, holding up one shoe.

Lincoln stared at her with squinty-eyed confusion like she hadn't just explained the logic behind her actions.

"What?" she screeched with a grin.

"You're batshit crazy," he quipped before leaving the kitchen. "We leave in five!" he shouted from the hall.

Donna smacked her lips. "Crazy? Hmphh!"

She placed her shoes on the floor and slid her feet inside. "Whew! Gotdamn, that's cold!"

∼

"This is so amazing."

Donna took a sip from her fourth glass of Rosé while admiring the beautiful scenery. Their table was on a patio lit by candles, torches, and decorative lighting. They were enjoying dinner and wine with a perfect view of a lake. About twenty-five feet away was a beautiful bridge covered with what looked like thousands of twinkling lights, reminiscent of the Eiffel Tower after dark.

So far, her visit had been extraordinary—from the moment she landed, to the hot welcome to Georgia sex, the redfish cooked by the Gods, and the stimulating conversation and romantic atmosphere. Lincoln did not disappoint.

"I'm glad you think so. How's your Crème Brûlée?"

"Mmm. It's perfection," Donna gushed.

Her eyes went from Lincoln to the beautiful view. It was then she realized that she would've been happy without all the bells and whistles. They could've been having dinner at a hot dog stand, and she would have been content with just being with him. Unlike her sister, she didn't run from love. Bella had been hurt, so she avoided romance like the plague, but Donna was different. She was willing to find the one. Although, she knew that with the job she did, it was unlikely.

For months, she and Lincoln had been spending every moment of free time that they had with each other. In his eyes, she could see that he cared for her. His actions confirmed it. In her heart, there was absolutely no doubt that she was falling for him. However, the sad reality was that they both could be called away at any time, and neither could predict how long they would be gone. They'd never sat down and discussed the dynamics of their relationship, but she knew that the conversation needed to happen.

"Lincoln, I—"

Donna was suddenly hit by cold feet, not so literal as before. He placed the spoon on the table and looked pointedly at her, giving her his undivided attention.

"What is it, Donatella?"

She chuckled nervously, surprising herself. Nervous wasn't one of her personality traits. "Why do you insist on calling me Donatella?"

He smiled, showing off perfectly straight teeth.

"Because that's your name. And I told you I love your name. Now, what's on your mind?"

Donna cleared her throat. It was time to rip off the proverbial Band-Aid. "Well, about us…"

"What about us?"

"Okay. The thing is…if we were ever to try this relationship thing, our jobs—"

"Okay. I gotta cut you off."

Donna held her breath. Maybe she'd jumped the gun. They were having fun, and maybe that was all he'd intended for them. However, things between them had heated to a boil and naturally, she was thinking about the next step. But she might have just unintentionally ended their thing.

"What do mean, 'try this relationship thing'? Donatella, we're already in a relationship. Shit, I thought you were aware."

"Oh." She exhaled, feeling surprisingly relieved. "To be honest, I wasn't aware. That's not something we've discussed."

"What we have has been established by feelings, not discussions."

"So, how long have we been in this…relationship?" Donna asked with a raised brow.

Lincoln grabbed his spoon and dipped it in his bread pudding.

"Lincoln?"

He shoved a generous amount of pudding in his mouth and slowly licked the spoon clean. Donna found herself reminiscing about the way he had so thoroughly licked her earlier in the day.

"Stop playing," she chuckled.

"What? Okay. Truthfully, I've considered us in a relationship since I saved your ass at the Glory Gala."

"Oh, please!" Donna scoffed. "But, you're away a lot. When I'm working undercover, I'm unreachable. How do we do this?"

He reached across the table and held out his hand. Donna placed her hand in his, instantly feeling the warmth and security of his touch.

"It's simple, sweetheart. When I'm away, you wait for me. When you're away, I wait for you. See? Simple."

"Long distance relationships are—"

"Colonel Lincoln Creed, as I live and breathe," came purring from a woman standing over their table.

Donna looked up to find a tall, curvy, black woman with long, dark hair. Admittedly, she was well-dressed and attractive. The magnitude of her cleavage made Donna want to throw away her pushup bra.

Lincoln offered a tight-lipped smiled before looking up at the woman. "Valerie, hello. How are you?"

She smiled and leaned over, pressing her palms to the table, giving him an unobstructed view of her golden-brown cleavage. "I'm better now. Haven't seen you in a while. Been off saving the world?"

"You can say that," Lincoln muttered.

She turned to Donna, finally acknowledging her presence.

"Who's this?" she asked, looking at Donna but still talking to Lincoln.

"I'm Donna. It's nice to meet you, Valerie."

She smiled, but it didn't reach her eyes. "Donna, huh?"

Donna gave her the same sugary grin. "Yep, Donna. You know...I like the view," she told her, nodded at her cleavage. "Probably more than Lincoln does."

Valerie tried, but she couldn't hide her shocked reaction to Donna's salacious declaration.

"Is that so?"

"Ye-p," Donna responded with an extra emphasis on the P.

Lincoln laughed softly and cleared his throat. "Valerie, it was good to see you again. But my lady and I are trying to enjoy a romantic dinner. I'm sure you understand."

She turned to Lincoln with wrinkled brows. "Your lady? As in, commitment?"

"Yes. So please, enjoy your dinner."

She continued to stare as if she couldn't believe he'd just admitted to being in a relationship.

"Valerie... I meant, enjoy your dinner at *your* table."

She laughed nervously and pushed off the table. Though she was smiling when she stepped back, Donna could see the resentment in her eyes. She turned to walk away.

"Nice to meet you, Valerie!" Donna called out in a fake, cheery voice tone as she left the patio.

Once she disappeared inside the restaurant, Donna's focus lasered on Lincoln. She was no longer all smiles. As a matter of fact, she was downright aggravated.

"What?" he asked with a look similar to that of a deer in the headlights. "Donatella, listen. Valerie and I—"

"Naw, to hell with that!" she interrupted with a wave of her hand.

"Donatella, we just—"

Donna shook her head emphatically. She wasn't trying to hear a thing that came out of his mouth.

"See, I assumed you didn't know any better. But, clearly, you do."

Lincoln frowned, tilting his head with obvious confusion. "What are you talking about?"

Donna pointed to her head. "You've been with black women before, which means you knew damn well not to put my head under that water."

Visibly relaxed, Lincoln leaned back in his seat and grinned. "Baby, I've never stayed long enough to shower after," he admitted through laughter.

33

DONATELLA

Donna looked at herself in the mirror and sighed. She was dressed from head to toe in camouflage. "Linc, why do you have me dressed like I'm going to war?"

Lincoln laughed and walked out of his walk-in closet with another bag. Apparently, he'd been shopping his ass off for her so-called surprise date. He sat the bag on the bed and pulled out a bright orange vest. "You'd never go to war in this, beautiful."

"Well, am I going to be directing traffic? Is there a whistle and white gloves in there too?"

He narrowed his eyes and tossed her the vest. "Put it on, smart ass. I'm going to pack the truck. We're leaving in five."

Leaving in five must have been his thing. As she watched him leave the bedroom, she noted just how sexy he was in fatigues. The man was tall, full-bodied, gorgeous, and a perfect lay. A real giver. She couldn't believe her luck. Whether their *thing* survived the distance and the time apart or not, Donna's plan was to enjoy the ride until it ended.

"Come on, girl!" Lincoln shouted from the hall.

Donna grabbed the vest and frowned at the moose on her way out of the bedroom. When she got to the garage, Lincoln was holding the passenger door of his Dodge Ram open for her. She laughed as she walked around the car to get to the truck.

"What?"

"You look like one of those 2nd Amendment nuts with the beard, the fatigues, and the pickup."

He pressed his hand in the small of her back and provided support as she climbed into the big truck. Once she was tucked comfortably in her seat, she reached for her seatbelt. He closed her door and walked around the truck and climbed in the driver's seat.

"Babe?"

"Hmm?" she asked, looking over at him.

"I *am* one of those 2nd Amendment freaks."

"I can live with that. But I need to know who you voted for in this last presidential election. Sorry, I know I'm not supposed to ask, but in these times, I have to."

Lincoln chuckled. "I understand. Well, I will tell you this... I am a registered Republican, but I couldn't vote for the current administration."

"Whew! I thought this was gonna be the shortest relationship in history."

He laughed while backing out of the garage. "So, the Republican thing doesn't bother you?"

"Naw. Anyway, how do you know I'm not a Republican?" she asked in an accusatory manner.

"I don't know. I just assumed because most Republicans are what you referred to as 2nd Amendment freaks."

"Oh, okay. Well, no, the Republican thing doesn't bother me. And I'm a believer in the 2nd Amendment, but I can guarantee you that the right to bear assault rifles and automatic weapons was not what the forefathers were protecting."

"Agreed."

Donna blinked over at him, shocked by his concurrence. "*Really?*"

"Yeah. Why are you so shocked?"

"Don't you have an AR-15 and an M16?"

"Much more than that," he admitted with a chuckle. "But I'm a soldier. Those weapons were meant for me, not Grover the hillbilly, Kyle the skinhead, or Wee-Bey the banger."

Donna's eyelids stretched at the stereotypical hood name. "Excuse me? Wee-Bey?"

To be honest, she didn't give a damn about him stereotypically branding white people, but she wasn't feeling the Wee-Bey shit.

"Calm your little self down," he said through soft laughter. "I got that from The Wire."

"The Wire?" Donna frowned. "The TV show?"

"Yeah. You've never seen it?"

"Naw. I don't watch cop dramas."

They continued their political conversation, thankfully without disagreeing during the surprisingly short drive. They were only in the truck like five minutes, yet they were pulling over. As a matter of fact, they never even passed through the gate to exit the property. They seemed to have just circled the lake.

"Lincoln, are we still on your property?"

"Yes, ma'am."

"My goodness. How much land do you have?"

"A little under 400 acres."

"Geesh. That sounds like a lot of work."

"Well, I ain't doing it." He chuckled.

Lincoln killed the engine and hopped out of the truck. Remembering that he preferred to open her door, she sat and waited for him to come around. When he opened the door, she climbed out and looked around, wondering what he had planned. He closed the door and reached into the bed of the pickup.

"What are we doing here?"

He pointed straight ahead. "We're gonna go just beyond that tree line over there."

"And do what?" she probed. "What's beyond the tree line?"

"Deer."

"What?" Donna gasped just as he was handing her a rifle.

"This is a Remington 30.6. I think you'll like this one."

"What?"

He laughed at her apprehension. "Hunting, babe. We're going hunting."

"Hunting? Like, we're going in there to shoot deer?"

"Yep," he confirmed with a grin. His eyes lit up with excitement as he clutched his own rifle. "You once told me that you liked guns and shooting."

"In a shooting range!" she squealed. "I don't wanna shoot Bambi."

"Sweetheart, Bambi and his mother died a long time ago. Don't worry I'll get you through it."

Donna slipped her arm through the shoulder strap and slung the rifle over her shoulder. She looked out at the tree line and wondered what other kinds of creatures were running around in those woods.

"Lincoln, I'm a city girl. I'm not really into—"

"Come, babe. You'll never know want you're into if you don't try new things."

He grabbed her hand and lifted it to his lips. His soft lips against her skin were comforting. He held on to her hand as they started toward the trees.

September in Chicago was unseasonably warm, but it was hotter than Satan's nut sac in Georgia. Lincoln had her dressed from head to toe in hot ass camouflage. How soldiers survived in the desert in fatigues, she didn't know.

Soon, they were engaged in small talk while trekking through tall trees. They walked for about five minutes until they were passing a small clearing. On the other side of the small piece of bare land was more forest. Lincoln stopped and pointed to a large tree with what looked like a small deck-like treehouse. It wasn't very high up, but Donna didn't have tree climbing skills.

Lincoln led her to the other side of the tree. Thankfully, there was a ladder attached to the thick trunk.

"We'll post up just past here," he said, pulling her gun from her shoulder. He nodded his head toward the ladder. "Climb."

Donna looked from him to the tree. She was having an inner debate about whether or not to climb. On one hand, the only thing she liked about nature was the view. She didn't need to be smack dab in the middle of it. On the other hand, she did have an adventurous side that was screaming, "Go for it!"

Her adventurous side won. She walked over to the tree and climbed the ladder. When she got to the top, she stepped onto the wooden planks that served as a floor. Lincoln climbed up after and handed her the rifles and a small cooler before joining her on the deck.

"What's in the cooler?"

"Beer, of course," he chortled.

Donna exhaled. "Drinking and shooting, great combination," she mumbled under her breath.

"It's for after," he said with a boyish grin. "To celebrate your first kill."

She didn't know how she felt about his excitement for her to kill.

He walked around the tree and came back, rolling two chairs. He rolled one over to her and sat on the other.

"Now what?"

"Now, we wait. Hunting is all about waiting. We can talk, but must do it quietly."

When Donna sat in the chair, he handed her the rifle.

"You ever fired one of these?"

"Nope."

"Ever fired any kind of rifle?"

"Nope."

"Well, you're gonna love this. Hand it here, I'll give you a crash course."

For thirty minutes, they spoke softly. She learned so much about Lincoln, his upbringing, his college life, his military career, and his love for his family. She'd had time to share her reasons for becoming a cop, going undercover, her Native American heritage. She'd even tried to explain the extraordinary bond between her and Bella. They started discussing past relationships when they heard the sound of snapping twigs. He held his hand up to silence the conversation. He grabbed the rifle Donna placed on the floor next to her foot, handed it to her, and gestured for her to point.

Donna stood quietly and placed the butt of the weapon in the crook of her shoulder. She waited quietly until a deer appeared in the small clearing. After lining her sights, she placed her index finger on the trigger. The deer was still, seemingly surveying its surroundings.

Donna held the rifle steady. She had a perfect shot. She began to gently squeeze the trigger. Then she suddenly pictured the innocent animal's flesh exploding.

She eased off the trigger and lowered the weapon. "I can't do it, Lincoln. I can't kill this animal for no reason," she whispered through a breath.

"What do mean for no reason?" he asked with wrinkled brows. "We're gonna eat that deer."

Donna closed her eyes and shook her head. She placed the riffle on the wooden floor.

"I can't do it," she huffed. Then she opened her eyes and glared at him. "You're not gonna do it either."

Lincoln smiled and pulled her into his arms. She relaxed her head against his chest, relieved that she hadn't shot the defenseless deer.

"It's okay, sweetheart. I understand."

"Thank you." She exhaled a cleansing breath and hugged his waist.

"I gotta better idea. And we're already dressed for it."

Donna raised her head and looked at him suspiciously. "Dressed for what?"

"Paintballing!" he exclaimed with excitement.

Donna laughed. "Now, you're talking. I don't mind shooting you," she joked.

"Alright, let's get outta here."

As soon as they separated, the feeling of loss was palpable.

He grabbed the cooler and rifles and jerked his head toward the ladder. "Be careful," he urged as she climbed down the ladder.

He climbed down after. Once he landed on earth, he smirked with a raised eyebrow.

"What?" she probed with narrowed eyes.

"You know I'm not feeding you any more meat, right?"

"Whatever, Jethro! Our ancestors created a world where I could eat the meat without having to kill it."

Lincoln laughed and teased her about her epic hunting fail all the way to the truck.

34

TAYLOR

"My Lord, that man is fine," Taylor breathed.

"He is a beautiful boy," Tabitha Creed agreed.

They were at the Rosemont Park Hall watching Victor go head to head with the Democratic candidate, Bill Thornton, in the Illinois Governor's Debate. Taylor, her mom and dad, along with Victor's entire family were watching from a monitor backstage. Watching her husband so eloquently rip his opponent to shreds was definitely an aphrodisiac. But, then again, at seven months pregnant, everything was an aphrodisiac. She'd never been hornier in her entire life, but her obstetrician assured her that her excessive need for sex was normal.

Due to scandalous photos in the paper, and possible indictments, it had been such a tiring campaign for Victor. Most of his time was spent governing the state, campaigning, or putting out political fires intensified by the media. Thankfully, he was still ahead in the polls. But neither he nor Taylor trusted the polls. So, over that last few months, they campaigned hard.

For two hours, she listened as Victor answered the question about his disdain for the current president, his social interactions with members of a Sicilian mafia, the school system, the overwhelming homicide rate in Chicago, and even potholes. With each question, his response was precise and intelligent. Not to mention that his blindingly good looks and irresistible charisma were casting a dark cloud over his opponent. Taylor couldn't have been prouder.

She placed her hand on her rounded belly and mentally told her unborn child how wonderful his or her father was. She was thinking of just how blessed and happy she was when the moderator's voice came through the monitor.

"Thank you for joining us for the Illinois Governor's Debate. We now have time for a short closing statement from each candidate. We'll begin with Counselman Thornton and close with Governor Creed."

"Thank you, Mark," Thornton said. "To the detriment of Illinois, my opponent has openly opposed the current administration, who happens to be a Republican. At every turn, he has betrayed and belittled his own political party, therefore creating discord with the president of these United States of America. His insolence could very well be counterproductive to the great state of Illinois. You need a candidate that can work well with others in a bipartisan capacity. I'll leave you with this… the incumbent governor's wife is a registered Democrat. If his own wife doesn't believe his, or his political party's aspirations, why should the good people of Illinois?"

Taylor recoiled and turned to her mother. "Did he just put me on blast?"

"Hmph! He sure did," she responded with a huff.

A portion of the crowd applauded the councilman. When the applause died down, the moderator looked to Victor for his response.

"Mark, thank you. Hmm… my democratic opponent wants nothing more than to be an apprentice to the president, who, by the way, happens to be a Republican. Yet, he speaks of loyalty to a political party. I am most certainly an avid supporter of my own party. However, Councilman, my loyalty will always lie with the people of Illinois. Therefore, Republican or not, I will never bow down and kiss the ring of a misogynistic, Führer-reflective dictator who openly supports radical racially motivated hate groups.

"His very presence in the Oval Office has sparked the momentum of every Skinhead, White Nationalist, and Klansman in America. That brand of hatemongering, bullying, and aspirations of dictatorship is something that I will *never* be willing to cosign. And, in closing...Councilman Thornton, with your dismal public record, I can guarantee you one thing. With you as the Democratic candidate for governor, my beautiful wife won't be the only registered Democrat voting Republican this election."

Thunderous applause surpassed the crowd's roar of laughter. Victor stepped back from the podium and casually stuffed his hands in his pockets. His charm and magnetism were irrefutable, and the audience was eating it up. Victor was a Rockstar.

Taylor socialized with her family backstage, not so patiently waiting for the commentator to wrap up the televised debate. She was delighted that Victor had destroyed his opponent in the debate, but truthfully, she was exhausted. Her ankles were swollen, and her butt and lower back were aching. However, that didn't stop her from rising to her feet when Victor walked backstage. She hurried over to him with a giant smile and her arms opened wide. His face was etched with concern as he clutched her shoulders.

"Slowdown, sweetheart," he implored.

"Oh, honey, I'm fine. Oh my God, you were inspiring." She was gushing excitement.

"Yeah?" he asked with a smile. "I did good, huh?"

"Baby, you slayed that dragon. Straight up destroyed his ass."

"He was alright," Lucas teased.

"Shut up your face, Lucas. He was awesome," Taylor defended.

Victor looked to his father. As a politician himself, his opinion was extremely important to him.

Victor Sr. smiled and placed his hand on his son's shoulder. "Taylor's right, Son. Your points were clear and concise, your intelligence and confidence were overshadowing, and those good looks you got from me didn't hurt."

The family was praising and congratulating him on a job well done when his opponent approached.

Thornton nodded respectfully to Victor Sr. "Senator, it's good to see you."

"Bill," Victor Sr. acknowledged.

Thornton turned his attention to Victor. "Now it's up to the voters," he said with his hand out.

Victor accepted his hand and shook.

"May the best man win," the councilman remarked.

Victor chuckled. "Sure."

When Taylor shifted uncomfortably, Victor frowned and pulled his hand from the councilman.

"Come on. Let's get you home."

"Victor, I'm good."

He nodded at Gregor who pulled out his phone and, no doubt, called Victor's new driver to bring the car around.

Taylor walked over and grabbed her purse from a chair. She knew there was no sense in arguing with him. His mind was made up.

Kena grabbed her coat from a rack and handed it to Victor. After tucking her into her coat, he placed a hand at the small of her back and led her toward the door.

~

TAYLOR SLIPPED the soft cotton nightshirt over her head and wrapped her hair with a satin scarf. When she walked out of the bathroom, Victor was standing in the middle of the room, staring intently at a sheet of paper that was in his hand.

"What's that?"

"Carlotta sent over your itinerary for next week. Kena printed it out and left it on my desk."

Taylor sighed. "What's my week looking like?"

"Like this." Victor tore the paper in half and placed it on the dresser. "It's been a crazy campaign. You've worked hard, made every single appearance without so much as one complaint. Thank you, sweetheart, but now I just want you to rest."

Taylor certainly wasn't going to argue. The pain in her lower back from carrying what couldn't have been a normal sized baby was on Victor's side of the dispute. Besides, the way he looked standing there shirtless and in pajama pants was a distraction. Forming a logical argument would be nearly impossible. All she could think about was running her fingers over his solid chest and chiseled abs. His thick, dark hair was pushed away from his handsome face, and the dark-rimmed reading glasses sitting on his nose slid far enough for her to be spellbound by the jade of his eyes.

Victor's smirk let on that he noticed her admiration. He pulled the glasses from his face and moved to place them on the nightstand.

"Assume the position," he instructed in deep, sultry tone that filled her with hope of a gratifying night.

Taylor was almost giddy when she pulled back the linen and climbed into bed. She rolled on her side, turning her back to him. After climbing in on his side of the bed, he slid her nightshirt over her hips and massaged her lower back.

"Mmmm, that feels so good," Taylor moaned.

She closed her eyes and melted against the pillow as he massaged the tension from her back. When she heard him squeezing lotion into his hand, she knew she was in for a treat. His hands moved to her butt. As he kneaded the tight muscles, the mood of the massage switched from maintenance to foreplay. The heat of his touch rushed to her core. Her sex throbbed with need. Apparently, her husband was either reading her body, or her mind.

He allowed his hand to glide sensually over until it reached her breast. He toyed with her extra sensitive nipple. She inhaled a sharp breath when a jolt of sexual electricity shocked her pussy.

Taylor pushed her ass against his hard dick, ready to beg for him to enter.

"Damn," he whispered near her ear. "You want me in that sweet pussy, don't you?"

"Yesssss," Taylor hissed. "Please."

His hand moved over her round belly, and his fingers found her clit. The small bundle of nerves went into a frenzy as he drew circles against the swollen bud. He pushed his dick against her ass while playing with her pussy. Taylor clawed the sheets as he fondled her to the point of orgasm. Her toes curled, her body tensed, and she cried out her release.

Victor slid his pajama pants down and spread her ass cheeks. He slid into her while her pussy throbbed through an intense orgasm. He slid an arm under her shoulder and used the other to grip her hip as he filled her completely with life-changing dick.

"Oh, *baby*... you feel so good," he declared.

But it was the way he was making her feel that made everything right in her world. She pushed her ass out, giving him more. The sound of his pleasure as he grunted through heavy breaths was fuel, motivation for her to please him more and more. She matched every stroke as he rodded her from behind until she was struck by an unexpected climax that rocked her to the core. He fucked her with fiery intent as her pussy contracted around his dick, secreting a release that made her go lightheaded.

"Aghhh! Fuck!" Victor croaked, as he pushed fiercely into her one last time.

He held her tight as he whimpered through his own eruption. Taylor could feel his strong thigh quivering against her skin. He slid his hand over her stomach and worked to control his breathing. For seconds, they rested without words until Victor broke the silence.

"You okay?" he asked with softness and regret.

Taylor smiled. No matter how many times she and her obstetrician assured him that sex wouldn't hurt the baby, he still worried after every lovemaking session.

"Yes, Victor, I'm perfect," she assured.

"Okay, good. I'll get you a towel," he said through a breath, seconds before she heard snoring.

35

ELECTION DAY...

DONATELLA

"Belladonna tells us you're dating a Creed? The soldier?" her dad asked from across the dinner table.

Donna looked over at her bigmouthed sister with a scowl. She raised a hand in her defense.

"What? You are," Bella squealed through laughter.

Donna rolled her eyes and stabbed a chunk of meat from the delicious Hunter's Stew she'd begged her mom to cook. "Do you ever get tired of talking about me?" she muttered.

"Nope," Bella quipped.

"He's so handsome," her mom commented as she walked into the room. She placed a plate of sliced cornbread on the table and took her seat next to her dad. "Although, I am concerned about you getting serious with a soldier."

Donna and Bella both looked at her mom. Surely, with two daughters who were cops in the most dangerous city in America, she couldn't have been serious.

"I'm just saying. Well, you two don't know what it's like to have to worry about someone every time they go to work."

Donna shrugged with a chuckle when Bella looked at her with a wrinkled brow of confusion. "So, Mom, you don't think I worry about

Donna when she goes to work? And you don't think she fears for my safety too?"

Their mom rubbed her chin. She seemed to be thinking of the possibility for the first time.

"Hmm, I guess you have a point. I honestly never thought of things like that. I just assumed you girls were fearless."

"Well, she is. I'm not," Bella pointed out. "She gets some kind of rush from working undercover."

"And you're surrounded by death," Donna rebutted.

"Whatever! Anyway...how do you and Linc do it? You have to leave, he's gotta leave. How do you spend time with each other?"

"We manage," Donna muttered, tired of talking about her relationship.

Bella exhaled a frustrated breath. "Why are you always so secretive when it comes to your dating life?"

"Leave your sister be," their dad interjected. "She ain't gotta tell y'all her business."

"You're right, honey. We're just glad to have you both for dinner at the same time."

"That's right, baby. And dinner is delicious."

"Thank you. Besides...I'm just glad she's with a man," her mom muttered under her breath. "For a while, I thought she was lesbian."

Donna glared at her mother, Bella erupted into laughter, and her dad dropped his head and shoved a potato in his mouth.

∼

EVEN WITH BELLA and her mom's lighthearted teasing, Donna was really enjoying the time she was spending with her family. She missed them when she was away, and she was away so much. In fact, she'd just been assigned to a new undercover investigation. She had no way of knowing when she'd see them again. Or Lincoln, either for that matter. For months, they'd been in a long-distance relationship. And surprisingly, it was working for them. They talked on the phone when they could. He visited Chicago.

She visited Fort Benning. They were even able to take a quick vacation to Cancun.

"You sure you guys don't wanna come to the Four Seasons with us?" Donna asked.

Victor, Taylor, and the rest of the Creeds were holed up at the fancy hotel where they'd be waiting for the election results.

"We're sure," her mom confirmed cuddling closer to her dad. The look she gave him was a look Donna had seen many times.

"Oh, God," Bella gasped. "Can't y'all wait for us to get out of the house?"

"Hmph, we have before," her mother mumbled.

"I'm outta here. Donna, can you grab my plate? I'm about to go warm up the car."

"Yeah, I got it."

Bella went to kiss their parents. She leaned over and kissed their mother. Before she could kiss her dad, he pushed himself off the couch.

"Now, you know damn well I'm not letting you walk to the car by yourself." He grabbed his coat from the rack and threw it on. "Gimme your keys."

Bella shook her head and handed him her keys. "Daddy, you still treat us like little girls," she chuckled.

"No, ma'am. I treat you like ladies. Any man that would let you leave their house after dark without walking you to your car is not a man. Besides, you and your sister will always be *my* little girls."

Her dad's words made Donna smile. When they walked out of the house, her mother asked, "Is that Creed a man like your daddy?"

"Yes, ma'am. Well, as close as you can get to somebody as perfect as Daddy."

Donna laughed with her mother until a pain powerful enough to make her fall to her knees pierced her skull. She screamed and pressed her palms to her temples, hoping the pressure would bring relief. Instead of running to her aid, her mom jumped to her feet and ran toward the front door.

The shrill of her mother's screams drove Donna to her feet. She pushed through the door, and what she saw when she got outside almost took her back down to her knees. Bella was lying on the ground with a small puddle of blood pooling under her head, and her mother was on all fours, pushing against her father's bloody chest. She was performing CPR.

Donna, instinctively ran to her twin as she screamed for the neighbors who had quickly gathered to call 911.

VICTORIA

"I don't know why his team keeps repeating that I'm all but guaranteeing him the black vote. What I can guarantee is that black men all over Illinois are side-eyeing and throwing big shade."

"Facts!" blurted Victoria from across the room. She smiled at the young server who was attempting to refill her glass with champagne and took the entire bottle from his hand.

"I'll serve the champagne if you go find me a bottle of Jack Daniels."

Taylor laughed at Victoria while she negotiated with the server. He was terrified to leave his assigned post in search of her whiskey. Once she convinced him to agree, she actually walked around and refilled everyone's glasses. It was strange watching a woman with billions serving everyone with a smile. Once she was done, she flopped down on the sofa next to her. Victor, the rest of the Creeds, and key members of his staff were in the adjourning suite.

"Where's your *friend*?" Victoria asked sarcastically.

"Girl, you know she's your friend now too," Taylor joked.

Victoria frowned with pursed lips. "Friend? I mean, we ain't trying to kill each other, but I definitely wouldn't call us friends."

"Well, I'm working on it. But, that's a good question. She texted me an hour and a half ago, saying she was on her way." Taylor stretched her hand toward the cocktail table across the room. "Hand me my phone."

Victoria smacked her lips. "Why you leave your phone all the way over there if you couldn't get your round ass up?"

Taylor's mouth flew open. "Don't be hurtful, Victoria. Get the goddamn phone!"

"Ugh," she groaned as she got up from the sofa. She grabbed the phone and handed it to her just as another waiter was entering the suite.

"Can I interest you ladies in some food?"

"Yes, thank you," Victoria responded with excitement.

"Dang, you hungry, huh?"

"Girl, I haven't eaten all day. As soon as I left the office, I rushed home and cooked for Jack and the kids. But I didn't have time to eat."

Taylor looked at her with shock and awe. "Wait, you work all day at Storm Enterprises, then you go home and cook?"

Victoria blinked over at her. "Yes! Don't you cook?"

"Every now and then, but our housekeeper or the chef does most of the cooking. Victor does a lot of the cooking too."

Victoria shook her head. "Mm-mm. No, ma'am. I'm not eating *nothing* Jack cooked."

"You mean to tell me there's something Jack can't do?" Taylor asked through laughter.

"Go figure. Me, Mrs. O'Malley, and his cousin, Gianni, are the only people who've ever cooked in my kitchen."

"What about Natasha?"

Victoria covered her mouth and laughed. "Shit, we hardly allow her in the dining room because it's so close to the kitchen."

They were enjoying a hearty round of laughter when both their phones chimed. Victoria ignored her phone, but Taylor swiped the screen. It was a KRS tabloid news link, sent by her sister. The original message read: "Oh, my God, Sis," followed by a line of sad emoji faces.

Since it was from Nicole, she started not to open it. She'd had the worst attitude ever since Lincoln tossed her dirt bag fiancé out of their penthouse. She didn't understand her sister's desperate need to hold on to his creepy ass. Even after Linc and Donna explained that he was hiding in a dark corner, jerking off to them having sex, she continued to throw a hissy fit in his defense. It got to a point where Taylor had to ask her to leave. She'd been getting shady texts and voice messages until Nicole got tired of communicating with her altogether and stopped reaching out.

Taylor rolled her eyes and prepared herself for the negative energy that her sister was throwing her way. Unfortunately, there was no way to prepare for what popped up on the screen. Her mouth flew open, and her eyes nearly popped out of her head.

"What it is?" Victoria asked, leaning over to see.

"Oh, my God," Taylor gasped.

"What is it, Taylor?"

"Me," she whispered with disbelief. "Um...it's um...us."

"What are you talking about?"

Taylor stared at her phone, horrified by a video that showed her on her knees with Victor's penis in her mouth.

"Oh, shit!" Victoria gasped, covering her mouth. Her eyes were wide with shock as the porno played out on the screen. Since Taylor was too shocked to move the phone, Victoria looked away.

The video was edited to shorten their tryst. It jumped from frame to frame, displaying them in each position. He was fucking her from behind while she was bent over his desk. She was lying on her back with her legs in the air. They even had full frontal footage of her spread out on his desk while he licked between her legs. Horrified wasn't a strong enough word to describe what she was feeling. There wasn't a word.

Taylor grabbed the arm of the sofa. With Victoria's help, she pulled herself to stand. Tears had covered her cheeks and she ran into the connecting suite. Victor frowned when she saw her running toward him.

"Honey, don't run." His face twisted with concern when he noticed the moisture on her cheek. "What's wrong?"

Taylor pushed her phone in his hand.

"Who is it?"

"Look at the phone, Victor!" she shrieked.

Regardless of his state of confusion, he looked down at the phone. Since the video was playing on a loop, he didn't have to swipe the screen. He looked down just as the video jumped to the frame of him fucking her from behind. At the bottom of the video was a rolling news ticker.

THE PEOPLE OF ILLINOIS ENDURE TAX INCREASE FOR GOVERNOR TO BANG WIFE WHILE ON THE CLOCK!

"WHAT THE FUCK?" he roared, startling every person in the room.

He gaped at the screen with an open mouth.

"Victor, I—"

She suddenly interrupted by a splash of warm fluid on her legs and feet.

"Victor, I-I think... my water. I think my water just broke," Taylor stuttered.

She wasn't sure. Hell, she might have just pissed herself. Even with birthing classes, childbirth was something she would have to play by ear. But a pain equal to a bullet shot through her back. She winced and fell against Victor. He lifted her in his arms and hurried her to a sofa.

"Mom! Help!"

Tabitha was soon standing over her. "Taylor, honey, can you hear me?"

She opened her mouth to speak, but pain and fear had rendered her speechless.

"She said her water broke!" Victor told his mother.

She looked at Taylor's legs and then she turned to look at the floor where she Victor had just been standing.

"Victor, that's not amniotic fluid. It's blood. Call 9-1-1," she said with a calmness that Taylor could tell was forced.

36

DONNA

"Come on, Momma you gotta let them work," Donna urged, pulling her mother out of the way.

She hugged her from behind and promised her that their family would be okay. They were still outside of her parents' house, surrounded by concerned neighbors, first responders, and flashing lights from countless emergency vehicles.

From what it looked like, someone had driven or walked up and opened fire on Bella. Her dad pushed her to safety and jumped in the line of fire. Bella was unconscious but breathing. Her heart rate and blood pressure were normal, but she had a large gash on the side of her head. Presumably, when she was pushed, she hit her head on the large, blood-covered decorative boulder near the walkway. She was hurt, but she would more than likely recover fully.

Her dad, on the other hand, was not breathing. When the Emergency Medical Technicians arrived, they took over. One used a heart monitor to check for heart rhythm, while another started an IV. The EMT with the monitor shook her head, so a third resumed CPR.

Donna's hysterical mother was praying out loud while digging her nails so deep into her hands, she was beginning to draw blood. But Donna couldn't think about the pain. She was too busy watching with disbelief as paramedics worked to keep her dad alive. The EMT stopped compressions so the other could check for heartbeat.

"No sinus rhythm!" the paramedic shouted.

Donna's heart dropped when they resumed CPR.

"Christ Hospital!" a paramedic shouted from the ambulance Bella was being loaded into.

"Ma, why don't you go with Bella? I'll stay here with dad."

Her mom turned and looked at her like she was the one that hit her head. "I will never leave my husband. Bella will be fine. My husband is dying!"

Donna's heart nearly stopped. The thought of her father not surviving was inconceivable.

"Daddy is not dying!" she gritted.

"Push a round of Epi!" said one performing compression.

"Epi's in," said another.

Once again, they stopped CPR to check for a heartbeat.

"I got a pulse. Let's get him intubated."

The words brought instant comfort. She and her mother simultaneously breathed a sigh of relief. Thankfully, her mom retracted her claws from her hand. They watched as a tube, meant to breathe for him, was inserted into her dad's mouth and guided down his throat. When one of the EMTs looked up at them, Donna could see the relief in her eyes as she said, "We're gonna transport him now."

"Mamma, you go with Daddy. I'm gonna ride with Bella."

Her mother cupped her face and kissed her. Her mom's eyes were red and swollen from crying.

"I'll see you at the hospital," she promised before following behind her dad.

Donna ran to the other ambulance and caught them just as they were pulling away. The vehicle came to a halt and the back door flew open. She climbed in and sat across from her sister. Bella was still unconscious, but her heart rate was normal, and she was still breathing normally on her own. Donna grabbed her hand, careful of the IV, and talked to her sister all the way to the hospital.

"Donna?" Bella called out in a pained voice.

Donna hurried over to her sister while her mom ran out to get a doctor. The fact that she'd been unconscious for hours was terrifying. She had become consumed with a fear of Bella never waking up.

"I'm here," she whispered.

Her entire head was swollen. Her dad might have saved her life, but he did a number on her nugget.

"Aye!" Bella squealed. "My head."

Donna winced from simply imagining her sister's pain. "I know, Sis."

Without lifting her head, Bella's eyes wandered the room. "Dad," she whispered with wide frightened eyes.

"Dad is gonna be fine, Bells."

"He...was shot," she whispered hoarsely.

"Yeah, he's in surgery, but he's gonna be fine."

Bella closed her eye and exhaled. "Mom?" she mouthed more said.

"You've been out for a while. Mom went to go find the doctor. Bella...what happened? What do you remember?"

Bella covered her eyes with her hand.

"I remember everything. Donna, can you turn off some of these lights, please?"

"Do you know who shot at you?" Donna asked before walking over to the light switch. She turned the knob to dim the light. "Is this okay?"

"Yeah. It was two women, but I didn't recognize either of them. They pulled into the driveway like they were using it to turn around. Then one just pointed a semi-auto out the window and opened up. One was a middle-aged woman. I think she was white. The other one, the one with the gun, was a white girl with green and blonde hair."

"*What?*" Bella gasped.

"Ummm...I couldn't see the make of the car."

"It's okay, Belly. You should get some rest."

"What?" Bella asked with a frown. "Didn't you just tell me that I've been out for hours? Why the hell would I need sleep? I'm trying to give you a description. Now, listen, the older one said something before the young one started shooting. No...wait. She asked a question."

Bella's brow wrinkled as if she was trying to remember.

"Oh, yeah. She asked, 'Do know what broke the heart of Jesus? When we didn't answer, she answered for us. She said, 'The betrayal of a friend.'"

Donna dropped her head in shame and worked to keep the tears that were pooling in her eyes at bay. Sadly, she was unsuccessful.

"What's wrong, Sis?"

Donna didn't respond. She couldn't. As soon as the first sob escaped, she found herself outright balling. Bella grabbed the handrail and rolled over enough to caress her head.

"What is it, Donna? Please, tell me," she encouraged.

"I know who it was," Donna admitted.

"What?" Bella breathed.

Donna looked up and faced her sister. "I worked those women in my last undercover investigation."

"What investigation? And, if you say something like you can't tell me, I'm gonna get up and beat the hell out of you."

Donna swiped the tears from her cheek and gently pushed at her sister's shoulder, urging her to lie down. Thankfully, she didn't put up a struggle and relaxed against her pillow.

"Long story short...I was detailed to a federal task force assigned to take down a religious cult. We did, but I got made at court."

"A religious cult?" Bella grimaced with disbelief.

"The Blood of The Chosen."

"Church people shot at us?"

"Bella," Donna whispered. Her faced heated from the overwhelming guilt she was feeling. "They thought you were me. They were trying to kill me."

"Oh, Donna," Bella breathed. "You can't blame yourself for—"

She was interrupted when her mother entered the room with the doctor in tow. The doctor slid her stethoscope from around her neck and hurried over to Bella. Donna slipped out of the room during the doctor's examination. Once in the hall, she fell back against the wall and slid to the floor. She tucked her head to her knees and wept. Even though Bella tried to tell her that she wasn't at fault, she knew she was culpable. After running into Vera at the courthouse, she should have taken some sort precaution to protect herself and her family. It was irresponsible of her not to know that Vera finding out that she was a cop was dangerous. She was naïve for not seeing her as a threat. Because of failure to act, her father was in surgery, and her sister was suffering from a severe head injury.

"Are you okay?" Donna felt a hand on her shoulder. She wiped her face and looked up in search of the soft, feminine voice. It was Dr. Camorra, the surgeon that had operated on her dad. She hurried to her feet. Ignoring the doctor's inquiry, she asked. "How's my dad?"

"It was work. We had to remove his spleen and a small portion of one of his lungs, but I'm pretty confident he'll make a full recovery."

Donna exhaled a sigh of relief. Had her father died because of her, she didn't know how she would go on. For certain, she would never be able to face her family again. Even with him being on his way to a full recovery, she found it difficult to look them in the eye.

"Thank you, Doctor," she said with sincerity.

"You're welcome. Will you join me in telling your family?"

Donna shook her head. "No. You go. I gotta make some calls."

When the doctor nodded and entered Bella's hospital room, Donna dug her phone out of her pocket and dialed Lucas. The least she could do was make sure Bella recovered with as much support as possible. When he didn't answer, she left a message letting him know that Bella was in the hospital, sure to tell him that she was okay. Just in case he didn't already know, she left the address for Christ Hospital before hanging up.

Donna stuffed the phone back into her pocket and walked toward the elevators.

37

TAYLOR

In record time, Taylor had been whisked from The Four Seasons hotel to Northwestern Memorial Hospital. As soon as they arrived, a team made of nurses and hospital administrators were waiting to take her directly to Labor and Delivery.

When they transferred her from the gurney to gurney, Taylor noticed the large puddle of blood that she'd left behind.

"*Victor!*" she said through a terrified breath.

Her entire body was trembling with fear. Victor clutched her hand and jogged along the gurney. Even though he seemed calm, he couldn't hide the horrified look in his eyes.

"You'll be fine, sweetheart. They're gonna take good care of you and the baby."

A nurse began to take her blood pressure as they rolled her into an elevator. The concerned look on the nurse's face did nothing to ease Taylor's fears. The doors separated when they reached the 4th floor. Dr. Jacquelyn Crane, her obstetrician, was waiting in the hall.

"Suite 32," she instructed the nurses with a trained calm. She smiled down and Taylor. "I'm gonna take a quick examination, then we'll get you all straightened out."

Taylor nodded and squeezed Victor's hand. She tried to remain calm as they rolled her to her room. Dr. Crane grabbed a pair of latex gloves from a box on the wall and walked over to the hospital bed. Taylor was transferred from the gurney to the examination table. Dr. Crane's tranquil disposition changed immediately when she noticed the amount of blood on the gurney.

"Get me an OR ready! Get me an anesthesiologist! I think Dr. Takashi is on call!"

There was not one bit of calm in her tone as she shouted orders to the hospital staff. Taylor was freaking out. She pulled at Victor's arm until he was holding her. The doctor frowned. She seemed to realize she was scaring the shit out of them. She took a deep breath, but Taylor was holding hers. Noticing her distress, Dr. Crane moved closer and placed a hand on her shoulder.

"Mrs. Creed, judging from the amount of blood loss you've suffered, I can safely diagnose you with a condition called Placental Abruption. It's when the placenta detaches from the uterus. Right now, your baby is being denied oxygen, and you are running the risk of bleeding out. So, we need to perform an emergency caesarian."

"What causes something like this?" Victor asked.

The doctor shrugged. "We really don't know. Your wife's lifestyle is inconsistent with the listed possible causes. Some causes are listed as drug and alcohol use, smoking, or some sort of trauma. From my understanding, you told the EMTs and the nurses that you hadn't suffered any trauma. So, there's really no way of knowing." She turned to one of the nurses. "Paula, please get Mrs. Creed on a fetal monitor and get her prepped for surgery."

Taylor sighed and looked up at Victor. He smiled, but it didn't reach his worried eyes.

"Please, don't worry, Governor and Mrs. Creed." Dr. Crane implored with a smile. "I am the Michael Jordan of maternity. Not only am I gonna get that angel out safely, but I might even give you a little tuck while I'm down there."

The return of the doctor's confidence helped Taylor to relax a bit. However, the sharp pain in her lower back rendered her peace short lived. It was a pain like no other. It felt like God was reaching down from heaven, squeezing her insides. When she screamed from sheer agony, Victor nearly jumped out of his skin.

"*What is that?*" he yelled at the doctor. "*What is happening?*"

"That sounded like a contraction, Governor," Dr. Crane responded.

Taylor was groaning, Victor was freaking, and the nurses were gathering the materials needed to prep her for surgery. When the contraction passed, the doctor gave her shoulder a squeeze.

"I'll meet you in the operating room," she said with a smile.

When she left the room, three nurses remained. They politely shooed Victor out of the way and started removing Taylor's clothing. Once they were done, they slipped two cloth belts under her back and attached them to two round monitors, one to measure the contractions, and the other to monitor the baby's heartbeat. The sound of her baby's heartbeat brought her instant comfort. She looked up at Victor and smiled weakly.

"He's gonna be fine," she assured.

"He? Do you know something that I don't?" he asked with a grin.

"I know God wouldn't dare give me a girl to raise," Taylor joked.

One of the nurses laughed and snapped her into a hospital gown. They left the strings untied and stuffed her hair into a surgical bonnet. The nurses were polite and engaging, but it didn't go unnoticed how fast they were working.

After slipping a pair of hospital socks on her feet, one of the nurses went out and came back with a clean gurney. They transferred her to the gurney by pulling the sheet she was lying on to slide her over.

"I'm sorry, Governor. In cases of emergencies, dads are not allowed in the operating room. But you can accompany your wife as far as the double doors," one of the nurses nervously conveyed.

To Taylor's surprise, Victor was the most cooperative she'd ever seen. As she began to roll, she reached for his hand. Victor waited until they cleared the narrow doorway before covering her hand within his.

"Sweetheart, do you realize the next time I see you, you'll be a mom?" When he smiled that time, not only did it reach his eyes, but his eyes were lit with excitement.

"And you'll be a dad to the third Victor Creed."

The corner of her mouth twitched from the beginnings of a smile, but the contraction that ripped through her lower abdomen would allow nothing but a loud groan. Taylor was squeezing Victor's hand so tight she was sure that she heard him groaning along with her.

When they reached the operating room, she could swear he seem relieved. Once the contraction subsided, she released his hand. With a guilty smile, she mouthed, "Sorry."

"No worries, baby. I'll be right here, waiting for you and my daughter," he said with the sweetest, boyish grin.

The nurse rubbed a magnetic key card to the automatic lock and opened the double doors to the operating room.

"I love you, sweetheart," Victor told her as they wheeled her inside.

"I love you."

As soon as she entered the hall and the double doors separated her from her husband, Taylor's anxiety returned.

"Don't worry, Mrs. Creed. Dr. Crane is the best. She can perform a cesarean with her eyes closed," one of the nurses assured.

"You just make sure she keeps her eyes open while she's cutting on me," Taylor quipped.

They made a turn which took them into the operating room. The large lights and medical tools and equipment were intimidating. More than anything, she wished Victor was there to hold her hand.

"You made it! Welcome," Dr. Crane greeted.

She was wearing a surgical mask, but Taylor could tell she was smiling from the crinkle of her eyes. One, of a whole new set of nurses, used an alcohol pad to prepare the skin of her hand for an IV. After a tiny prick, the nurse inserted the tiny hose that would be pumping fluids into her intravenously.

"Hello, Mrs. Creed. I'm Dr. Takashi. I'm your anesthesiologist. Since we need to move quickly, I'm gonna put you to sleep right now."

Taylor could feel her legs trembling as they transferred her to a bed directly under the lights. She didn't know what was going to happen, but the idea of sleeping through it all took the notion of control away from her. Dr. Takashi inserted a syringe full of medicine into the injection port of the IV. Within seconds, she was feeling no pain. Her entire body seemed to melt into the bed.

"Mrs. Creed, when your girlish figure returns, what color will your first bikini be?" Dr. Takashi asked.

"Ohhh... yeahhhh, white," she slurred.

"Any second now," he said to someone. "Mrs. Creed, can you count backward from ten?"

"Yep." Her own voice sounded like it was coming from an intercom. She was in a deep, deep haze. "Ten... nine... eiiiiiiiiiiii..."

LINCOLN

There was very little chatter in the waiting area. Both the Montgomerys were visibly concerned. Everyone in the room appeared anxiously impatient as they waited for news of Taylor and the baby. In order to create some sort of distraction, Lincoln slid a cigar into Victor's shirt pocket. "Hold on to this, brother."

Victor smiled and pulled the cigar from his pocket and examined it. "Cuban, huh?"

"Since you're gonna be the first dad among us, I feel like you've earned it."

"Well, not exactly the first," their dad chimed.

Lincoln passed his dad a cigar. "There's always a Cohiba for you, Pop."

"Thank you, Son."

Lincoln noticed his dad watching his mom. She was on pacing nervously on the other side of the waiting room.

"Let me go see about your mom. She's not accustomed to being on this side of waiting."

When Victor Sr. walked away, Lincoln put his hand on Victor's shoulder. It wasn't hard to see that his brother was worried about his wife and child. Even though he was surrounded by family, without being able to lay hands on his wife, he must've felt powerless and alone.

For about forty-five minutes, Victor had been standing near the door, waiting for someone to come in and share his wife's progress. And, for forty-five minutes, Lincoln had been standing right next to him. Since Victor had forbidden them all from speaking to him about anything going on in the outside world, the conversation was kept to a minimum. Under no circumstances was anyone to mention anything about the election, and especially, the leaked sex tape.

"What's going on with Luc?" Victor asked with a frown.

Lincoln had been so busy watching his oldest brother, he hadn't noticed Lucas. He was on a phone call, and judging from his stressed expression, the news he was receiving wasn't good. Since he didn't want Victor to be bothered by whatever was going on with Lucas, Lincoln excused himself and walked over to his other brother. As soon as he approached him, he ended the call. The look on his face was cause for concern.

"What's going on? Who was that?"

"That was Donna."

The mention of her name, and the fact that she was calling Lucas instead of him, gave him a feeling of dread.

"Their family was ambushed outside of her parents' home," he said as if he didn't believe the words that were coming out of his own mouth.

"*What?*" Lincoln breathed.

"Bella suffered a head injuring from a fall, but Mr. Devereaux was shot four times."

"*What?!*"

Whatever small amount of chatter that was going on in the room ceased with Lincoln's outburst.

"He shoved Bella to the ground and used his body as a shield. He just got out of surgery and is expected to make a full recovery. Bella has a concussion, but she'll be fine."

"Donna?" Every single nerve in his body had awakened.

He held his breath and waited for his brother to respond.

"Donna was unharmed."

His somber tone provided no comfort. Lincoln was sure there was more to tell. Since he was too nervous to speak, he gave his brother a look that urged him to continue.

"She's physically okay, but she didn't sound too good."

Lincoln exhaled. "That's expected. Her dad was shot, and her sister was hurt."

"Those bullets were meant for her," Lucas revealed sympathetically. "The shooting was retaliatory."

"Retaliatory from whom?"

"The BOC."

Lincoln's mouth flew open. He knew the Blood of the Chosen was easily capable of committing unthinkable crimes, but he had to admit, he didn't see murder as one of them. But why not murder? They were capable of human trafficking, horrible child labor practices, and physical abuse. How very naive he'd been to have not been more concerned for Donatella's safety.

"Where is she? What hospital?"

"The family is at Christ Hospital on the southside, but Donna left. She said she couldn't stay anymore. I think the guilt is getting to her."

Lincoln nodded. The guilt might have been getting to her, but that definitely wasn't why she left.

"I'm headed out," Lucas told him. "Call me when we have news."

Lincoln shook his head. "Can't, I gotta make a run. Do me a favor... speak to dad. Ask him to call us when there's news."

"Why can't you—"

The door opened, cutting off Lucas' protest. A woman, presumably the doctor, entered. The smile on her face elicited sighs of relief throughout the room.

"Mom and baby are doing well," she happily announced.

Victor exhaled a heavy breath. He seemed to breathe freely for the first time since he'd arrived at the hospital. They all did their best to provide comfort, but comfort would not have come until he was assured that his wife and child were doing okay.

The doctor was beaming with pleasure. "Governor, how would you like to meet your daughter?"

Victor's smile grew wide. "I'd like that very much," he responded with a relieved chuckle.

"Alright, then. Please allow us to get your women all cleaned up. I'll come back and get you in about ten minutes."

"Ten minutes. Yes, Doctor," Victor happily agreed.

When the doctor left the waiting room, Victor turned to their family, happier than Lincoln had ever seen him.

"It's a girl!" he celebrated.

As Lincoln and the rest of his family hugged and congratulated Victor, a familiar female voice shouted, "Congratulations!"

Everyone in the room turned to the voice.

"Naomi?" Victor questioned with furrowed brows. He looked to Gregor, who was dressed in jeans and appeared to be off duty. "How did you get past security?"

"I have my ways, Governor," she bragged with a cheeky grin.

Lincoln took long strides to get to the CIA agent. He'd warned her to stay away from his family. Had she listened, she wouldn't have had to worry about being dragged into one of the empty hospital rooms to have him snap her thin neck.

Tahira took a quick step back and held her hands up in surrender.

"Ah... ah... ah! Wait a minute, Colonel. I come bearing gifts."

Lincoln continued to charge until his fingers were wrapped tightly around her neck.

"*Lincoln Creed!*" his father bellowed, probably at the sight of him manhandling a woman, but Tahira Raji was no ordinary woman. She was a weapon. More specifically, a weapon that seemed to be trained on his family.

Lincoln's brother pried his fingers from her neck and pulled him away. When Tahira clutched her neck and gasped for air, she was actually smiling.

"What the hell is wrong with you?" Victor asked him. "Was there something between you and Naomi?"

Lincoln shook his brothers off of him and turned to Victor. "Her name is not Naomi!"

"What? Then, what is her name?"

"I can't tell you that," Lincoln growled.

Tahira cleared her throat and stood up straight. "I can help you understand. That is if the Colonel here will give me a chance."

Victor pulled the back of Lincoln's shirt until he was facing them.

"I don't have time for this shit. Tell me what the hell is going on."

"As I said, Governor," she interjected. "I come bearing gifts. But I must speak to you in private. Well, he can come." She pointed at Lincoln. "And Gregor can wait just outside the door."

Lincoln could feel his brother's eyes burning into him. He felt that he had no other choice but to divulge a small portion of classified information. He leaned close to Victor and whispered, "CIA."

The short acronym immediately got his attention. With an angry scowl, he barked, "Let's go!"

Victor stormed out of the waiting room. Lincoln held the door open for Tahira so they could follow. After locating an empty hospital room, they entered. As soon as Lincoln closed the door, Tahira began to speak.

"I can't tell you my name, but I can tell you that it's not Naomi. The information that I am about to give you is classified. It must not be shared."

Victor folded his arms and waited for her to continue. However, his expression read anything but patient.

"I'm behind the investigation into your PAC funds. And, I'm also the one who killed the investigation once I got what I needed."

Victor frowned and shook his head. "What do have to gain by getting me indicted?"

"I can't tell you that. I'm sorry."

"Then what the fuck can you tell me? Why are you here?" Victor was visibly irritated.

"I told you, I'm here to apologize in the form of gift giving."

"Get on with it!" Lincoln snapped.

Victor pushed past them to leave. Lincoln would imagine he was anxious to see his wife and daughter.

She sighed and rolled her eyes. "I found the man, or men, behind your *very* impressive sex tape."

Victor's steps halted. When he turned his angry glare on Tahira, Lincoln could see the fire in his eyes.

She threw a hand on her hip and narrowed her eyes. "I said I found the guy. I'm not responsible for the video. *This time...*I'm not the bad guy."

"Go on," Victor pressed.

"I tracked the IP address where the video was uploaded to a house in Chicago Heights. Turns out, this wasn't just any ole house. It was a whore house. *And*, this was not just any ole whore house. This whore house is known to accommodate those with special proclivities."

"Special proclivities?" Victor repeated with frown.

"Yeah. You know like... choking, whipping, pissing, shitting. Stuff like that."

Victor grimaced and looked over at Lincoln. "How does this help me?"

Since he didn't have an answer, Lincoln could only shrug.

"Governor, after a brief interview with Michelle Young, the owner, and operator, I learned the identity of the men responsible for uploading the video."

Lincoln knew exactly what Tahira meant by *brief interview*. He'd bet a finger that some form of torture involved.

"*Who?*" Victor inquired impatiently.

Tahira crossed her arms. "Why, your opponent, of course," she responded with a raised eyebrow.

Victor stuffed his hands in his pockets, something he'd been doing since he was a boy to control his rage.

"You're telling me that Bill Thornton put that video out?"

"Yep."

Although Lincoln didn't doubt her story, it just wasn't adding up.

"How did he get the video?" he asked.

"Now, here's the kicker..." She shook her head with a faint chuckle. "There's a traitor amongst you."

She must've noticed that each pause for effect was getting on Lincoln's last nerve when she blurted, "Jeffrey Morgan!"

"*What*?!" Victor raged.

"He used his City Hall credentials and familial connection to get into your office so he could plant the cameras."

"That motherfucker," Lincoln muttered under his breath.

"It turns out...the Councilman found out about your soon to be brother-in-law's voyeuristic proclivities and capitalized on it. It seems that Jeffrey Morgan is a very ambitious man, and Thornton promised him a position in the Governor's office once he was elected."

Victor shook his head with disgust. "And... how do you know this?" he asked.

"I conducted a brief interview," she responded with a wicked grin.

"Mmm...I see. Alright, I gotta go." Victor moved to leave.

"Wait! There's more!" Tahira blurted.

Victor blew out a frustrated breath. "More?"

"I told you, I came bearing gifts. I pulled the video. Now, I can't erase the memories of everyone who's already seen it. But, within fifteen minutes of it being up, I managed to plant a virus. So now, if someone tries to open or share the link, it will disintegrate their entire hard drive."

Victor's eyes narrowed as if he was trying to decide whether or not to believe what Tahira was telling him. It was clear that he didn't trust her, and Lincoln couldn't blame him. He didn't trust her either. She'd stepped in and turned Victor's life upside down. Then she showed up and presented herself as some sort of savior.

"You've just admitted to fabricating false accusations against me. So why, all of a sudden, are you being so helpful?"

"I owed you one," she admitted with a shrug. "Look, believe it or not, Governor, I'm a great admirer of you, your dad, and even your angry violent brother." She glanced over at Lincoln. "I have a job to do. Sometimes, it's not pretty. But it's never personal." She walked toward the door and opened it. With a smile, she turned around. "I'm sorry for any inconveniences I may have caused. Congratulations on your baby girl."

She pulled the black hijab from her coat pocket, covered her head, and walked out of the room. Victor turned to him for an explanation of the tornado that had just swept through his life. But, before he could utter a word, the door flew open. Tahira peered inside with a grim.

"Ohhhh, I almost forgot. Congratulations on your election victory. You won by a landslide. I, personally, think the sex tape won it for you."

She winked and dipped out of sight. Victor stood frozen. He hadn't even inquired about the election the whole time they were at the hospital. And if he had, Lincoln wouldn't have had answers. He hadn't had a chance to check. With everything that was going on, it just seemed insignificant.

"Good job, bro. Congratulations!"

"Wow," Victor gasped. "It's been a helluva day."

"Yeah, it has. Go see your kid. I gotta take care of something."

Lincoln hurried out of the room in search of Tahira. He needed to take advantage of her repentant mood by asking for a huge favor.

38

BELLADONNA

Since she'd lost the battle with her nurse, Bella was being wheeled by chair into her father's room. As a precaution, he'd been transferred from a recovery room to a room in the Intensive Care Unit. In order to aid in his healing, he was kept heavily sedated. But that didn't stop her mom from carrying on a full-fledged conversation with him.

Bella's excitement over seeing her dad deflated as soon as she saw his big, strong body, lying helpless in a hospital bed with a tube in his mouth. The nurse must've noticed the change in her disposition. She placed a hand on Bella's shoulder and leaned to whisper in her ear.

"Your dad is breathing on his own. His heart is strong, and his blood pressure is on point. The tube is there simply as a precaution. He's doing well."

The nurse's assurance brought relief.

"Thank you."

"You're welcome."

The nurse wheeled her close enough to hold her dad's hand. The warmth radiating from his skin was encouraging. She placed his hand to her cheek and thanked God that she still had a dad. Now that she was able to see that he was alive with her own eyes, her fears were focused solely on her sister.

Donatella hadn't returned and she knew, as well as she knew her own name, her sister was plotting revenge. It wasn't as if she didn't understand why she wanted to make someone pay for what happened to them. However, she would've preferred that she exercised a little patience and included her in the plan. Bella wanted in on the revenge. And had she known where her sister was going, she would have abandoned the hospital bed to join her.

Bella placed her dad's hand back on the bed and rested her face against it. She didn't know if sedation meant that he couldn't see or hear, but she convinced herself that he could feel touch. When she felt hands gripping her shoulders, she didn't need to look back to know that it was her man. Not only could she recognize the clean, masculine aroma of pheromones that had allured her to him since the moment they met, but she had gotten to a point where she could actually sense his presence.

She sat upright and placed her hand over his. "I'm fine, babe. Just a headache," she softly assured.

Lucas leaned over and kiss the top of her head, then each temple. "All better now?"

"I think so," Bella lied with light laughter.

TAYLOR

"Honey, is she not the most beautiful baby in the world?" Even though Victor was speaking more to his daughter than to Taylor, she agreed. "She is."

"Is that Daddy's girl?" he cooed.

Taylor looked up at her family and smiled. Victor looked like a giant, cradling their tiny 5lb. 6oz. baby girl in his arms. Less than an hour before, she had gone to sleep not knowing whether or not she and her baby would be okay. But when she woke, and the fog cleared, a nurse was placing her perfect little girl in her arms. She couldn't wait for Victor to see the beauty they'd created. And when he met her for the first time, it was nothing less than love at first sight. The tears that fell from her husband's eyes brought her to tears. The beautiful display of love and raw emotion from her strong as oak husband was precious and heartwarming.

They introduced her to their waiting friends and family as Victoria Nicole Creed. Even though their little angel was named after her father, grown-up Victoria was tickled pink, begging to be present when they told Bella.

Once everyone had a chance to see that she and the baby were fine with their own eyes, they didn't stay long. Once they were gone,

Victor filled her in on everything she'd missed. Sadly, she learned of the attack on the Devereaux family. And, to her shock and horror, she found out that it was her sister's fiancé that had been responsible for filming them making love and uploading it to the internet. Thankfully, Lincoln's friend was some kind of a computer geek and was able to quickly remove the video. Unfortunately, Taylor knew all too well that once in the Cloud, always in the Cloud.

"Sweetheart, when are her eyes gonna turn green?"

Taylor laughed. It was Victor's 4th time questioning his daughter's blue eyes.

"I told you a lot of babies are born with blue eyes. They'll change."

"Xander and Jay are walking around high-fiving each other. Even got Mom doing it."

"Honey, whereas I do recognize that strong Creed blood, I did put in half on this baby. She might get my brown eyes."

Victor looked up from his daughter with a grin. He placed the baby in the little hospital bassinet and carefully slipped in bed next to her. He slid his arm behind her and eased her to his chest.

"Everything that she gets from you is what will make her beautiful," he whispered against her forehead before kissing her softly.

39

DONATELLA

Since she wasn't stupid enough to burst in through the front gates, Donna walked through the trees until she could see the pond. That was where she would enter without being seen. She was locked and loaded, dressed in black, ready to exact revenge. Robert Lee Khal and the rest of the Kool-Aid drinkers were out of their fucking minds if they thought they could attack her family and get away with it.

Donna played dumb with the police on the scene and the ones that showed up at the hospital, and she knew that Bella would do the same. And, she'd make sure that their parents kept quiet as well.

She leaned against the tree. After racking the slide of her Smith & Wesson 9-millimeter, she patted her hip, unnecessarily checking the clip holder for the tenth time, to ensure that she had extra mags. She inhaled, then exhaled a deep cleansing breath. She pushed off the tree, ready to wreak havoc. If she had to, she was going to kill every last bible beater on the property to get to her enemies.

The snap of a twig kept her still. She listened, hoping it was an animal. But if it wasn't…if it was an obstacle in the way of retribution, it was dead.

"Don't shoot." The sound of the familiar masculine baritone had her lowering her weapon. She looked around but didn't see him.

"Lincoln!" she called in a too loud whisper.

"I'm here." Her ears told her that he was directly in front of her. She squinted, trying to find him. It wasn't until he moved closer that she realized that he was standing right in front of her. He too was dressed in all black, and his white skin was covered in what looked like mud.

"Lincoln, what the hell are you doing here? How did you find me?"

"Oh," he chuckled. "You thought it would take a genius to know where you'd be?"

"You gotta get outta here!" Donna pushed him in the chest, but he didn't even rock backward.

"Donatella, what are you here to do?"

Not having time to answer stupid questions, she glared at him with narrowed eyes. "You know what the fuck I'm here to do," she sneered.

She turned to continue along her path, but Lincoln grabbed her elbow and whipped her around to face him.

"No, baby. I don't think you understand. I'm asking you for the plan. I'm here to help."

Donna looked him in the eye, studying him with a furrowed brow to gauge his seriousness. He released her elbow.

"Gimme your weapon."

"*What?*"

"Your weapon. Give it to me."

With great hesitation, she handed her 9mm to Lincoln. She prayed that he wasn't trying to stop her from doing what she had gone there to do. If that was his plan, she'd have to rely on the backup piece she had in a secure ankle holster.

"Just like I thought," he said with a grimace. "You gonna kill people with your duty weapon? Did you at all plan on getting away with this?"

"I don't care, Lincoln! They shot my fucking father!"

He shook his head as if disappointed. "So, your dad comes home from the hospital just to discover that his baby girl is in prison for being stupid? That's your plan?"

"Lincoln—"

"No," he interrupted. "Just listen."

He took off the backpack he was carrying and dropped to one knee. He opened the bag, put her gun inside, and pulled out a different one. He handed it to her and said, "Use this one."

Donna accepted the weapon and studied it. She held it in her open hand to test the weight and pointed it to check the sights.

"A Desert Eagle," she whispered, more to herself than him. Lincoln might as well had just handed her Tiger Wood's driving iron. It was a beautiful weapon, but was he trying to trade places by going to prison instead of her?

"But, you—"

"It's clean. And, just so you know, right now Donatella Devereaux is boarding a flight to Georgia, and I'm picking her up from the airport."

Donna's breath hitched. He had so thoughtfully done something she was too angry and reckless to do. He thought ahead.

"Use this," he said, handing her a silencer.

Donna acquiesced and twisted the tool on the weapon.

Lincoln zipped the bag and swung it around his back. After tucking his arms in the straps, he pulled his own weapon out of the holster. Together, they continued through the trees.

"Lincoln?"

"Yes?"

"Don't kill anybody. They're mine."

"Okay, I won't," he whispered.

"I mean it. Promise me," Donna pushed.

Lincoln chuckled softly. "I promise I won't kill anyone."

"Thanks, babe."

When they broke from the trees, Donna clutched the grip of the

Desert Eagle. She was ready to see how much damage the semi-auto could do.

"Oh...Linc?"

"Yep?"

She turned to him with a smirk. "Let this be the last time I see yo ass in 'blackface'."

LINCOLN

Lincoln laughed quietly and shoved her to walk ahead. Since he didn't know where exactly to go, he needed her to lead the way.

He followed her to her old dormitory. She said Vera would be the easiest target. Well, she would've been had she been there. When they arrived, they discovered she wasn't in their old room, but Donna said she had an idea where to find her.

They crept quietly through a field of grass until they reached a house made of brick. Since her enemies lived on a compound secured by a tall gate with armed guards, Donna must've assumed that they felt secure enough to leave their doors unlocked. She was wrong. Lincoln nudged her aside and pulled a knife from the sheath attached to his belt.

"I got it," he whispered.

He slid the knife in the lock set, jimmied it open, then slowly turned the knob until he heard the click. He gradually eased the door open until it was wide enough for them to step inside. Donna stepped inside and waved him in. As quietly as possible, they tip-toed across the hardwood floor until they reached a hallway with wood paneling. Before they made it to the end of the hall, they could hear raised voices.

Lincoln couldn't quite make out what they were saying, but the conversation sounded heated. When they reached the door at the end of the hall, they were better able to make out what the voices were saying.

"I tried! He jumped in front of her!" came from a female voice behind the door.

"Then, he clearly loves her more than you love me," came from a male voice.

Donna readied her weapon and nodded for him to open the door. Lincoln twisted the knob and gently pushed the door. Once he realized nothing was barricading the door, he flung it open and rushed inside, weapon ready, with his angry woman by his side.

To Lincoln's surprise, he'd just walked into a room with a swimming pool. Khal was lounging naked in the pool. He was leaning back with his elbows resting on the edge. Clara and the other woman were fully clothed standing near the edge.

Khal was the first to notice their presence. When he looked up, there was a smile on his face, but hatred in his eyes.

"Welcome, Judas!" he shouted.

His greeting prompted the women to turn in their direction. Donna moved forward with her gun aimed at him. Lincoln moved to the other side of the pool. In case she was unable to carry out her revenge, he was ready to do it for her. And he had a feeling that he might have to. Donna was tough, but she was no killer. After all, she couldn't even shoot a deer.

"You here to arrest me, Kateri? Or, should I say...Donatella?" Khal challenged.

For some reason, he was arrogant enough to think that Donatella was there in a police capacity.

"You should say whatever you want because it'll be the last thing you say," Donatella seethed.

The hatred in her eyes out measured the hatred in his by light years. The young blonde raised her hands and moved closer to Donatella.

"Please, Kateri, I—"

Donatella put a bullet in her chest before she could finish her plea. Then, she fired another, hitting her before she hit the ground. She quickly turned her rage to the "Messiah's" righthand woman. Clara looked down at Khal through narrowed eyes. "You and your *fucking* Pocahontas fetish! You're a goddamned idiot!"

She turned to Donatella and raised her arms in defiance. "Fuck you!" she spat, before a 50 caliber round met her head, causing it to explode like a melon. Donatella kept firing as if the woman with no head was still alive. Banking on her being occupied, Khal scrambled out of the pool and made a run toward a door opposite the pool. Lincoln lowered his sights and fired, shooting him in the leg. He hit the floor with a thud and continued to inch toward the door. Since he promised not to kill anyone, he shot him in the other leg.

Khal was on his belly, wailing in agony when Donatella stalked over to him.

"Roll over!" she shouted.

Khal didn't comply right away, so she kicked his wound until he did. There he lay, wet, naked, and afraid. He was trembling like an abused puppy while pleading for his life. Unfortunately for him, Donatella was not feeling very merciful.

"When you get to Hell, dear Messiah, say hello to your *real* father."

"Wait!" he squealed in a high-pitched, almost feminine manner.

Without the slightest hesitation, she opened fire, and she didn't stop until the slide of her weapon locked to the rear. Her weapon was empty and the Messiah was dead. The woman couldn't shoot a deer, but she hadn't hesitated to put very large holes in three human beings.

LINCOLN

TWO MONTHS LATER

Lincoln peeped around the huge boxes he was carrying and frowned. "Why are you emptyhanded?" he complained. "What happened to all that women's lib shit?"

"Please," Donna scoffed. "I only care about that in the workplace. Besides, you know I just got my nails done."

Lincoln hit her with a blank stare. One minute, she was a hardcore tomboy, boxing and drinking men under a table. Then, the next minute, she tried to pull the girly girl on him. Donatella was whoever she needed to be when she needed to be.

"Whaaat?" she screeched with a playful grin.

"Ring the bell, lady."

"Yeah, let's get you some help with all that," she teased, ringing the bell.

Lincoln juggled the packages without help from Donatella until Bella finally opened the door. Her eyes grew wide.

"Oooh, what did you do, buy the whole store?" she squealed.

"Do you plan on letting us in?"

"Of course, come on in." She opened the door wider and stepped to the side. "Donna, why you ain't helping him? Gimme one of these boxes."

Bella grabbed two boxes from the top of the pile and carried them inside. He greeted other guests as he followed her to the dining room table where she placed them next to the other gifts. Lucas walked over with a wide grin.

"It's a beautiful day for miracles, Brother."

"Luc, what are you talking about?"

"Bella and Victoria, working together to throw this baby shower for Taylor."

"Why is that a miracle?"

"You're kidding, right?" Lucas asked with a furrowed brow. "You do know they don't like each other, right?"

"How would I know that?" he asked with a squint. "I don't hang out with the women. Why do you know that?"

"It's common knowledge."

"Why don't they like each other?" he asked, but he really didn't care.

"I'm not sure. I heard it was because Bella didn't like the way Victoria treated Donna when they were a couple."

Lincoln tilted his head, studying his brother to see if he was joking. It didn't seem so.

"Donna and Victoria were a couple? Victoria Storm?"

"Yep. You didn't know? Do you guys actually talk to each other?"

"We don't talk about past lovers."

"Do you even remember the names of any of your past lovers?" Lucas asked through laughter. "Seriously, I heard they were together for a while."

Lincoln frowned. "Listen to yourself, *'I heard.'* You're a woman," he chuckled as he turned to walk away. He didn't get far because Lucas grabbed his arm. He grimaced at the death grip his brother had on his limb. He was trying to get to Donatella so he could get more details about the fling. Even though he wouldn't admit it to Lucas, he did wonder why she never mentioned a relationship with Victoria. He knew she'd had experiences with other women, but relationships were different.

"Wait, I wanna talk to you about something," Lucas whispered conspiratorially.

Lincoln sighed. He supposed he could talk to her about it later. "What's up?"

Lucas reached in his pocket and pulled out a ring box. Before his brother could utter a word, Lincoln shook his head emphatically.

Lucas glared at him with furrowed brows. "What? Why are you shaking your head? We love each other."

"I don't doubt that, but have Bella's views about marriage changed?"

"What views about marriage? You think her first marriage turned her anti-marriage?"

"Ugh...*yeah!*" Lincoln scoffed.

Lucas' eyes narrowed. He shoved the box back in his pocket. "I don't even know why I asked you. You don't know shit about relationships."

Lincoln laughed and looked over at Donatella. "I don't know, Big Bro. I think I'm doing pretty good."

Taylor was wearing a smile as she walked over to them.

"What are you two over here talking about?"

Lincoln pulled her close and gave her a bear hug. "How are you, Baby Sis? I haven't seen you since you had the baby. Where is my niece? I wanna meet her. I hear she's got Mom's eyes."

Taylor laughed. "Your brother is still waiting on them to turn green, but it ain't looking good."

"Where is Princess Victoria?

Taylor slapped his arm. "Shhh!" She looked around the room, confusing the hell out of him.

"What is wrong with you, woman?"

"Every time someone says the baby's name, Bella starts pouting and rolling her eyes. So, we've been calling her Vicky."

Lincoln laughed. "She is definitely gonna have to get over that. Besides, she's about to have bigger issues." He smirked at Lucas. "Go on. Don't be shy. Tell her what you got planned."

His brother's angry glare told him that if looks could kill, they'd be spreading his ashes.

"Go on. Show her the ring," Lincoln pressed.

Taylor's mouth flew open. She was surprised, but not necessarily in a good way. In fact, she seemed a bit horrified.

"You're gonna asked Bella to marry you?" she asked in a hushed tone.

"That's the plan," Lucas muttered.

"Not here, in front of everybody? Maybe you should do it privately," she urged.

"Why? So, you think she's gonna say no too?"

Lincoln laughed when Taylor offered him a sad smile as if he'd already been turned down.

"Oh, ye of little faith. Bella is going to marry me. She loves me."

"Whaaat's love got to do... got to do with it?" Lincoln sang.

Without a word, Lucas walked away wearing a scowl. Taylor narrowed her eyes and pinched him on the arm.

"Ouch!"

"Stop teasing your brother and be supportive." Her lips twitched as if she was trying her best to suppress laughter.

"He's gonna need it," she blurted, unable to help herself.

Lincoln laughed and pulled his vibrating phone from his pocket. He wrinkled his brow, wondering who was calling him private.

"Excuse me, Sis," he said before swiping to answer.

"Hello," he said into the phone.

"Turn on the news," came from a familiar voice.

"Tahira?"

"Turn on the news," she repeated before hanging up.

TAYLOR

Taylor left Lincoln to his call and went to Bella's bedroom to check on Victor and Vicky. He was sitting in her comfy La-Z-Boy, feeding the baby. She stood in the doorway and watching the way he interacted with their daughter made her love him a million times more than she thought possible.

Vicky let out a little squeak when he pulled the near-empty bottle from her mouth. He tossed a burp cloth over his shoulder and lifted her to his chest. She squirmed in his arms and stuck her little butt out.

Victor was a natural. The way he protected her head while burping her would make it hard for someone to believe he was a first-time dad.

"You are so much better at this than me," she said from the doorway.

"I know," Victor teased.

"Haha. You might wanna put the baby in her bassinet and go check on your brother."

"Which brother?"

"Lucas. He's gonna propose to Bella."

Victor threw his head back with a sigh. "Ohhh, my God," he groaned.

"There she is!" Victoria crowed, pushing past her. "My little namesake."

Carefully, she stole Vicky from Victor's arms. Without even speaking to them, she walked right out of the room. Victor sat, still holding his baby-less arms up.

"Well, damn," he marveled.

Taylor grinned and sat in his lap. "Oh, I get to hold my other baby," he flirted before tucking his face in the crook of her neck. She giggled between kisses, thinking they were never gonna make it to her six-week checkup without having sex.

"Babe, is Nicole coming?"

Taylor's smile fell. She hadn't spoken to her sister in months. "She was invited, but I doubt she'll show."

"I'm sorry, sweetheart."

Taylor shrugged. "It is what it is."

Lincoln rushed into the bedroom, grabbed the remote from the footboard, and turned on the local 24-hour news station.

"What's going on, Linc?" Victor asked, puzzled by his brother's behavior.

"Watch."

Taylor got up from Victor's lap and went to sit on the footboard. Her mouth flew open when footage of Bill Thornton and her sister's fiancé being perp-walked out of their homes. Sadly, she could see Nicole crying in the background. After everything Jeffrey had done to Victor, she had no love for him. Frankly, she hadn't liked him before that. But she loved her sister, and never wanted to see her in pain.

"City officials, William "Bill" Thornton, and Jeffrey Morgan, were arrested in a south suburban brothel after video of deviant sexual behavior lands into the hands of the authorities."

As Taylor listened to the news anchor, her heart went out to Nicole. But Nicole wasn't taking her calls, and she'd made it very clear that she didn't want to talk to her. And there was nothing Taylor could do to change that. That didn't stop her from trying again.

She reached behind her and grabbed her purse from Bella's bed. She fished her phone and dialed Nicole. As expected, she was sent to voicemail.

"Couldn't have happened to better people," Victor muttered. "Now, I'm really gonna enjoy the party." He stood to leave but stopped at the doorway. "You okay?"

"Yep." Taylor hopped to her feet and followed Victor down the hall.

DONATELLA

After casually scanning the room for the third time, she finally spotted Lincoln. He was coming from the back of the house with Taylor and Victor. She walked over to him and pressed up against his big body.

"I missed you. What's going on back there?"

"I'll tell you later." He wrapped an arm around her shoulder and kissed the top of her head.

Donna would have pushed, but the sight of Lucas dropping down to one knee had her speechless. Her eyes went buck and her jaw dropped. She pulled away from Lincoln, horrified for Lucas. Bella was about to crush the man's dreams. She felt bad for Bella. Hurting Lucas wasn't gonna be easy.

After looking around the room, at all the terrified faces, she realized everyone was scared for him and prepared to console.

"Marry me, Bella," was all he said.

Bella seemed so confused, as if she had no clue what dropping to one knee meant. Her hand flew to cover her mouth.

"Shit," Lincoln cursed under his breath.

"*Yes!*"

Donna's breath hitched. She was in total shock, and not sure she heard her right. And she clearly wasn't the only one in shock. The loud chorus of, "*What*?!" was the first clue.

Lucas slipped the impressive rock on her finger and jumped to his feet. He looked over at Lincoln and shouted, "Ha!"

"Thank you, baby. I love you," he declared as he pulled Bella into his arms.

Overcome with excitement for her sister, Donna started clapping and jumping up and down. The love she shared with Lucas must have been extremely powerful. Since her divorce, Bella had vowed that she would never marry again. As Donna watched her sister, smiling from ear to ear and crying tears of joy, she realized that not only did she feel her pain, but she also felt her happiness.

THE END

Made in the USA
Coppell, TX
14 June 2024